MW01537112

TRANSGRESSOR

TEN GIFFORD MYSTERIES BOOK TWO

JOE SCHOLES

To Matt,
Enjoy my favorite character,
NanC !

Joe Scholes

JOE
SCHOLES
AUTHOR

TRANSGRESSOR

A novel by Joe Scholes
Copyright © 2017 by Joe Scholes
All rights reserved.

Published by:
JDS Literary Services, LLC
PO Box 57172
Oklahoma City, OK 73157

This is a work of fiction. Names (except where with permission), places, incidents and characters are the product of the author's imagination. Any resemblance to actual events, locales or persons (living or dead) is coincidental.

ISBN-13: 978-1-63478-016-2
ISBN: 1-63478-016-7

This book, whole or in part, may not be copied or reproduced by electronic or mechanical means (including photocopying or the implementation of any type of storage or retrieval system) without the express written permission of the author, except where permitted by law.

Cover Art by The Cover Counts

For Jay Brand, Lonny Bridges and Lindsay Torres.

ACKNOWLEDGMENTS

To my sisters Dianne Jantzen and Denise Wright, my nephew Justin Wright, and to my friends Mark Stout, Jeff Zielny, Greg Rowland, Larry Omans, Debra Salazar, Jerry Owens, Nick Owens, Price Brown, Norm and Carmel Jackson, Nancy Anspaugh, Robbie Rickey, Paul Eller and Silvio Kimmel, ***thank you***. I truly appreciate your contribution to the book.

Many thanks to my entire family in America and Australia, including the ones no longer with us. All were and are, major contributors to my growth, happiness and success.

A special thanks to Connie Suttle, who has encouraged me from the beginning to accomplish my dream of publishing. I truly appreciate your support, friendship, talent and generosity of the past forty-plus years.

ABOUT THE AUTHOR

Joe retired from the US Postal Service in 2010, after thirty-six years. Not long after, he became the proofreader and jack of all trades for author Connie Suttle, a long-time, very close friend.

With Connie as his inspiration, Joe decided to become a writer.

Joe lives in Oklahoma City, Oklahoma, USA, with his two kids, Dingo and Ringo, both of which are miniature long-coat Chihuahuas.

For more information, please visit Joe's website at JoeScholesAuthor.net or find him on his Facebook page at Joe Scholes Author

BOOKS BY JOE SCHOLES

Ren Gifford Mysteries:

Malefactor

Transgressor

CHAPTER 1

Warren Millpond
Aboard the Adelaide II
Port Adelaide, South Australia

Call me in the next two minutes, Warren, or you'll be dead in three. —M

I'd just entered my cabin for a short nap when my phone chimed. The blood drained from my face as I read the text message.

I closed and locked the cabin door. As far as I knew there was no one else in crew quarters, but I couldn't risk being overheard. I sat on the bed to make the call.

"Very good, Warren," said a man whose voice I didn't recognize, yet I had no doubt who was speaking.

"What do you want from me? I thought we were done. Blake said you released me," I whispered harshly.

"Well, now. We know what happened to Blake, don't we?" he purred. "One final *project* and I promise you'll never hear from me again." He stopped and waited for my response.

Finally, I mumbled gruffly, "As if I have a choice. What is it?"

"Don't be petulant," he barked through the phone. "You'll get what you're due when I'm done with you. And don't give me any shit about

1

crossing your friends. We both know you don't have the backbone to refuse me, or to confess anything to Ren."

I remained silent, hating myself because I knew he was right. He sighed heavily, then continued.

"Get rid of the others this evening, no later than five o'clock. I don't care how you do it, but get them away from the marina. Make sure they're gone for at least two hours."

"We're going to dinner around then anyway, so that shouldn't be a problem."

"Good. You, however, will remain on board and wait for one of my associates to contact you."

"How will I know when and who?"

"You'll know," he said with a chuckle, and ended the call.

~

M Dekker

Several hours had passed since I pressed Warren into service once more. I relished the fear and hatred I heard in his voice. He'd do as I demanded, however, no matter how distasteful he found it. The thought made me smile.

My surveillance teams reported the group was split up. Ren and Terry were in Oklahoma City. Russ and the rest were bunking aboard their new yacht in Port Adelaide while it was nearing the end of its refit.

Hunched over the tablet I'd stolen just hours ago, I squinted at the single line of text on the screen, my finger hovering over the send button. To ensure the message would be read immediately, I used Ren's personal email account, which my staff found exceedingly easy to hack. Nodding to myself, I tapped it. *Sent.*

The game's afoot as my favorite fictional detective would say. I had much to do before Ren got involved.

~

Glen Moreland
Aboard the Adelaide II
Port Adelaide, South Australia

Russ, Alex and Warren went ashore for dinner. I could have gone, but I preferred the alone time so I could drink in quiet. Besides, Russ liked one of us to always be aboard the yacht whenever it was docked. I volunteered, as I usually did.

Not that I didn't have company. Dunkin was lying on the lower bunk, snoring softly, while I was sprawled across the top bunk with one leg dangling over the side. The half-empty bottle of vodka, lying on the pillow beside me, nearly lured me into a nap; I was drowsy.

The boat was almost motionless, tied securely to the dock. Most of the refit was done, with just a day or two left to finish some interior decorating. Jacko, the marina owner, was anxious to be paid for the refit, so he practically perched on the foreman's shoulder like a parrot, barking orders and supervising much of the work over the past couple of weeks.

I looked forward to leaving Port Adelaide; I felt much more comfortable at sea, away from the public and large crowds. Russ and Alex assured me that when we had a charter, I'd be able to stay out of sight and keep to myself while the guests were up and about. I was nervous about meeting the yacht's crew, too. I don't like meeting new people. They're not trustworthy.

Half a year after I managed to elude the Malefactor, my heavy anxiety finally diminished. At least I was functional. Alex still complained that I drank too much, but I only had to nod in Russ' direction to shut down his good-hearted and kindly-delivered reproach.

I like to drink. I want to drink. I'm gonna drink, so get over it. That was my attitude. I would only curtail my habit if Russ told me it was interfering with what little I could do to be useful on the boat.

These thoughts got tangled in my sleepy head and I was soon snoozing in the small crew cabin I would eventually share with Warren when the rest of the crew were aboard. Hours later I was startled awake by Dunkin barking furiously at the closed cabin door.

"Quiet, Dunkin," I said as I slid off the bunk to the floor. He whined, but quieted as I rubbed him behind one ear. I strained to hear any unusual sounds, but there was nothing. I downed the remaining vodka and crawled back onto the top bunk, quickly falling asleep.

~

Warren

Aboard the Adelaide II

Despite my efforts, I couldn't get Glen to go to dinner with Russ and Alex. I begged off at the last minute, feigning an upset stomach—which wasn't much of an exaggeration. It was in knots since talking to *him*.

Russ and Alex left the marina at a quarter to five. At exactly five o'clock, I received another text.

Walk to the security booth at the front gate.

I padded quietly downstairs to crew quarters to check on Glen. I tapped on his door, but there was no response, other than a soft whine from Dunkin. Good. That meant Glen was passed out.

Setting a casual pace, I headed along the pier toward the parking lot and approached the guard. Biscuit was on duty, as usual for this time of day.

"Evenin', Warren. Jus' saw Russ and Alex leave. Headed to dinner, I reckon." I nodded and stood quietly with my arms folded across my chest. He took another biscuit from a pocket and started nibbling on it. "You didn't go along, eh."

Such a keen observer, I thought. "Nah. Had an upset stomach, so I'm just hanging out here this evening."

"Hang on, mate," he said distractedly. "Someone's yammerin' on the radio." He put it to his ear for a few seconds to listen, then his eyes grew round.

"Yeah, yeah, I heard ya. I'm comin'," he said irritably, putting the walkie-talkie back on his belt. "Sorry, but one of the rookies is in a panic about nothin', I reckon, but I gotta go check it out. Talk to ya later." He shut the door to the guard booth, ambled the few steps to his golf cart, climbed in and took off across the parking lot.

Once he'd disappeared from sight, my phone chimed again.

Open the gate. When the car is inside, close the gate and follow the driver's instructions.

I looked toward the gate where a dark sedan approached. Pulling on the booth door, I was surprised Biscuit had left it unlocked. I reached in and pushed the green button, so worn from wear I could barely make out the word *open* on it.

When the car cleared the track, I closed the gate and then closed the booth door. The driver parked the car in a space close to the pier and stepped out.

"Come on, we don't have all night," he barked, motioning for me to come to him. He popped the trunk. "Grab one of those boxes and lead me to the yacht." We each carried one of two heavy boxes, labeled Extra Virgin Olive Oil, aboard the *Adelaide II* and set them on the deck.

"Right," he said. "Leave the boxes here. Go get a change of clothes, your passport and whatever money you've got. Don't bring anything more than you can carry in a backpack." Then he pulled a gun with a silencer attached from a hidden holster behind his back. "Where's the drunkard?"

"What? No, he's passed out. He doesn't have a clue what's going on. There's no need to kill him," I pleaded. His eyes narrowed as he glared at me, as if he were distracted. He nodded once and put the gun away.

"Get your kit and meet me outside the gate. And hurry—some serious shit's about to go down," he instructed.

I stood still for a moment, wondering if I should try to call Russ. My phone chimed.

Go, Warren. Go now.

Shit. I went as quietly as I could to my cabin and stuffed what I could into a backpack. I could hear Dunkin barking inside Glen's cabin, but I didn't have time to deal with it. I scrawled out a brief note and left it on my pillow, then locked the door behind me.

The car was idling outside the gate. The driver waved from the window for me to hurry and get in the car, so I trotted in that direction, looking around to ensure I wasn't seen.

I sat in the front passenger seat and he slammed his foot on the gas before I could close the door. Moments later, I heard—and felt—an explosion behind us. Looking over my shoulder, I could see a large plume of smoke and fire rising from a warehouse on the far side of the marina.

The driver handed an envelope to me.

"What's this?"

"Since I'm takin' ya to the airport, I reckon it's an airline ticket." Heavy on the sarcasm.

The envelope wasn't sealed and contained instructions how to claim the e-ticket on an app on my phone. The departure was soon and the destination was Honolulu, Hawaii, via Sydney. *Fuck.*

There was also a note and a key. *When you arrive in Honolulu and exit Customs, take a shuttle to the HNL Locker Depot and remove the contents of the locker with the enclosed key—the locker number is on the key. Then proceed to the hotel. Additional instructions will be provided. —M*

I knew Ren and Russ decided to sail the *Adelaide II* to Hawaii once the refit was done, which was expected soon. Considering that I was being shipped to Hawaii, it was fair to assume the Malefactor wasn't done with me yet.

The driver slowed to a speed unlikely to attract attention as we headed toward the airport. We made the trip in complete silence. I soon found myself standing on the curb at the departure terminal with my backpack in one hand and the envelope in the other.

"I'd get a move on, if I were you. Your flight leaves in less than an hour," the driver said through the open window, then slowly merged into the traffic, disappearing in the flow. Numb, I looked at the ticket and took in my surroundings, then turned to walk to the nearest entrance.

The domestic flight from Adelaide ended in Sydney, where I would have to transfer to the international terminal to catch the flight to Honolulu. I would have many hours in transit; plenty of time to dwell on my misdeeds, now and the recent past. If I survived this, I hoped I could confess to Ren and, somehow, gain his forgiveness.

~

Russ Garrett

Port Adelaide

Alejandro leaned against my side in the backseat of the taxi on the way back to the marina. Dinner was exceptional, and we'd had plenty of wine, making us relaxed and comfortable. I wouldn't admit it to Warren, but I was pleased when he decided to stay behind. Alejandro and I seldom had a quiet evening to ourselves, and we'd both enjoyed it. I hoped it would continue once we were in our cabin.

The driver interrupted my thoughts. "I'm not sure I can get you into the marina, gents. There's been an explosion there and the place is locked down tight," he explained.

"When did that happen?" Alejandro asked, as we both sat up straight in our seats.

"Don't know exactly. They just mentioned it on the radio a few minutes ago. Evidently, a warehouse exploded."

I pulled my phone out and called Warren, but the call went straight to voicemail.

"Damn."

Alejandro squeezed my arm. "I'm sure they're okay. I don't recall there being a warehouse near our pier, and they wouldn't have any reason to be anywhere but on the *Adelaide*," he assured me. I nodded in agreement.

As we approached the entrance to the marina, we were waved to the side by a police officer, who motioned for the driver to open his window.

"Marina's closed," he said gruffly.

"I'm just dropping off these guys," the driver explained, pointing toward us with a thumb over his shoulder.

The officer bent down to peer through the window into the

backseat, flashing his light in our faces. "What's your business here, then?"

"I'm the captain of the yacht *Adelaide II*, which is undergoing refit. We're just coming back from dinner," I responded.

Just then, Biscuit walked up beside the officer, chuffing with the effort. "They're okay. I can vouch for 'em. They're due to depart in a couple of days."

The officer glanced down, noticing Alejandro's hand resting on the inside of my thigh. "Hmph," he grunted, then turned toward another officer at the gate. "Let 'em in," he called. Then back to us, "don't venture toward the crime scene," he instructed.

As we exited the taxi, Biscuit waved me over. "Russ, do me a favor. When you see Warren, tell him the police want to speak to him. He was visiting with me at the guard booth when I was called away just a few minutes before the explosion."

"You don't think he had anything to do with it, do you?" Alejandro asked with eyes wide. Biscuit paused to retrieve a partially eaten cookie from his pocket before responding.

"No, but the explosion destroyed the electronics closet in the warehouse. We don't have access to any of the surveillance videos as a result. We need to find out if he saw anyone or anything unusual."

"Ah, yeah. Okay. Was anybody hurt?" I asked. Biscuit bowed his head.

"Sadly, one of the rookie security guards was killed. I reckon I should'a taken him more seriously when he radioed for help."

"We're sorry to hear that. Let me know if there is anything we can do, all right?" Biscuit nodded, and we turned toward the pier, walking in silence.

~

Glen

Aboard the Adelaide II

When I awoke, Dunkin was agitated. He sat by the cabin door, anxious to go. I figured he needed to relieve himself, so I dropped down to the floor. Just then, I heard footsteps on the main deck above. The guys were back.

"Come on, Dunkin, let's go say hello."

I led him out of the cabin and up the stairs to the main deck, where Russ and Alex had just stepped off the gangplank. Russ looked extremely worried.

"Hi guys," I said quietly. Russ nodded hello. Alex waved from behind Russ.

"Has Warren come back aboard?" Russ asked. "Security said they saw him shortly after we left for dinner."

"I thought he went with you two," I replied. Russ shook his head.

"He canceled at the last minute because he didn't feel good. You didn't talk to him?"

"Uh, I've been sleeping for a while," I said sheepishly. "Maybe he's in one of the other crew cabins? Dunkin woke me up at least an hour ago, maybe more. We were alone in our cabin. Maybe it was Warren."

"What good does it do to leave you on board when we're gone if you're just gonna get drunk and fall asleep with the deck unsecured?" Russ grumbled.

My face flushed at his rebuke. "Move," he huffed, and brushed past me as he headed for the stairs to crew quarters. I stared after him.

Alex followed Russ, but whispered as he passed, "Don't worry about him, Glen, he's just pissy."

"Don't apologize for me, Alejandro," I heard Russ growl over his shoulder.

A couple of minutes later, they were back.

"His cabin's locked and he's not answering—if he's there," Alex reported.

I hesitated to ask, since Russ was apparently miffed about something, but I did anyway.

"What's going on, guys?"

Russ ignored me, too occupied with thoughts of Warren.

Alex sighed, then explained. "You didn't hear the explosion?" That confused me completely, and I shook my head. "Well, evidently a warehouse here in the marina exploded not long after we left. You must have been seriously drunk if you slept through that," he said softly.

I dipped my head, embarrassed. "No worse than usual," I mumbled.

"I'm going to our cabin to get the master key and open Warren's door," Russ said, and walked quickly toward the stairs to crew quarters. "I'd hate to think he's had a heart attack or something, and just lying on the floor waiting for help." Alex and I watched him leave and didn't speak for a couple of minutes.

"He's not in his cabin and some of his things are gone," Russ reported as he rejoined us. "All of my calls keep going to voicemail. Somethin' ain't right, guys. I found this on the bed," he added, waving a piece of paper toward us.

"What is it?" Alex asked, and Russ handed it to him. Alex read it aloud, "*Russ, I'm sorry.* That's it?" Russ nodded. "What's he sorry about? Do you think he had anything to do with the explosion?" Alex handed the paper back to Russ.

"No idea," Russ replied as we all pondered what this meant.

"Where'd you go to dinner?" I asked, to fill the silence.

"The Bistro Ballroom at the Palais Hotel in Semaphore. You know, the place Jacko's wife, Carmel, recommended. Russ said he had one of the best steaks he's ever eaten. I told him it was kangaroo, and he nearly choked on a mouthful," Alex said, laughing. "It was an excellent meal and now the evening's ruined, coming back to this cockup," he complained.

"Where'd you say the Bistro Ballroom was?" I asked lamely. Before Alex could reply, Russ raised his eyebrows and looked at me with a deadpan expression.

"You know where we saw that cruise ship in the harbor when we arrived a few weeks ago?" I nodded, remembering it vaguely. "Well, it's nowhere near there." Damn, he did it to me again, but at least his sense of humor was returning.

"Come on, li'l buddy," he said, less harshly. "Let's go to the bar and talk about what to do."

Russ gestured for us to take a seat at the bar and he went behind to pour drinks. He grabbed the whiskey and three highball glasses and filled them a third full. I started to raise my glass in our usual silent first toast, but Russ already had his glass to his lips and sucked down half its contents.

Alex and I followed suit, glancing at each other over the rims of our drinks, then Russ poured refills.

After a moment, Russ mused, "I should probably report him missing to the local authorities. I've got a bad feeling about this, guys. *Dammit.*"

We practically gulped our whiskey. Russ' phone beeped and he pulled it from his pocket. I was grateful for the interruption and wondered if it might be Warren.

"Who's that?" Alex asked.

"It's an email from Ren," Russ replied, and opened it. There was only one brief sentence, and a website link.

Russ, check this out. –Ren

Russ showed the screen to Alex and me, then tapped the link. While it was loading, Russ came around the bar to stand between us so we could see the phone.

The link took a moment to load, but then showed a video of Warren. First, he was walking quickly out of the marina entrance and getting into a dark sedan, and again as he passed through airport security with only a backpack.

"Fuck," Russ exploded. The video image zoomed in on Warren so we could get a good look, then panned above his head to a digital clock. It read seven-thirty p.m. That was hours ago.

"That's the Adelaide Airport," Russ said, taking another drink from his glass. "What the hell is he up to?" The video went blank for a moment. "And who the hell made this video?" he said as an afterthought. "It certainly wasn't Ren." Then the video displayed a single line of text that sent chills up my spine.

Make no mention of Warren's absence to the authorities if you want him to live. See you in Hawaii. I'll be in touch. –M

～

Russ Garrett

Aboard the Adelaide II

The moment the video ended, Glen's eyes glazed over and I watched panic flood his pale face. He knew as well as Alejandro and I did who wrote that line of text. The *Malefactor*. I glanced at Alejandro, who wore a concerned expression as he focused on Glen.

Alejandro went behind the bar. "Here. Drink this," he said, and handed Glen a bottle of cold water he took from the mini-fridge under the bar. Alejandro looked at me, nodded toward Glen, his expression telling me to say something. Anything.

Glen was slouched over his now-empty glass, ignoring the water Alejandro offered. He merely pushed his glass toward Alejandro for a refill, his hands shaking.

"Russ. Alex. What the hell is happening? Is this real?" Glen whispered. He looked as if he were about to collapse.

"I don't know, man. We have to figure this out. And I need to talk with Ren, but not until we've left Port Adelaide."

"I'm going to bed, guys. G'night," Glen said, and slid off the barstool. Alejandro and I looked at each other, then followed a moment later to make sure he made it to his cabin.

Alejandro knocked softly on the door before opening it and stepping inside. Dunkin leapt onto the lower bunk and snuggled between Glen and the wall, his snout resting on Glen's hip bone. We knew he'd watch over Glen.

We dimmed the lights and left the door ajar. I wanted Dunkin to be able to paw the door open if Glen needed us.

∼

Ren Gifford

Oklahoma City, Oklahoma

I was exhausted. The weeks during the *Malefactor* ordeal and the months after had taken their toll, physically, mentally and emotionally.

In that brief period, I outwitted the Malefactor's front man, losing one of my closest friends in the process. I became privy to crimes I had no way to prove, with no tangible perpetrator to deliver at the end. My bank account had grown to eight digits, although scrutiny of the details would certainly raise serious questions as to how that happened. I made some lifelong friends, married my partner of four years and honeymooned in Hawaii, Australia and New Zealand.

While Terry and I honeymooned, Russ was busy shopping for luxury yachts. A couple of months after the honeymoon, we joined Russ, who'd selected three yachts in our price range to visit.

Of the three, we settled on a beauty manufactured by Trinity in 1994. She would need a refit, including being updated with modern electronics and interior decor, but otherwise she was in very good shape.

The yacht was docked in Fremantle, near Perth, Australia, when we saw her. I engaged Beau's attorney, Walter Evans, to handle the international sale, leaving the details for him, Russ and the seller to work out. Terry and I returned home, leaving Dunkin with Glen, who'd become attached to the Norwegian Dunker.

I had yet to decide what I wanted to do with the investigation business, now that we were independently wealthy. I'd given serious thought to throwing in with Connie. She's the one who sparked my interest in being a private investigator to start with. She had her own one-woman company, Subtle Investigations, here in Oklahoma City, and was considering opening an office in Tulsa. I resolved to set aside some time to discuss this idea with her.

Terry needed to find gainful employment, just for his own sanity. I still encouraged him to work with me as an investigator, but he hadn't decided, yet. His first immersive experience had not improved his opinion of it as a career choice. He hadn't ruled it out, though, so I remained hopeful.

On a bittersweet note, Mr. Evans managed to expedite the transfer of Beau's assets to me. I detested how I came into such a windfall, but was delighted to put it toward a new endeavor, one which I was sure Beau would bless.

When the yacht purchase was concluded, Russ wasted no time

getting her registered as the *Adelaide II*. It was fitting—and convenient —to sail her to a wonderful marina on the Port River in Port Adelaide, South Australia for the refit and remodeling she needed.

A few weeks later, Russ arranged a FaceTime call so he could introduce me to the crew. Technically, I had equal say in who was hired, but I left those decisions where they belonged—with the man who knew the right people.

The internet connection was surprisingly clear during the call.

"Hey, Ren, how are things going?" he began.

"We can't complain," I answered simply. I was tired and not in the mood for small talk. "Do you have your crew with you?"

"Yeah. The senior crew, at least."

"Okay, let's get started, then."

"I thought Terry would be with you."

I shook my head. "No, he's in bed. It's late, here."

Russ nodded and turned the tablet toward a man who appeared to be in his mid-thirties, with an authoritative air about him. "This is Mack. He and I worked together in the past and he's had experience as a captain on a smaller vessel. He's the First Mate."

I nodded my head in greeting, which he returned. "Nice to meet you, Mack. Russ tells me he also gave you the responsibility of choosing most of the rest of the crew. You okay with that?"

"Absolutely. I only recommended people to Russ whom I would have hired to crew my own yacht, if I had one," he asserted. I gestured for him to continue and he turned the tablet away.

In sequence, Mack introduced the rest of the senior crew; Dale Albright, the chief engineer, and JT and Kat, the bosun and chief stewardess; a married couple. Mack briefly covered their qualifications before turning the camera back to Russ.

"I'll wait to introduce the rest of the crew once we're together. All that remain are the chef and the two additional stewardesses," he explained.

"All right. With Glen, Warren and Alex added in, that makes eleven crew members. Does the *Adelaide* have room that many?"

Standing behind Russ so I could see him, Mack nodded once and said, "No worries. It'll be tight, but manageable. I can go over the cabin assignments if you like."

"Let's knock off for now," Russ interrupted. "We've covered the important stuff, and this call is a strain on all of us, considering the time zone differences."

"Sounds good to me, guys. We'll see you in a few weeks," I said, and ended the call.

CHAPTER 2

$\mathcal{A}$aron Jeffries
FBI Headquarters
Washington DC
Present

It's been five months since my friend Beau Richards' death. After three hours at my office desk reading the case file, I felt drained.

I slid my dark-rimmed glasses off my nose and made a call on my cell phone.

"Hi Jerry, how are you," I said when he answered the phone.

"Hey Aaron, I'm good, man, I'm good. What's goin' on with you?"

Jerry's a CIA data analyst. Our paths crossed several years ago when we were on a joint CIA/FBI cyber-attack task force. About ten years younger than I, we hit it off immediately. We shared the same interest in gadgets and technology, although we disagreed consistently when it came to sports teams. All in fun, though. He and his wife became close friends with Sophia and me.

"Ah, well, I've got a favor to ask, but I don't want to talk about it over the phone. I need to clear it with Sophie, but do you suppose you and Kristal could come over for dinner this weekend? Lenny is welcome, too, of course," I added.

Without hesitation, Jerry said, "Yeah, man, that could happen. We don't have anything going on this weekend, so work out the details with Sophie and get back to me. But I reckon the kid will stay home. No offense, man, but he gets bored at your place."

I smiled. Sophie and I didn't have kids; had never wanted any, so our home lacked the games and interests kids were into nowadays. "No problem. I expected as much. Okay, I'll talk to Sophie when I get home and call you tomorrow. 'Bye."

A few moments later my phone beeped; Sophie texted, *Just got off the phone with Kristal. She and Jerry will be over Saturday around three. I told them we'd grill steaks.*

Huh? Then a follow-up message. *Jerry called Kristal after you and he talked and she called me. We figured we'd get the party started.* She punctuated her message with three smiley-faces.

Sounds good, I replied. *I'm leaving the office now and should be home in about an hour.*

Three days later, Saturday was upon us. I grilled steaks; the women giggled over wine in the kitchen while working on the side dishes. Jerry and I talked about some recent efforts by foreign countries to hack into American computer systems, but on a layman's level, omitting the top-secret details that we couldn't discuss around anyone, including our families.

Sophie and Kristal dished up Italian cream cake and brandy, while Jerry and I put away the dishes and cleaned the kitchen. After dessert, Jerry and I excused ourselves to talk privately in my study. Just as I was about to close the door, Sophie followed us into the room with two mugs and a pot of hot decaf.

"Here ya go, gentlemen. Try not to stay locked in here all night, okay?" Without waiting for an answer, she left the room, closing the door behind her with a soft click.

I walked silently to the bar and held up a brandy bottle in a silent question. Jerry waved no, so I poured coffee and joined him at the small conference table.

Jerry is probably one of the most patient people I know. He sipped his coffee in silence while I gathered my thoughts, deciding where to begin.

With a heavy sigh, I lead with, "Do you remember my friend Beau?"

"Of course. Isn't he the one who died under mysterious circumstances not long ago?"

"Not so mysterious. He was murdered," I responded. I shared what little information there was to be had.

"The official report held a lot of detail, and Beau's killer, JC, is in custody, but his information only leads to more dead bodies. He's been cooperative, but I believe he knows very little about his real boss. The whole thing is suspicious."

"Remind me how you and Beau met," Jerry prompted.

"Ah, well. Shortly after graduating from the Academy, I was assigned to Beau as his partner. I'd never met anyone other than you who had the computer and analytical skills Beau did. We worked together for almost eight years before he retired, and that was eighteen years ago. Two years later, I accepted a promotion to headquarters.

"Beau and I stayed in touch, of course, but as often happens, we drifted apart over the years. I regret that; Beau was a wonderful mentor and a close friend. I should have made more of an effort to see him."

"Water under the bridge, my friend."

"Indeed. But, maybe I can make up for some of it by solving his murder."

"No progress on the case, I take it." he said.

I shook my head. "No. The local field office there and the homicide detective on the Oklahoma City Police Department tracked every lead to a dead end—no pun intended. The investigation's still active, but has gone cold.

"Still, there are people involved in this that I want to interview personally, and that means taking some time off and traveling to Oklahoma. I'm particularly interested in a couple of Beau's closest friends; Darren Gifford and Terry Franklin."

Jerry and I sat in silence across from each other, he with his elbows on the table and his fingers steepled beneath his chin. I'd shared the significant details of Beau's death and answered what few questions he had. Now I waited while he mulled the information over.

"So, what's your plan, Aaron? You can't insinuate yourself into the investigation. Anything improper will only serve to fuel the defense attorney's case for his client."

I nodded in agreement. "My request for time off has already been approved. The boss offered to send me officially to help, given that the case had gone cold, but I felt I could be more effective on the sly. Being on leave then, he also warned me not to interfere in the official investigation." Jerry nodded slightly in approval.

"But I refuse to simply let it go," I continued. "My plan is to start interviewing those closest to Beau who were also involved in some way. Yes, they've all been interviewed by the local authorities—with a couple of exceptions, and had nothing useful to offer."

"Oh? Who were the exceptions?"

"Glen Mooreland, Russ Garrett and Alejandro Martinez. They're mixed up in this somehow, but were out of the country when the murder took place. I still want to talk to them, if I can arrange it."

"What can I do, my friend? Aside from taking time off and coming with you. That would raise more than a few eyebrows," Jerry said.

"I was hoping I could count on you to ply your skills with computers and networks, if need be. I think there is much more to this investigation than has been discovered so far. I may need some, uh, unofficial technical support, shall we say."

"That's the favor you need?" Jerry laughed. "That's a no-brainer, Aaron. Before you leave, I'll set up several secure channels of communication just for us. I'm sure that between the two of us, we can fly under the radar of all the monitoring systems."

"You mean the systems *you* designed?" I asked with a smile.

"Nah, you give me too much credit. I was just the head of the team. But I do know more about them than just about anyone else. And I can hide our tracks with no problem."

"Thank you," was all I could say as relief flooded through my mind.

Jerry leaned back and gazed into the middle distance between us, reminiscing. "Do you remember the time you introduced me to Beau? I forget why he was in DC, but you brought him to my office in Langley. I was staring at a code module on the computer that had me bumfuzzled for days. With you having inflated his reputation, as far as I was concerned, I asked him to take a look at it."

I nodded, remembering the incident well. I'd been surprised Jerry had so freely allowed Beau to see something that was very likely highly classified—way beyond Beau's or my clearance levels.

Jerry shook his head; his smile sincere. "Hmmph. He lifted his glasses that were hanging from a rainbow-colored lanyard around his neck and slid them onto his face, then peered down at the screen. He studied it, oh, for perhaps three minutes. Then he took up pen and paper from my desk and scratched out three lines of code." Jerry stopped and just shook his head.

"And? Beau never explained what that was about, and I pressed him hard for the details. What did he give you?" I prompted.

"All I can tell you is that those three lines of code blasted through a roadblock that had stalled my entire team for almost a week. I called him a week later to thank him, and all I got was that hysterically infectious laugh of his over the phone."

"He never told me you called," I said, surprised.

"I know. Beau was a man of rare talents and had the widest streak of discretion I've ever seen in anyone. I never doubted that he would keep secret that block of code, or that he helped us through it. Hell, I couldn't even give him credit."

"Ah, but he wouldn't have wanted that anyway," I added.

Jerry looked at me then and said solemnly, "You're not considering taking justice into your own hands, are you?" My silence was response enough. A moment later, he continued. "You go to Oklahoma, or wherever you need, to figure out why Beau was killed by that scum in prison. Keep in touch with me and I'll do whatever I can behind the scenes to help. I'm putting my ass on the line, here, you know that? The CIA is forbidden by law to operate inside the United States."

I raised my hand. "No one will ever know of this from me. And I can't thank you enough."

We stood and shook hands, then he asked, "When are you leaving?"

I shrugged. "Not sure. I've got a few irons in the fire I need to hand off before I can go, so it'll be a few days. I'll let you know when I have a firm date."

∽

Terry Franklin
Oklahoma City, Oklahoma
Present

Brandi was one of those outgoing, blustery, eyes-set-on-high-beam realtors you always want working for you but with whom you seldom wanted to socialize. Ren and I met her at one of Beau's parties years ago.

She was outrageously successful and when I told her we were going to sell, she immediately thrust herself into the job at a reduced commission, as a tribute to Beau. She batted eyelids heavily laden with mascara at me as I signed the contract, then breezed out the front door with a promise to have interested buyers on our doorstep in no time.

I was surprised when she called two hours later.

"Terry? Uh, this is weird. There's a lady who wants to tour the house this afternoon. Will you be home?"

"Sure, I'll be here. Why is it weird?"

"Nancy is her name. She called a few minutes ago asking about the house. Terry, I haven't had time to enter it into the system yet. When I asked how she knew the house was for sale, she said something, but the phone went all static-y and I couldn't understand her."

"I dunno, Brandi. I hardly think it's weird. Ren and I have made no secret of the fact that we're planning to sell. She could have heard about it from just about any of our friends," I offered.

"Well, okay, I guess. But how'd she know I'm your realtor?" I thought it over, but had no response. "Also," Brandi continued, "she wants to come on her own and have you show her around, not me. What do you want to do?"

"I guess it's okay," I agreed slowly. "I'm already home and wasn't planning to go anywhere. Tell her two o'clock is fine. I'll call you after she leaves."

"Okay," Brandi said. "If you're sure," and ended the call.

Putting the phone in my pocket, I looked around the living room. It was clean, but cluttered. I went through the house quickly. I couldn't tell if I was straightening up or just rearranging the clutter.

The back doorbell rang, then I heard a faint, "Hi-eeee."

I walked through to the kitchen and the back door. When I opened it, there stood a diminutive, colorfully dressed woman with bright, watery-blue eyes and a friendly face that defied an age estimate. She could be anywhere from fifty to seventy.

She stepped into the room uninvited, taking my hand in a firm grip. "Mr. Franklin, I am *excited* to meet you." She held my hand warmly between hers as she looked up at me expectantly. She couldn't be more than five-feet tall.

Her eyes squinted as she regarded me, but her smile never faltered. I still hadn't spoken. She released my hand with a gentle squeeze, pulled the bright-red scarf from atop her head and let it droop over her shoulders, revealing short-cropped, unkempt hair in a gunmetal hue.

She grinned at me and said, "What's the matter, Terry? Cat got your tongue?" Her laugh was unrestrained, but not unkind.

It was as if I came to myself once she dropped my hand. "Yes, hello, ma'am. Nancy, is it? Come in. Please excuse my manners. I was surprised you came to the back door."

"Well, it's the most frequently used entrance to this lovely home, isn't it? I shouldn't wish to enter any other way." Before I could respond, she asked, "Since we're already in the kitchen, might I impose upon you for a cup of tea? I'm sure you have something herbal to my liking; you choose. Plain please, no sweetener or cream."

Nonplussed, I gestured for her to have a seat at the breakfast table and turned toward the stove to put the teakettle on to boil. While the water heated, I went through my herbal tea selection. Nancy sat at the breakfast table and began to ramble.

"Such an odd saying, don't you think? *Cat got your tongue?* We've all used it at some point in our lives, I suppose. I know I did when I was a child. Oh, and I'm fifty-five going on seventy, in case you were wondering. I read somewhere the phrase was first found in publication around 1911, but I can tell you, my family dates back to the Middle Ages—as does that silly phrase," she stated with authority.

I turned toward her, crossed my arms and leaned back against the countertop, waiting for the water to boil.

"Oh, my, yes," She continued. "Such nonsense, back in those days. They used to believe that cats were drawn to the smell of milk on a baby's breath and would cuddle up and smother them. So much superstition placed at the paws of felines over the centuries." Her eyes meandered around the room, as unguided as her rambling chatter while she spoke.

"You're a very handsome young man, if you don't mind me saying."

The kettle whistled, drawing my attention. I loaded it, mugs and a selection of herbal teas on a tray and carried them to the table.

"Oh, please, Terry, sit next to me in the warm sun while we relax and talk. I do hope I'm not keeping you from anything important."

I smiled and said, "No, the cat doesn't have my tongue." She beamed at my non-sequitur. I couldn't help but smile back at her. She was oddly *comfortable*, as if I'd known her all my life. "And thank you for the compliment."

She dipped her eyes toward the table as she repeatedly dunked a peppermint teabag in the water. "It's okay to be reticent. I often have that effect on people when we first meet." She raised her eyes to mine then. "But this doesn't feel like the first time we've met, does it?"

I shook my head. "You said your family dates to the Middle Ages. What is your family history, then?"

She blew gently on her tea before taking a sip, then replied with a twinkle in her eye. "Well, my parents were Gypsies, of Romany descent. We immigrated to America when I was still an infant."

I must have looked at her skeptically, because she chuckled as she admonished softly, "Terry, not all Gypsies are tramps and thieves." She was quite pleased with herself when I laughed aloud.

I chose chamomile tea, and added a teaspoon of raw honey. "And I suppose Nancy is a widely used and cherished name among the Romany Gypsies," I teased.

"Ah, that. No. My given name is Nanevra C'Doe, which is a minor modification of my birth name. My parents changed it to help me *fit in*, or so they said. I suspect there were more traditional reasons for the change." She shrugged and sipped her tea.

"It was my own choice to go by Nancy, you know, N-A-N from my first name and C from my last," she spelled, then brightened. "Did you know through its various derivatives over the centuries, Nancy means 'grace,' or 'full of grace?' Describes me perfectly, wouldn't you agree, dear?" she coaxed.

"Well, yes, NanC. I've only known you a very short time and already I can't think you're full of *anything* but grace," I said. It was her turn to laugh aloud, one wrinkled hand demurely covering her mouth. I refilled her mug with hot water and we sat in silence while she dipped her teabag again.

Her focus turned inward for a moment, then she squinted at me over the rim of her mug. "It's so sad about your friend. The one who passed a few months ago. And disturbing, I might add, that it was under such violent circumstances. When one gets to be his age—and mine soon—one begins to think the end of life will be due to illness or old age; certainly not by intentional violence. How are you and your partner coping?"

This tiny human being was as full of surprises as she was grace. I refilled my own mug while pretending not to be caught off guard by her question.

"You know, NanC, you have a way of putting people at ease, and I think that leads one to believe we've been friends for a very long time. But I'm sure we've never met. Please tell me how you know about my friend's death, and about my partner."

She turned her head toward the window then, and closed her eyes while the midafternoon sunlight bathed her face in warmth. When she turned toward me again, her eyes held a worrisome look.

"I'm not sure I should confess the truth of that. Not so early in our *lifelong* friendship," she said with a tight-lipped smile. "But at the risk of ridicule or skepticism, I'll share with you my little secret."

She glanced over my shoulder and nodded toward a door on the liquor cabinet. "Perhaps the tale will come more readily if I had something to fortify my tea, dear. Cognac?" I raised an eyebrow, but didn't speak while I retrieved a bottle of Martell Cordon Bleu and two snifters from the liquor cabinet. I set the stemware on the table, poured an appropriate amount of cognac for each of us, and returned to my seat.

NanC raised her glass toward me in a toast; I followed suit, wondering where this was heading.

"May your phuro's spirit abide in happier times," she said softly, and clinked her glass to mine. We sipped.

"Phuro?" I asked.

"Ah. Sorry. It means a wise elder whom you love and respect. The toast is one my parents used after the passing of non-Gypsy friends," she explained, "so it's somewhat nontraditional." Evidently my question sparked another meandering train of thought, because she shot off into a somewhat shallow introduction to Gypsy beliefs and traditions.

When her cognac ran dry, so did her tongue. She looked at me with eyes that glistened more than when she began. She twirled the snifter by the short stem between her fingertips, which I took as a signal for a refill. She nodded her thanks as I poured.

"I suppose after all that, you think I'm somewhat eccentric, eh?" I was relieved to see she was sipping from her second glass more slowly.

I smiled and waved away her comment. "Nah, you're fine. However, after such a rapid-fire delivery of the various Gypsy terms and traditions, I will be able to tell Ren that our first interested homebuyer had a vowel movement in our breakfast nook."

Her eyes crinkled with amusement as she laughed aloud once

more. "Oh, dear, you *are* a delight. It isn't lost on me, though, that you mentioned your partner as a polite reminder for me to explain how I knew about him, and your phuro." She paused long enough to have another sip of cognac before shrugging her shoulders and stating flatly, "It's quite simple. I'm clairvoyant."

I could only stare at her in silence. I'd never met anyone who claimed paranormal abilities, but I didn't necessarily disbelieve they existed. I had no reason to think she was dishonest; deluded, perhaps, but not dishonest.

After several moments of silence, NanC spoke softly. "It's okay to be skeptical. I've dealt with it for fifty-plus years and it doesn't hurt my feelings. I can't tell you how I know things; I just know them. They come to me at the oddest times, both good things and, let's say, unpleasant, things. It's as if the ability exists outside my spirit and merely *informs* me."

I opened the cognac and poured myself another portion, but she waved her hand when I moved to do the same for her. We sipped from our glasses.

"I'm not exactly skeptical. It's just that I've never met a clairvoyant and I'm unsure what to say or believe," I told her, holding her gaze with mine. "Give me some time to adjust to the idea."

She sat back in her chair and folded her hands in her lap, turning her face toward the sunlight again. "By all means, young man. No hurry. However, I do want to leave in the next hour or so before it starts to rain."

I raised an eyebrow and smiled. "You sense that it's going to rain?" I asked.

"Oh heavens, no, Terry. I saw the weather forecast on the noon news before coming over," she replied, and we laughed aloud.

I took the kettle back to the stove to heat the water once more, then poured for us. She chose chamomile this time, but without the honey I liked in mine.

"Six months or so ago, when I decided to move to Oklahoma City, I awoke one morning with the vague knowledge that the perfect house would be waiting for me, but under less than ideal circumstances. I visualized what it would look like, where it was located and the wonderful people who currently owned it.

"I knew something terrible would happen that would affect the owners' decision to sell, but not when it would happen or when the house would go on the market. I simply bided my time, knowing I would be *informed* at the appropriate moment."

She paused to sip her tea, so I interjected. "Why did you decide to move to Oklahoma City?"

"Ah, yes. I visited close friends here not long ago, and they convinced me I should move. I've lived alone all my adult life, and only have a few acquaintances in Arizona. Being clairvoyant is off-putting to some people. So, I didn't have a good reason *not* to come. At least I have friends here, and that's not such a bad thing at my age—to have friends nearby."

"I assume your parents have passed." She nodded. "No siblings?"

"Unfortunately, no. My only sister, Doe, died in childbirth. My parents gave up on having more kids after that."

"That's understandable," I agreed. "Her name was Doe? As in Doe C'Doe?" I grinned. We both chuckled.

"Well, my parents were ignorant of the humor in the name at the time, and her name was seldom mentioned as I grew up, given the circumstances."

I nodded, encouraging her to continue. "Sorry to interrupt. You were saying?"

"Yes, well, I put my house in Prescott Valley on the market, said goodbye to the altitude and dry air and headed this way. I'm currently staying at the Lakeview Plaza Hotel on Northwest Expressway. I knew it would be relatively close to my future home, so I wanted to get to know the area.

"It didn't take me long to find the neighborhood I'd envisioned, and even less time to find this house. I've driven past it every day for the past two weeks, waiting for it to go on the market. When I saw the For-Sale sign in the yard this morning, I called the realtor immediately." She paused at the amused look on my face. "What?" she asked.

"The realtor's name is Brandi. When she called to tell me you were coming by, she was puzzled how you knew the house was for sale so quickly after we signed the contract, because she hadn't entered the information in the system yet. In fact, she was completely baffled," I explained. "I was beginning to think your clairvoyance had *informed* you."

"My, my, no," she laughed. "My gift comes of its own accord; I can rarely *will* it to manifest. No, I'm at the mercy of mundane methods most of the time, but I can see how you would think that. Did she not recall putting the sign in the yard and realize a passerby might notice it?"

I shrugged. "I don't know. She didn't mention it."

"Then you'll have an amusing story to tell Ren," she said with a smile. "And yes, my talent informed me of your partner, although nothing so specific as his name. All I get is that you're a happily married couple dealing with the death of a very close friend. And I know that the circumstances, as foul as they apparently were, resulted in a financial windfall for you. Would you care to tell me what happened?" She leaned forward in anticipation.

Surprised by the request, I replied quietly. "Ah, not right now. Perhaps later, after you've met Ren."

"Certainly. I didn't mean to pry." She patted her palms firmly on her knees, leaned forward, then said, "Well, shall we have a stroll about this wonderful home that is soon to be mine?" she asked with warmth in her eyes.

I stood and offered her a hand, then led her toward the den, her hand taking my arm at the elbow. Half an hour later, we stood where we'd started, at the back door to the kitchen. NanC suggested I call Brandi and ask her to prepare the contract.

"I certainly will," I said. "Thank you for your full-price offer. How long will it take to arrange the financing, if you don't mind my asking? We haven't found our new house yet, and may need some time for that, and to arrange the sale."

She donned her red scarf and light jacket before turning to me. "It'll be a cash sale, but I'm in no hurry to move in. I have a feeling everything will work out. I still have to return to Prescott Valley to complete the sale of my home there and arrange to transport my belongings."

With that, she gave my hand another squeeze, smiled at me and let herself out the door. Without looking back, she raised a hand and waved at me. "Bye-eee."

I called Brandi to fill her in on the details. She made a comment about feeling guilty for taking a commission on the sale, considering the only thing she'd done up to then was put a sign in the yard. Which reminded me to ask her to take it down right away.

Outside, thunderclouds roiled overhead and it started to rain.

I looked forward to sharing today's events with Ren, and even more to introducing him to NanC.

~

Oklahoma County Jail

Oklahoma City, Oklahoma

"What happened to this fucker?" The captain wondered aloud as he looked over the shoulder of a young Detention Officer.

"Not sure, except that he died," the DO said snidely, before looking at the man who'd asked. That's when he noticed the man's rank on his uniform, and although he didn't recognize him, he snapped to a more formal demeanor in the captain's presence.

The captain grunted his disapproval. "Great. Now we'll have to deal with another damn investigation—and the press, no doubt. Don't let anyone touch the bars or go inside until the crime scene guys are finished collecting evidence."

"Yes, sir. Who is this guy, anyways? Why'd anyone want to kill him?"

"Remember a few months back when that retired FBI guy was murdered in the northwest part of town?" The captain shrugged and tilted his head toward the jail cell. "That's the guy who done it. Don't know why he was killed and don't much care. That investigation's gone cold anyway."

The DO nodded in agreement. "Then good riddance, I'd say."

"True dat," replied the captain as he strolled toward the elevator.

~

M

I listened to the brief report on the phone.

"Well done."

That's one less loose end to deal with later.

~

Ren

Oklahoma City

It was quiet in the office. Too quiet. I locked up and called Terry as I slid onto the driver's seat and shut the car door.

"Hey, I'm on the way home," I said, when Terry answered the phone.

"Great! I think I have some good news for you, but I want to wait until you're here to tell you about it."

"Okay, hon." An incoming call interrupted me; I looked at the phone. "Hey, Russ is calling me. I'll see you in a few minutes." I switched over to take Russ' call.

"Admiral Russ. What's up? Everything okay with the *Adelaide II*?" I asked, using the nickname old Jacko gave him.

"She's fine, but we have a few developments. We finalized the refit except a few minor touch-ups. You'll need to get Evans to send the final payment to Jacko." I could hear the urgency in his voice and knew something was wrong.

"Tell me what's going on."

"I rounded up the new crew. You know that shake-down cruise we planned? Looks like it's going to be longer than I originally thought. We're on the way to Hawaii; just left Port Adelaide."

"And?"

I listened in silence while he told me about Warren's strange behavior and sudden departure.

"And if that wasn't odd enough, I also received an email, *from you*, telling me to check out a link. I'll forward it to you, but the link leads to a video showing Warren at the Adelaide airport boarding a flight to Sydney. I don't have any proof, but I'm pretty sure he's headed to Hawaii. Even if he isn't, we have to get the *Adelaide* to the US west coast anyway, so we're on the way."

"How long will it take you to get to Hawaii?"

"Weeks, I'm afraid. Even at maximum speed and fair weather, four to five weeks."

"Hell, Warren could be anywhere by then. I don't have any way to track him right now. What did you mean when you said you received an email from me?" I was puzzled.

"It looked like a genuine email from you, which is why I opened it immediately. Glen managed to trace it to an IP address at a hotel in Key West, and I know you weren't there. The kicker is, at the end of the video was a short, typed message signed by *M*. Just the initial. You know who that's gotta be."

I sighed.

"Yes. What was the message?"

"*Make no mention of Warren's absence to the authorities if you want him to live. See you in Hawaii. I'll be in touch.*"

"Fuck."

"Exactly," Russ agreed.

31

CHAPTER 3

❧

*R*en   As I approached the driveway I noticed a car parked along the curb in front of the house. The porch light was on, which probably meant Terry was waiting for me to arrive. Whoever was here must have arrived in the ten-minute interval it took for me to drive home from the office, or Terry would have mentioned it.

I parked the car, strode around to the back stairs and let myself inside. I heard Terry excuse himself to meet me. A moment later, he stepped into the kitchen, a frown darkening his usually sunny features.

"What's up?" I asked quietly as I leaned in for a quick kiss. His hands rested comfortably on my waist. *Not* our usual hello. His eyes closed briefly while we kissed before he responded.

"There's a guy here from the FBI," he said softly. "He wants to talk to us about Beau's death. Says he was a friend of Beau's."

I followed Terry back to the den. A stocky man in his late-forties or early-fifties rose from his seat as we approached. His smile was genuine, but guarded.

"Hi, I'm Ren," I began.

"Yes, of course, Ren Gifford. I've heard much about you over the years," he said as he shook my hand warmly. "Beau spoke very highly of you, always. He thought of you as a son. I was just telling Terry how sorry I am that I couldn't make it to the funeral. I was unfortunately occupied with urgent matters elsewhere," he said apologetically.

"And you are?" I prompted.

"Yes, sorry. I'm Aaron Jeffries. I worked with Beau when I first hired on at the FBI, for the last eight years before he retired. I hoped he might have mentioned me to you."

"He made a few references to his partner, but never went into detail. He was a man of extreme discretion, as you are probably aware," I commented as I gestured for him to return to his seat.

"Yes, yes, most certainly. In fact, just the other day a close friend in the CIA said the same thing, in almost those exact words." He smiled at Terry and me as he settled into the chair.

"I was just about to brew some tea. Would you care for some? Or coffee?" Terry asked.

"Hot tea would be nice, thank you," Jeffries replied. I nodded my head in agreement.

"I'll be back," Terry said as he turned toward the kitchen. I took the chair opposite Jeffries', while considering how to handle his sudden visit.

"So, Mr. Jeffries, what can I do for the FBI? Oh, and would you mind showing me your credentials?"

"Please, call me Aaron. I'm not here in an official capacity," he said while fishing his ID from a pocket and handing it to me. It was genuine. "After reading the report on Beau's death, and given that the case is going cold, I thought I would take some time off and see what I could discover, uh, off the record, as it were," he explained.

"By the way," he continued quietly, "did you know Beau's killer was found dead this morning in his cell at the county jail?"

"What?" He'd caught me off guard; a clever tactic by an experienced investigator. "No, I had no idea. How did he die?"

"Looks like homicide, but it's still too early to be certain. He wasn't on suicide watch and there was nothing in his cell he could harm himself with. There were no bullet or knife wounds, and no blunt force trauma. I have a feeling they'll find he was poisoned when the toxicology report comes back."

Terry returned then with a tray, carrying a teapot, three mugs and sugar.

"Did you hear that?" I asked Terry.

"Mmm-hmm," he hummed as he set the tray on the table between us and poured.

"And you're here to ask where we were at the time of his death, I assume?" Terry asked.

Jeffries shook his head emphatically. "No. As I told Ren, I'm not here in an official capacity. I don't give a damn how he died or who killed him. There was no doubt as to the man's guilt; the video evidence was ironclad. If someone else hadn't killed him, I was planning to do it myself." He stared at us pointedly as he paused to sip from his mug.

"I have no doubt there is more to Beau's murder than what I read in the report. Someone with significant resources is behind his death, and I'm here for however long it takes to find the bastard and put him behind bars."

Terry and I exchanged a worried, sidelong glance as we digested this abrupt and disturbing turn in the conversation.

~

Warren

Waikiki Beach, Hawaii

I hadn't slept much on the long flight from Sydney, and I was exhausted. I paced the aisles of the plane until the flight attendants told me it was time to return to my seat.

In spite of my lack of sleep, I went to the storage locker the moment I cleared Customs, as instructed. Inside was a leather satchel; sturdy but weathered. Without opening it, I headed for the Hilton, checked in and went to my room overlooking Waikiki Beach.

I sat heavily on the bed, dropping my backpack and the satchel on the floor at my feet, and fell back. As tired as I was, I couldn't sleep, so after a few minutes I unpacked my toiletry kit and showered, letting the hot water run down my back until the muscles began to un-bunch and I thought I could face whatever awaited me in the satchel.

Returning to the bedroom, I pulled open the leather closure on the satchel and peered inside. Naturally, there was an envelope stuffed with cash and several prepaid Visa gift cards. There was also a cell phone with a note wrapped around it.

I know you've checked into the hotel. Turn on the phone and wait for a text message from me.

When the phone came on, a text came through immediately.

Your room is paid in advance. You'll be there four to six weeks, until the Adelaide II *arrives, depending on how long it takes them to cross the Pacific. You'll have one final task before you are released from my service.*

DO NOT contact anyone you know, especially Ren, Terry, Russ or Glen.

Do not leave the Waikiki area.

Do nothing to draw attention to yourself.

Failure to follow these instructions will result in terrible consequences. You know I can deliver on this threat.

You will receive additional instructions when I am ready to send them. —M

I sprawled across the bed, exhaustion finally overtaking me. The phone made a soft noise as it fell from my relaxed grip and thumped onto the carpeted floor. I closed my eyes, asleep in seconds.

~

M

I am very pleased with myself. Warren is settled at the hotel in Waikiki awaiting my instructions. Glen and his family, as he calls them, are *en route* to Hawaii. Ren and Terry will soon learn of the destiny I have planned for them.

I reclined in the comfortable leather office chair and closed my eyes. I longed to be at home where, so very faintly, as a seraph might strum a harp to beguile the devil, I occasionally heard the Great Stalacpipe Organ. It was so easy to relax there, as it would lull me, serenade me, seduce me into the comfort of guiltless sleep. Soon. Very soon.

~

Aaron
Oklahoma City, OK

I thought I would regret the words the moment they left my mouth, but I realized they were true. The idea of killing Beau's assailant had floated in the darker regions of my mind since I first read the file on his death. I almost felt cheated that someone beat me to it. The way Ren and Terry looked at each other only confirmed they knew more than they'd reported to the authorities.

"JC, Beau's killer, provided no help in the investigation and was bound to be executed eventually," I continued. "The only reason I can think of for killing him now would be for his secretive, top-level employer to ensure his ass was covered. As I said earlier, it would take someone with significant resources to accomplish this; Beau's death and that of his killer, especially while he was in jail."

Ren nodded, whether in agreement or as simple acknowledgement of my assessment, I didn't know. Our time together was too brief for me to read his signals, except in a general way.

"I apologize if my confession shocked you, but it was sincere. If someone hadn't already done it, I would've killed JC myself. Fortunately, I won't have to deal with that, now. Beau and I were very close. He was my mentor and my friend, and the thought of someone getting away with his murder is simply not acceptable."

"I wasn't particularly shocked, Aaron," Ren said. "The idea has crossed my mind, too." He looked at Terry, then, to gauge his reaction. Terry simply nodded, encouraging Ren to continue. "As much a part of my life as Beau was, though, I don't think I have the constitution for revenge killing. It might be satisfying in the moment, but it would be a hollow, immoral victory for me. That's a path I dare not tread."

"I understand," I said. "Usually, I would agree with you, but let me ask you this; are you satisfied knowing the real culprit behind Beau's death is still at large?" Both shook their heads.

"Neither am I. While I wouldn't ask you to *actually* kill someone, I do need your help. I think you know much more than you've admitted so far; things that could help me bring Beau's true killer to justice. And, in the end, that may bring the closure you need."

We sat in silence for a moment, then Terry said, "Would you excuse Ren and me for a few minutes? I'd like to talk with him privately."

"Certainly. Take all the time you need."

They rose together and left the room. I refilled my cup and sent a text to Jerry while I waited. *I think I'm onto something,* I tapped out. *I'll bring you up to date later.*

His reply was immediate. *Looking forward to hearing about it.*

~

Ren

Terry and I went upstairs, our footsteps heavy with the weight of new circumstances on our shoulders. We walked into the bedroom and sat side-by-side on the bed.

"What do you think?" I asked.

Terry sighed heavily.

"I think we should trust him."

"Are you kidding me?" I interrupted. He raised a hand to stop me.

"Hear me out." I fell silent. His eyes were clouded with concern.

"You've been in a dark daze since Beau died. I know it's been eating at you that you haven't made any progress finding M. You've tried to busy yourself with other things to keep your mind off it, but I know you, Ren. You won't rest until the rat bastard is out of business. It isn't just that he orchestrated Beau's death, it's about all the other lives he's ruined with his manipulation.

"Look what happened to Glen; an already fragile spirit, virtually destroyed emotionally. He's only now getting back to a semblance of normalcy. What?" he asked, seeing anger flash across my face.

"There's an update from Russ and the crew on the *Adelaide* I need to tell you about, but that can wait 'til later," I explained. He nodded, then continued.

"And that's just an example. M even killed his front man because you beat him at his own game. Blake was dedicated to M, for reasons known only to him, but he died anyway. M, or his scurvy crew, killed Glen's neighbor, Old Jim, and almost killed Dunkin. Now what? What's so funny?" He asked, irritated with my smirk.

"You said *scurvy crew*. That's cute," I said, laughing lightly. He smiled grimly in return, but his mood lightened somewhat.

"Listen, handsome, I know you're only thinking of me and you've been worried about me since Beau died. I understand. Truly, I do. But when I said *are you kidding* I didn't mean we shouldn't work with Aaron. I was just surprised that you bought in so quickly." Terry nodded, put his arm around my waist and rested his head on my shoulder. "I think we should trust him, too," I added.

Terry nuzzled against me, his voice muffled against my shirt collar. "I hoped you'd say that. You're a better judge of character than I am, but I've had nothing but good vibes from Aaron."

"And think of the resources he has at his disposal. With the information Glen gave us and what we can share, too, Aaron might be able to do what has stymied me from the beginning."

He squeezed my waist and looked at me, relief flooding his troubled eyes. I gave him a smooch on the tip of his nose.

"Okay, let's go downstairs and fill Aaron in on M and his *scurvy crew*," I said, and he chuckled softly.

"Wait. What's the update from Russ?" Terry wanted to know.

"I'll tell you later, but for now let me just say that M's meddling has returned." Terry fell silent as we descended the stairs.

I was already thinking ahead to how much I should confide in Mr. Aaron Jeffries. If it became necessary to reveal my involvement in some of the deaths associated with Beau's, I wanted to do it without implicating Terry in any way. Aaron might have been Beau's friend, but he was still FBI.

Not that I doubted the veracity of Aaron's desire to avenge Beau's death; I just felt there was more to it. It sounded like something I would say to entice someone into dropping his guard and reveal possibly incriminating information. Aaron is no fool. If I'd say something like that I'm sure he would, too.

I stopped on the middle landing and pulled out my phone.

"What are you doing?" Terry asked.

"Hang on," I said. "I need to send a quick update to Russ while I'm thinking about it." A minute later, we walked back into the den where Aaron had helped himself to bourbon.

Alex Martinez

Aboard the Adelaide II

Bass Strait, between Melbourne, Victoria and Tasmania

What a mad rush it was, leaving Port Adelaide. Russ was anxious to get under way. The crew, except for two stewardesses, were aboard. They'd join us when we stopped in Sydney.

Glen was introduced to the crew present, but refused to socialize with any of them, preferring to stay in his cabin or hidden in a secluded area up top. Dunkin was his constant companion. Glen had accepted his role as part-time deckhand and kitchen help with no comment or complaint.

The ship's bosun, JT, didn't have a problem with Glen; they appeared to get along well enough. JT trained Glen in some of the more complicated parts of the job; Glen was a quick study—when he was sober.

Mack and Russ spent a lot of time in the wheelhouse, but Russ let Mack run things while he spent his time plotting the route across the Pacific Ocean.

Russ, never one to remain in a foul mood for long, rebounded after Warren's exit and the message from the Malefactor. Glen hadn't mentioned the video or the Malefactor since that night, and handled it with what appeared to be grim acceptance.

JT's wife, Kat, appeared to be bored, with no guests to pamper.

Dale, the engineer, was content to stay below decks getting acquainted with his beloved engines.

Aside from Mack and the inner circle, the rest of the crew were unaware of our urgency to get to Hawaii. Russ preferred to keep it that way and instructed us not to talk about Warren, M or the recent past with anyone. We also avoided talking about it in Glen's presence, as it only fueled his paranoia and his desire to drink.

My crew radio squawked and I heard Russ say, "Alejandro, please meet me in our cabin in fifteen minutes."

"Aye-Aye, Admiral," I replied.

"Knock that shit off," came the terse response, but I knew he secretly liked the nickname Jacko gave him.

I arrived at our cabin before Russ, so I brushed my teeth and rinsed quickly. He didn't say why he wanted me to meet him, but I wasn't discounting the possibility of an afternoon quickie. When he opened the door, however, I knew he had other things on his mind.

"What's going on?" I asked. He took me in his arms for a quick hug, then motioned for me to sit on the bed while he went to his desk. "Did you hear any more from Ren?"

"Yeah. But look at this," he said, handing his phone to me. It was an email, from an anonymous address. Like the one he received a few days ago, purportedly from Ren, this one was brief.

Safe travels. −M

"He knows we're on the move. So, what? We know he's got eyes and ears everywhere," I said. Russ sighed and leaned back in his chair.

"That just came in, so I thought I'd show it to you. It's not the reason I wanted to talk to you privately, though." I nodded for him to continue.

"I received a text from Ren. Looks like we may have some major firepower lining up behind us to help with M. Ren, Terry and an FBI friend are flying to Sydney to meet us. My original plan was to collect the remaining crew, stock up and refuel before continuing. That's all changed, now," he explained.

"Ren wants to meet with Glen and us, and introduce us to their friend, so we're going to stay at least one night in Sydney Harbour. After we talk privately with Ren, we'll regroup."

"Are they sailing with us to Hawaii?" I asked, my hopes rising. I enjoyed their company, and I knew Glen would feel better seeing Ren and Terry again.

Russ shook his head. "No, they're just flying in for a couple of days to meet with us and see the results of *Adelaide*'s refit. They'll fly back to the States. Too much going on for them to be away the length of time it'll take us to get to Hawaii."

I was disappointed, but it made sense.

"Okay. What's the plan for now?"

"Mack already knows about the layover in Sydney. Dale, too, and he's going to use the time to get some spare parts. I've told them not to mention it to anyone else, and I'd rather you didn't say anything to Glen."

I nodded. "Okay. Do you want me to let Kat know so she can have guest cabins ready?"

"Nah. Let Mack take care of the details. I just wanted you to know so you're not blindsided by the change in plans."

I reached across the short distance between us and pinched the tickle spot above his kneecap playfully.

"That's so sweet of you. Why don't you come over here and get comfortable and let me show my appreciation for your thoughtfulness," I cajoled.

Russ pulled his crew radio off his belt and radioed Mack to switch to a private channel.

"Yes, sir?" Mack said.

"Alejandro and I will be in our cabin for a while. I don't want to be disturbed unless something urgent comes up."

"Understood. Mack out."

"Did he just say *make out*?" I teased.

"We'll get to that," he grinned.

Russ turned the volume down on his radio and pulled his shirttail out.

"No, let me do that," I said with a leer. He relaxed his arms. Once I had him out of his clothes, I positioned him on his stomach on the bed and started a full-body massage, concentrating on his shoulders and back. By the time I worked my way to his waistline, he was snoring softly.

I undressed, dimmed the lights and slid in bed beside him, pulling a light blanket across us. God knows he needed the rest. I'd finish where I left off when he awoke.

Resting a hand at the base of his spine, I closed my eyes.

Softly, almost a whisper, Russ said, "I love you, Alejandro," then began breathing slowly and deeply.

CHAPTER 4

Ren

"Why the somber look, boys?" Aaron asked when we entered the room.

"We have a lot to talk about. Unfortunately, we can't do it here. That old saying *the walls have ears* may have originated in this house," I replied.

"Ah, yes. I may know a guy who knows a guy who can help with that," he said, taking a sip from his drink.

I smiled and poured drinks for Terry and myself. "That would be very helpful, actually. Beau had a friend locally who helped us before, but I don't have his contact info. Beau called him Bill Murray, because he, ah."

Aaron nearly choked on his drink, he was laughing so hard. "I know exactly who you mean, and I will get in contact with him the moment I leave here. If you like, we can move this meeting to my hotel. They have a quiet lounge where we won't be disturbed."

I opened the contact app on my phone and handed it to him. "If you don't mind, just put everything in there," I suggested, and waited while he did so. When he handed the phone back, I sent him a text message with Terry's contact information so he'd have our numbers.

"Would it suit you to meet at your hotel in a couple of hours? I need to put some information together for you before we continue."

"Perfect. Message me when you're on the way and I'll meet you in the lounge."

He finished his drink in one swallow, then stood to shake hands again. We walked him to the door and saw him out.

When I closed the door behind him, Terry took me in his arms for the long embrace he normally greets me with, which had been denied us earlier due to Aaron's presence. The hug felt good and I savored the moment. Thoughts of a hot shower together crossed my mind, but we didn't have time. I had a lot to do before we saw Aaron again.

~

M

The phone jarred me awake with its incessant ringing and I looked around. When I realized I was safe, I answered the phone but didn't speak. I listened to the report until the caller fell silent, then ended the call. I felt vindicated and irritated at the same time. I hadn't expected this from Ren so soon.

~

Terry

While Ren worked in his home office assembling a portfolio to give to Aaron, I puttered in the kitchen, cleaning and putting away the teapot and mugs. After an hour or so, he found me in the den watching the evening news.

"Are you ready to go?" he asked. He sounded distracted.

"I'm ready when you are, hon."

"Do you mind driving?"

"Uh, no. I usually do when we go somewhere together, don't I?"

He nodded, but didn't say anything. I turned off the TV; we walked to the back door to pull the car keys off the hook.

"Where are we going?" I asked, as we backed out of the driveway.

"Hmm," he pulled his phone out of his pocket. "The Founders Hotel, on Northwest Expressway, between May and Portland."

That's when it hit me. NanC was staying at the Lakeview Plaza Hotel, less than a half-mile east of there. With the major distraction of Aaron's arrival and the discussion in the late afternoon, I'd forgotten to tell Ren about the purchase offer on the house.

"How would you feel about a quick trip to Sydney?" Ren asked casually, derailing my thoughts.

"Huh? When?"

"Soon. Like day after tomorrow, or maybe the next day."

"Sounds okay, I guess, but why on such short notice?"

"Let's wait until we're with Aaron for me to explain, because I'm going to ask him to come with us."

Ren spent the rest of the drive mostly in silence, texting and reviewing documents on his tablet. I didn't press him. I knew he was preoccupied in thought and wouldn't appreciate the interruption. He'd share his thoughts when he sorted them out. I reached over, squeezed his inner thigh, and kept my hand on his leg the rest of the drive.

Dusk overtook us as we made the short drive to the Founders Hotel and parked in the lot east of the building. Ren must have messaged Aaron, because he was waiting for us in the lobby as we entered the hotel.

"Hey, guys. Come with me, I have a table in a corner of the bar," Aaron said, turning toward the bar with a slight wave for us to follow.

It was dim in the quiet lounge, with very few customers. We settled around the table as Aaron signaled the bartender. Once drinks were delivered, Aaron indicated Ren should start.

Speaking softly, Ren began. "This all started last winter when I received a call from a man who said his name was Ray Hanson. He was known by other names, but we eventually started calling him the Malefactor, or just M. Hanson asked me to fly to Washington DC to meet with him, to discuss locating a contract employee who had gone underground."

Ren continued for the better part of an hour. Aaron took notes on a tablet from the outset, but rarely interrupted Ren with questions. Ren described how he located Glen, and in the process, what Hanson was making him do.

"That's when I decided I would rather help Glen escape than turn him over to Hanson. I feared for Glen's life. When you meet him, you'll see he's a sad, gentle, damaged spirit."

"Do you have any proof of Glen's activities, or that Hanson was threatening his life?" Aaron asked. Ren nodded and opened his tablet.

"Here are a few of Glen's journal entries where he documented what he was doing. Let me warn you, some of it is graphic and difficult to read. There are also copies of several anonymous emails from Hanson, which Glen was never able to trace."

Aaron positioned a pair of reading glasses atop his nose and began reading the documents on Ren's tablet.

"And you believe Glen, because of your own dealings with Hanson and his field team," Aaron commented. Ren nodded.

"Where is Glen now?"

"He's with our friends Russ and Alex on a yacht we purchased, cruising north from the Tasman Sea to Sydney."

Aaron's shoulders drooped disappointedly. "I was hoping to talk with him in person."

"And you will, if you agree to come with Terry and me to Sydney for a few days," Ren said. "At my expense, of course."

"As I told you earlier, I'm here for as long as it takes to bring this guy to justice. Let me amend that to *legal or otherwise*. Going to Sydney is not a problem. In fact, with my official FBI passport, I should be able to expedite our entry into the country. When do you want to leave?"

Ren looked at me as if asking permission. "Day after tomorrow?" I nodded, although I was considering not going so I could continue with the sale of the house and the search for the next one. I didn't really see the need for me to go with them.

"That shouldn't be a problem," Aaron repeated. "So, you never located Hanson again, even after his agents dogged you while you searched for Glen? And how does all this play into Beau's death?"

Ren sighed heavily, then signaled the bartender for another round of drinks. When they were delivered, he continued.

"I feel responsible for Beau's death," Ren confessed, "because I went to him to get information on Hanson. That was before I knew of the Malefactor's reach and resources."

"You say that like Hanson and the Malefactor are different people."

Surprisingly, Ren smiled. "Aaron, I'm trying to employ some of Beau's world-renowned discretion, here."

Aaron looked at both of us, then, and said, "Guys, we need to put all our cards on the table." He and I both saw the squint in Ren's eyes. "What can I do or say to make you trust me?"

~

Ren

I took a moment to reflect. I didn't understand my own reluctance to confide in Aaron, other than the worry that M would follow through on his threat to kill everyone I cared about should I ever go to the authorities. Terry was my main concern, of course. He was pulled into this against his will, like so many others.

There was also the threat from M to release the video of me shooting Hanson to deal with. If our home was indeed bugged again, then M already knew I'd violated his instructions. As I was about to press forward, Aaron raised a finger and picked up his phone.

"Go ahead and take that, if you need to. I need some time to think."

"Hmm-mmm," he said. "It's not a call; it's a message." He put a Bluetooth headset in one ear and his eyes were locked to the phone's screen for several minutes. We sat in silence while Aaron watched his phone. Finally, he gave a brief grunt, removed the headset and put his phone face down in his lap. He motioned for me to continue.

I began again. "We were manipulated through a series of events into doing some terrible things. The Malefactor is truly evil in his intentions and actions. We have no way to find him, no way to evade him and no way to resist him. He has evidence of a crime I committed which he says he will release to the media and the authorities if I ever try to cross him.

"It's like a huge game to him. To me, it's a threat to the lives of everyone I care for. I have no doubt he had Beau killed because I asked him for help. And as you've already seen, he's ruined countless lives over the years. He has to be stopped." Aaron nodded for me to continue.

"I wish I could give you the details, because I have the sense that you are who you say you are and you were a friend of Beau's. But you are a federal agent, after all, and whether you condone my actions or not, you're obligated by your oath to uphold the law. I simply cannot take that chance."

The silence was thick between us while Aaron thought about my comments. Then he slid his phone across the table to me.

"Push play," he said, and sat back in his chair. Terry moved closer to me so he could see as well.

It only took a few seconds of video for me to recognize what I was seeing; the recording of me shooting Hanson to stop the electrocution of Terry and his brother. The color drained from my face and I felt light-headed. Terry took my hand in his and slid the phone back to Aaron.

"He sent that video directly to me. He evidently knows I am involved now, most likely due to your place being bugged." What he did next completely surprised me.

Putting his phone in speaker mode, he dialed a number. When his call was answered, Aaron said, "Hey, you're on speaker. I have Ren and Terry with me. An incriminating video of Ren committing a crime just came to my FBI email address. Would you do me a favor and destroy all copies of the video? Find out where it came from first, if you can, then wipe it from existence."

"Consider it done," and the line went dead. Aaron held up his phone so we could see it, and the video disappeared from the screen.

"Yes, my friend can even reach into someone's device and delete information." His phone vibrated; a text message this time. "He said all he could get on the video's origin is that it came from Honolulu, Hawaii. He's confident he destroyed it, however."

Terry squeezed my hand and I looked at him. His eyes were tender and encouraging, and he nodded his approval. I felt a knot of tension in my belly dissolve in relief. With a deep sigh, I continued sharing the events from six months ago with Aaron, until there was nothing left to tell.

My fate was now in the hands of Aaron Jeffries, a man who, until a few hours ago, I never knew existed.

∾

Aaron

By the time Ren was finished, I could tell he was exhausted. Terry added a comment occasionally, but mostly stayed quiet while Ren gave me all the details, including copies of emails from M; one showing a guy named Blake Thompson slumped over the steering wheel of a vehicle with a bullet wound to the temple. Ren repeated that Blake was the Malefactor's front man. All of this only confirmed in my mind that M also had JC killed in the Oklahoma County jail.

Ren was looking at me expectantly, as if he thought I would say something profound.

"Let me say this, guys. I believe you. I've seen enough and heard enough that I don't have any doubts about the Malefactor. Ren, I don't blame you for Beau's death. You had no way of knowing M's reach or level of depravity at the time you engaged Beau.

"I watched the video of you shooting Hanson from beginning to end, and I know you were only saving the lives of Terry and his brother. Hanson was a sick ticket in his own right." That's when I remembered Hanson was Terry's father. "No offense, Terry." Terry shrugged, as if to say *none taken.*

"While the video might damage you socially and professionally, I honestly believe that were you to go to trial for shooting Hanson, you would be completely exonerated. In fact, I don't think the District

Attorney would press charges. Fortunately, with the help of my buddy, we won't have to deal with that scenario."

"Your buddy certainly has skills," Terry observed.

"You have no idea," was all I was willing to say on that subject. "So, it looks like a trip to Sydney is in our future, and that M is trying to orchestrate a showdown in Hawaii. When do we leave?"

Ren glanced at his watch. It was almost ten o'clock. "Let me talk to Russ and find out exactly when they'll arrive in Sydney and we'll put together a plan. I'll call you tomorrow."

"That's an excellent idea. You look exhausted, and I know I'm tired. I'm sure you two have plenty to discuss. I'm glad I arrived when I did; it looks like M is about to transgress beyond his original promise to leave all of you alone. It will be a pleasure to throw a monkey wrench into the works while we track him down."

"Just remember what happened to Beau when he started helping us," Ren cautioned.

I nodded. "I'm aware."

We stood and shook hands; I walked with Ren and Terry toward the hotel exit.

"By the way," I threw out just as they were about to leave. "Bill Murray swept your home while you've been here. I apologize for not mentioning it before. He left the front door key on the counter by the sink. He said he found six listening devices but no cameras; he took them all out. He'll be happy to make regular sweeps until this business is over, but he'll need you to put the key back in the realtor lockbox on the front door."

The expression on Ren's face went from puzzlement to understanding to relief, then back to puzzlement.

"Realtor lockbox?"

"Uh, yeah. Sorry, that's on me. So much has happened since Aaron arrived, I never found time to tell you I arranged with Brandi to list the house today. There's more news in that area, but we can discuss it at home," Terry explained.

We said our good-byes and I headed for the elevator lobby. I imagine I sounded more positive than I felt. Someone with M's wealth and resources would be a formidable enemy. He could even have allies in the FBI or CIA. I'd have to share that information with Jerry, so he could protect himself, if need be.

$\sim$

M

I sent the video to his FBI friend, Jeffries, after my team identified him and phished his government email address. I had Dava driving by the house regularly, and she reported a rental car. That was all my team needed to trace the rental to Mr. Jeffries, and from there to his occupation and contact information. The fact that the video was traced to the seventh tier of servers and deleted from virtually everywhere confirmed my suspicions.

Ren had upped the ante in this game, whether he realized it or not. I'd already instructed my team to get all the information they could on his friend, but to take no action—for now. Jeffries had powerful connections, indeed, to be able to stop that video release. I wouldn't underestimate either of them again.

$\sim$

Terry

The moment we left the hotel, Ren fell into another thoughtful silence. As we pulled out of the back entrance to the hotel and drove east along 59th Street toward May Avenue, I asked, "So, do you want the details about the house listing now or after we get home?"

Ren stifled a yawn. "So, you got the house listed? That's good."

"More than that, handsome. I sold it."

"What? When?" he asked, incredulously.

"About four hours after signing the realtor contract with Brandi, today." I then gave him a short version of my meeting with NanC, leaving out the part about her supposed clairvoyant abilities.

"I mean, it's just a verbal commitment at this point, but I think it'll go through with no problem. Not long before you got home, NanC left and I called Brandi to prepare the sale contract. NanC is staying right here," I said, nodding toward the Lakeview Plaza Hotel as we passed the May Avenue entrance.

"Ren, she made a full-price offer, in cash. I really think I should stay here and work with Brandi to finalize the sale while you go to Sydney. I don't see how I can be of any help there, anyway."

"It'd be a comfort to have you close to me, for one thing. I worry about you being here by yourself. Besides, I know the guys would love to see you, especially Dunkin."

"But shouldn't someone be here in case Warren shows up?"

"Huh. I hadn't thought of that. Okay, let me talk to Aaron in the morning and see if he can arrange some protection for you. If nothing else, I'd like you to stay at a hotel while I'm gone," Ren insisted.

"That's overkill, don't you think?"

"Hon, in the space of three hours while we were at Aaron's hotel, Bill Murray swept our house and found six bugs. For all I know, this car may have them, too. No, I don't think it's overkill."

"Then there's NanC to consider," I added, when the thought occurred to me.

"What do you mean?"

"She'll be staying at the hotel until the sale is finished; who knows when that will be. I think she'll be okay, though. She's, ah, somewhat eccentric, but has a way of knowing things." Ren gave me a quizzical look. "I'll explain later. But we don't know how long the house has been bugged. No doubt M knows about her, too."

When we turned down our street, my eyes automatically scanned the cars parked along the curb for as far as I could see, but there were no suspicious vehicles. I knew Ren was doing the same.

"I just worry, though, that with M's penchant for harming people we encounter, I wouldn't want her to become his latest victim. I can't wait for you to meet her; she's quite the surprise," I added, with a smile in my voice.

Once inside, I found the front door key by the kitchen sink, as Aaron said I would, and put it back in the realtor lockbox, along with a note telling him to keep it until I asked for it back. Ren locked all the doors, pulled the shades and we went upstairs to the bedroom.

"I just sent a text message to Aaron," Ren said, pulling off his clothes, "Telling him you're staying here while we go to Sydney, just in case Warren shows up. Guess what?" I shrugged an *I don't know.*

"Warren's in Hawaii; Waikiki to be exact. After giving Aaron all the info tonight, he ran a search on Warren's cell phone and found it in Hawaii. Aaron's arranging to have him tailed. At least we know where he is and will know if he leaves. Aaron thinks it's a good idea for you to stay here, though. And he's arranging a protection detail; he says you'll never notice them." I was about to object but changed my mind as I undressed as well.

"Suddenly, I'm starting to feel a lot better about all this," I said.

"Same here," Ren agreed.

"Are you as tired as I am?" I asked, walking toward the shower. He smiled.

"Not too tired for *that.*"

As we slipped into bed forty-five minutes later and turned out the light, I said "Nichols Hills or Quail Creek?"

"Hmm?" Ren muttered sleepily.

"Where do you think we should look for our new place? Nichols Hills or Quail Creek?" I expanded.

"Whatever makes you happy, blondie," He said. I pinched him gently beneath his navel as I circled his waist with my arm.

~

Russ

Aboard the Adelaide II
200 Miles East of Batesmans Bay
Tasman Sea

Alejandro, Mack, Dale and I were having an impromptu meeting in the crew's galley.

"I want to fill you in on the plans for the next few days," I began. "Ren and an associate, Aaron, will arrive in Australia in three days.

They have some things to finish back in Oklahoma, then there's travel time. We're going to slow our pace and stay at sea rather than dock in Sydney and wait."

"Any particular reason, Captain? That'll expend more fuel than necessary," Dale commented.

"I want JT to have more time to work with Alejandro and Glen, training them on their deckhand duties. We're a man down in that department, after all."

"G'day," JT said cheerfully as he and Kat walked into the galley. "Wot's goin' on?"

Alejandro slid closer to me so they'd have a place to sit, and I filled them in on the latest update.

"Right, then," JT said. "Has anyone seen Glen? He didn't show up for duty this morning."

Alejandro and I glanced at each other, worried.

"I'll have a talk with him, " Alejandro said.

"No, mate, it's all good. He reports to me, so I'll handle it, if you don't mind," JT pressed. Alejandro frowned, but didn't respond.

"Good. Let me know if you have any problems," I said. JT nodded before leaving the galley.

He returned several minutes later.

"Captain, we've got a problem," JT said, his brow dipped inward toward the top of his nose.

"What is it?"

"Glen's bolted with Dunkin. The lifeboat's missing."

"Fuck." I flew into emergency mode.

"Mack, get to the wheelhouse and bring us around. Everybody else get your life vests and binoculars and take your stations. Dale, go see if the lifeboat's emergency beacon is working. If so, get to the bridge and help Mack get us to Glen."

I watched as everybody scrambled out of the galley.

CHAPTER 5

$\mathcal{A}$*lex*
Aboard the Adelaide II

Tasman Sea

Late morning was pleasant on deck, but I hardly noticed. Dale was unable to locate the lifeboat's beacon, so we were forced to retrace our route south along the coastline, back to where it was most likely that Glen abandoned ship during the middle of the night. Glen probably disabled the beacon so he couldn't be found.

Russ came along the railing to where I was standing, scanning the sea between us and the coastline.

"Anything?" he asked.

"No, dammit. What on Earth has gotten into him?"

"Hell if I know. But you know he's emotionally unstable where M is concerned, so I should have anticipated something like this. The Malefactor raises his ugly head again, and just when Glen was beginning to show progress. I figure he's trying to disappear in Australia so he can avoid M. I hope he knows what he's doing."

That's when it hit me.

" I don't think he's going ashore here," I said in a panic.

"Why not?"

"What was his destination when he first hired us?" I asked. Russ' eyes narrowed as he thought back to those first few days with Glen aboard.

"Oh, my God, Alejandro. He was going to Dunedin, New Zealand," Russ practically yelled.

"Would the lifeboat be able to make it that far?" I asked.

"Not even close. It would run out of fuel before he'd gone very far. Then he'd be subject to the ocean currents between here and New Zealand, and even with the best of luck, his journey would take several days, if he made it at all. And he'd run out of food and water— or booze—long before he got there."

Russ pulled his crew radio off his belt and hailed Mack. "Turn us out to sea, toward New Zealand, and step up the speed. I'll be there in a minute to explain." Turning to me, then, he said, "Please ask everyone to stay alert. I want to get as far as we can while we have daylight."

"Shouldn't you radio for help? Glen isn't a sailor, and he's probably drunk off his ass. It may be time to get someone better equipped to attempt a rescue," I said in a rush.

"Even Glen can survive twenty-four hours. If we haven't found him by morning, I'll call for help. I don't want to attract attention to us if I can possibly avoid it." I nodded and went to do as he asked while he joined Mack on the bridge.

~

M

"You may begin," I spoke into the phone.

~

Terry

When I awoke the next morning, with sunlight streaming through the east bedroom window, Ren was already up and about. I smelled coffee; that sparked a craving, so I got out of bed and slipped into some shorts. Ren was downstairs in the office sitting at his desk when I found him. Surprisingly, Connie was there, too.

"Hey, Connie," I greeted her with a smile. "How's the PI business treating you?"

"Mornin', Terry. Good, I guess." She was more serious than usual.

"Good morning, hon. Are you rested?" I asked, hugging Ren from behind and planting a kiss on his cheekbone. "How long have you been up?"

"A couple of hours. I don't know. Didn't check the time," he said distractedly. "Russ had a crisis and sent a text to alert me."

"What happened? Is the *Adelaide* okay?" I asked, concerned.

"She's fine. But get this. Glen got up in the middle of the night and highjacked a lifeboat, loaded it with food, water, whiskey and Dunkin, and decided to sail off to Dunedin, New Zealand."

"That's crazy. Did they find him? Is he okay?"

"Miraculously, yeah, they found him and he's okay; just dehydrated from drinking more whiskey than water. He's probably worse off from the tongue-lashing Russ gave him than from the actual experience. Russ figures the Malefactor's reappearance is what triggered this," Ren explained.

"You two need coffee refills?" I asked, grabbing their mugs.

"Sure, thanks," Ren answered for both.

When I returned, I asked, "So does this change your plans at all?" He sipped from his coffee before replying.

"Hmm-mmm. Russ said they were ahead of schedule anyway, so they reduced speed and will stay at sea rather than dock in Sydney Harbour. Aaron and I are leaving this afternoon. The best I could get on the flights on such short notice was a midnight departure from Los Angeles with a four-hour layover in Hawaii. Are you sure you'll be okay here by yourself?"

"Yeah, but it'll make me feel better knowing Aaron has arranged someone to keep an eye on me. And I feel better that he's traveling with you."

"Sorry, guys," Connie interrupted, "I've got to go." Closing her laptop, she stood suddenly and leaned across Ren's desk for a quick hug, then hugged me, too. As she pulled away from me, she slapped me playfully on the ass. "I don't know how Ren gets any work done with you parading around almost naked. Do you call that underwear, or a showcase?" she teased. "See ya, guys. Thanks for your help with the laptop, Ren." She let herself out the front door.

Ren continued as if she'd never been there. "It's the travel to and from Sydney that takes so long. We'll only be there one night to meet with them. Russ, Alex and Glen will meet with Aaron and me. Aaron has a lot of questions for them."

"I bet he does," I agreed. Changing the subject, I asked, "What's Connie doing here so early?"

"Oh, she needed some help with a software problem on her laptop. It was a simple fix."

"Are you bringing her into this fucked up mess?" I guess he heard the worry in my voice, because he stopped to look up at me.

"Not exactly. I haven't given her much information, but I did ask her to make herself available to you while I'm gone. And she'll be able to be here to let Bill Murray in, if you're out and about."

"I gave him a key."

"Yeah, I know, and I took it out of the lockbox. I left a note in it for him to contact you or Connie when he wanted to come in."

"Why? You don't trust him, even though he was recommended by Beau and Aaron?"

He hedged. "It's not that I don't trust him. It's just that I know M has bottomless pockets and a knack for luring people away from their personal convictions. I just don't want to take any chances."

The back doorbell rang.

"Did you invite Aaron over?" I asked, headed that way.

"Yeah, I did. He's checked out of the hotel and is going to leave some of his stuff here while we're gone. Get him some coffee, would you? And you should probably put some clothes on." I nodded.

Surprisingly, it wasn't Aaron at the back door, but NanC. My eyes must have widened in surprise, because she waved through the glass apologetically. I unlocked the door and invited her in.

"Hi-eee," she greeted.

"Good morning, NanC. I wasn't expecting you today," I began.

"Evidently, Mr. Terrance Franklin. Do you always answer the door in just a pair of undies? Rather skimpy ones at that?" she said reproachfully, but her eyes held their usual twinkle.

Embarrassed, I said, "Certainly not. If you'll excuse me, I'll get dressed. Please help yourself to coffee or tea." I headed up the back stairs to the bedroom.

By the time I returned, NanC had poured coffee for herself and wandered into the office. She and Ren were talking quietly. She'd pulled the guest chair around to the side of his desk so she could be closer to him while they spoke. For someone so tiny, she had a way of crowding one's personal space, and I could see a look of consternation on Ren's face.

"Terry, dear, would you help me please," she asked pleasantly. "I'm having difficulty convincing Ren to follow my advice on something that is extremely urgent." I could see the concern in her eyes.

"What's the advice?" I asked.

"I merely asked him to call his friend at the Founders Hotel and instruct him to leave the premises—*now.*"

The hair rose on the back of my neck.

"Ren. Do it. Now," I said, mirroring the urgency in NanC's voice.

Ren sighed in frustration, but made the call rather than argue with both of us.

"Okay, he's walking out the door now and should be here shortly. Are you happy, now?" he said, glaring at NanC. "And how did you know I had a friend at the Founders Hotel?"

I raised a finger to my lips, urging him to be patient. NanC slid back in her seat and took another sip from her coffee while she closed her eyes. After a moment, she visibly relaxed and said quietly, "Yes. Now I'm happy. As for the other, I'll let Terry explain."

I was about to do so when we felt what I thought was a mild earthquake, and the lights flickered.

"What the fuck?" Ren said, and turned on the TV.

"Oh, dear," NanC fretted. "This is going to be worse than I thought."

Ren scoured the TV stations, but nothing was reported—yet.

A few minutes later, the front doorbell rang and Ren and I hurried to answer. Ren opened the door for Aaron, who was standing there with a shocked look on his pallid face, just ending a phone call.

"Where's your luggage," Ren asked, motioning Aaron inside.

"It's in the car. I'm not leaving it here, and neither of you are staying here, either," he said breathlessly. "In fact, Terry, you should go pack; we need to leave immediately."

"But our flight isn't for hours yet," Ren started to protest.

"Not anymore it isn't. I've pulled some strings to get us out of Oklahoma and out of the country immediately."

"What time's our flight, then?" Ren pressed.

"In two hours," Aaron answered.

Aaron appeared to notice NanC for the first time and said, "Who's this?"

I made rapid introductions.

"Also, NanC is the one who insisted you leave the hotel immediately, but for whatever reason, I don't know," I offered lamely.

Aaron straightened his posture, took a deep breath and held out his hand to NanC. "If so, you have my profound thanks, ma'am," he said.

"It's true, Aaron," Ren added. "In fact, she insisted I call you. What's going on?"

"The top three floors of the Founders Hotel exploded," he said darkly. "If I hadn't left when I did, I would no doubt be buried in the rubble."

"Oh, dear," NanC said again, fear quavering in her voice. "Let's move to the kitchen, shall we?" She herded us like sheep quickly through the doorway with outstretched arms. "I could use a sip of cognac."

Then, the front windows of the house exploded inward in a powerful spray of bullets, fired from at least two automatic weapons. All of us ducked, dropping to the floor behind the heavy furniture. The gunfire felt like it lasted for minutes, but was more likely seconds. I heard a squeal as a vehicle sped from the scene.

After a moment of silence, we stood and dusted ourselves off.

"Is everyone all right?" Ren asked, looking around us at the damage.

"It appears so," Aaron replied for all of us.

NanC pulled a tissue from her sleeve and dabbed the corners of her eyes. "I hope you know, Terrance, this may have affected my decision to buy the house. And *not* in a good way," she announced sweetly. I couldn't help but laugh, but the others looked at me as if I were crazy.

We wandered through the house, checking the damage. It was extensive. The bullets were so powerful, some penetrated the walls in the living room and blasted through to the kitchen.

"Ren," I called. "We're gonna need a new refrigerator."

"Why?"

When he came into the kitchen, I pointed at the bullet hole in the top of the door and said, "This one's shot."

And that's how NanC and I wound up joining Ren and Aaron in the urgent escape from the events in Oklahoma.

~

M

I read Dava's text message; an update on her assignments. There were several fatalities in the hotel explosion, which I cared nothing about. As for the assault on Ren and Terry's home, it went flawlessly. She reported no evidence of any injuries, which is exactly what I knew would happen.

Go to Hawaii and await my instructions. Get someone to drive you to Dallas and fly from there. I don't want you appearing on video surveillance at the Oklahoma City airport, I sent.

Understood.

~

Alex

Aboard the Adelaide II

Thirty-Six Hours from Sydney Harbour

I can't describe the relief I felt when I spotted Glen's lifeboat in the distance, just as dusk settled over the ocean. I hailed Mack, who looked down at me from the bridge. I pointed in Glen's direction and watched as he held binoculars to his eyes. Moments later, we were at maximum speed, approaching Glen's location.

Glen was passed out drunk when we pulled alongside. Dunkin wagged his tail happily. I looked at Russ as he stood beside me while JT and Mack lifted Dunkin, then Glen onto the deck. Relief crossed his face first, followed by pity, then anger.

"Don't be too hard on him when he wakes, okay? He's safe and sound. I know you were just as worried about him as I was, but scolding him won't help. He was terrified and probably thought that if he were found with us, we'd all die with him."

His expression softened, but his tone was stern. "He put everyone aboard at risk, not just himself. I know he wasn't thinking; he was reacting in fear and paranoia. But I can't put the rest of the crew in these circumstances again."

"What do you intend to do, then?" I asked quietly.

Russ sighed heavily, shaking his head.

"I'm gonna be hard on him and I'll need your help. He has to get help or I'm done with him. We can't leave him alone, either. One of us has to stay nearby when he's not in his cabin. I'm not going to put the other crew members in that situation, so it'll be you and me. If he hasn't shown significant improvement by the time we reach Hawaii, I'm gonna leave him there, in the care of professionals. Is that understood?"

I nodded. I can't say I was surprised. Since Russ and Ren became co-owners of the *Adelaide II*, Russ and I had curbed our drinking significantly. We had much bigger responsibilities now. I think it's been very good for both of us.

"You're right," I agreed. "But it'll be hard for him. We've enabled his drinking for so long and I hate to say it, but it might be best if we found somewhere in Sydney to take him in. A quiet place where he can get the care he needs, including getting sober and undergoing therapy."

"No. I'll give him until we get to Hawaii. I'm not going to dump him in a foreign country."

"That's what he wanted anyway, remember? He was headed to Dunedin when we met him."

"I understand that, but no. He was headed there to drink himself into oblivion, as I recall his statement. When he wakes, I'm going to talk with him and make sure he understands what he faces. We care about him and he deserves the opportunity to work his way back, if he can. My only regret is that we didn't do this a long time ago."

"All right, then, Hawaii it is. I'll do everything I can to help."

"I know you will, li'l buddy. I know." He pulled me close to him, his arm across my shoulder and his hand resting on my chest. Our height difference made for some comfortable cuddle positions.

"Just out of curiosity, what made you suggest leaving him in Sydney?" Russ asked.

"He needs trained professionals who can help him emotionally. Some of the detox process requires medication, and the whole thing needs constant monitoring."

"Do you think a shrink is gonna believe his story about being manipulated into doing horrible things by an invisible, omniscient Malefactor?"

"I hadn't thought of that," I admitted.

"Let's talk about it with Ren when we get to Sydney. He may have another suggestion."

"And will Glen's wishes play into the decision at all?" I added.

"He's a grown man, Alejandro, not an indentured servant or a prisoner. If he chooses to leave of his own accord, which I doubt he will, I won't stop him."

I nodded silently as we watched JT and Mack carry Glen to his cabin, Dunkin following watchfully behind. Both needed baths. I'd take care of Dunkin while Glen slept off the booze. Then the tough love would begin.

~

Aaron

Above the Pacific Ocean

En Route to Sydney, Australia, via Melbourne

Ren gave me all the electronic data Glen collected during his five-year employment for the Malefactor. Much of it was useless due to its age. Some of the more recent data, including what Ren collected, I felt would be very useful. The Malefactor might have blocked Glen's amateurish attempts to track him, but I doubted he had the resources of the US Government. I had full confidence Jerry could make use of the information.

I arranged to have Warren Millpond followed, but he stayed in his hotel room most of the time, probably awaiting instructions. My opinion was that Millpond was a bit player, caught up in M's manipulations against his will, but I couldn't rule out the possibility that he was a willing accomplice. This merited further discussion with Ren.

We were hustled out of Oklahoma City from Tinker Air Force Base on naval aviation flying to Houston, with no record of our names on the flight. From there, we switched to a nonstop international flight to Melbourne, with a connecting domestic flight to Sydney. I hoped these arrangements would prevent M from learning our exact itinerary, but wouldn't know until we arrived. According to Ren, the Malefactor had deep resources and I had no reason to doubt that.

~

Ren

Above the Pacific Ocean

En Route to Sydney, Australia, via Melbourne

My opinion of Aaron rose significantly, with his quick orchestration of our departure from Oklahoma. During my first dance with the Malefactor, I attempted to avoid Blake's detection by arriving at Wiley Post Airport instead of Will Rogers World Airport.

With Aaron's connections, we hitched a ride on a military transport out of Tinker Air Force Base. I didn't know how high in the FBI Aaron was, but he has a lot of friends.

During the flight from Oklahoma City to Houston, Terry told me the story of Nanevra C'Doe, or NanC, as she preferred to be addressed.

We'd found an unlikely ally in this tiny woman, and I agreed with Terry that it was imperative we keep her existence from the Malefactor. That's why we'd hurriedly scooped her belongings from the Lakeview Plaza and brought her with us. She didn't raise a single objection, and I suppose her gift of clairvoyance *informed* her, as Terry put it, that this was the best thing for her.

Despite witnessing her talent firsthand, I still didn't put full faith in her abilities. Out of respect for Terry's belief that she was genuine, I kept my opinion to myself. Unlike me, Terry's first instinct in such matters was acceptance rather than skepticism.

Terry said she couldn't will it to manifest by her own admission, but it did appear that she was trying to protect us by herding us out of the path of the bullets that virtually destroyed the front of our house.

Aaron thought the attempts on our lives were orchestrated by M, and that he was trying to take us by surprise. I disagreed with the latter part of his assessment. I agreed M was trying to kill Aaron, without a doubt. You don't blow off the top three floors of a hotel unless you're seriously pissed. But as deadly as the attack on our house appeared, it was carefully executed so as not to kill anyone inside.

The trajectory of the bullets ran from low outside to high inside, indicating to me that they were deliberately firing above our heads. M wasn't trying to kill us; he was merely forcing us to rush our next move. In that, he'd certainly succeeded. After discussing it with Aaron, he agreed with me.

Aaron also managed to get the investigation of the hotel explosion and the attack on the house brought under FBI jurisdiction, since he was the intended target at the hotel. That would keep the Oklahoma City Police Department at a safe distance, and Aaron felt confident he could manage the investigation to insulate Terry and me. He'd already steered the lead investigator toward a terrorist attack theory. The media was eating it up.

Aaron had packed new phones for Terry and me in his luggage, which he gave to us on the way to Houston. These, he said, were encrypted at Department of Defense standards and he wanted us to use them from then on. In fact, he asked Terry and me to relinquish our personal phones, which we did. Aaron assured us he'd return them when it was safe to stop using the replacements.

While we awaited our departure in Houston, I used the new phone to message Russ. He was skeptical, since I was communicating with a new telephone number.

How do I know this is you? He asked.

Ask some questions only I would know, I responded.

When we made the deal to be partners in getting the new yacht, where were we?

That's easy. We were on the bridge of the Adelaide, offshore of the Easter Islands.

What activity had we done shortly before we shook on the deal?

I thought for a moment. *We scattered Beau's ashes at sea.*

One last question. What color was your swimsuit?

I laughed. *Well, after we shook hands, you wrapped me in a big hug. Which was prickly, pardon the pun, because we were both naked. I would have to say my swimsuit was flesh-toned!*

LOL. OK Ren. I believe this is you. I've never been called prickly!

After the quiz, I gave him Terry's new phone number, and as an afterthought, Aaron's contact information, also. Then I told him we were bringing a female guest with us. He was curious, I'm sure, but didn't pursue it. We confirmed our rendezvous time and location in Sydney, then said goodbye.

∾

Terry

Above the Pacific Ocean

En Route to Sydney, Australia, via Melbourne

I hated these long flights, mainly because I couldn't get much physical activity, and I never slept well on airplanes.

I was slumped to the left, resting my head on Ren's shoulder. He was busy on his tablet. When I sat up, it drew his attention. His eyes were bloodshot and he looked exhausted.

"What time is it?"

"I don't know," he answered. "But we're still over the ocean, and the pilot announced a few minutes ago that we'll be landing in Melbourne in less than four hours."

"Have you slept at all?" He shook his head. "Give me that," I said, taking the tablet away from him and putting it in a seat pocket. "Come here. Lay your head in my lap," I instructed, putting a pillow there first. Reluctantly, he did so. I turned off the overhead lights for both our seats.

"I have work to do," he mumbled.

"It'll wait," I replied.

I ran my hands through his hair and across his forehead until I heard his breathing relax into a regular, slow pattern. Whenever he stirred, even slightly, I resumed the forehead massage until he relaxed again. He needed as much sleep as he could get before we arrived in Australia.

Our business-class seats were on a row together, and NanC was across the aisle from me. I looked in her direction; she was asleep. Aaron was seated left of Ren, also asleep. Good.

I worried about NanC. As spry and enchanting as she was, she'd gone through some heavy stress before we left Oklahoma, and she was fifty-five going on seventy, by her own admission. All this couldn't be healthy for her. Not that fifty-five is old, but people wear their age differently depending on their lifestyle and experiences.

Even though I'd slept some, I yawned and closed my eyes. Maybe I could get another hour's sleep before we arrived.

～

Russ

Aboard the Adelaide II, *Anchored Offshore*

Sydney Harbour

We were ahead of Ren and company by nearly a day, which was fine by me. Alex helped the chef order fresh food and other supplies needed for the next leg of our journey.

JT and Kat went ashore to meet JT's parents for lunch. Mack had shared the fact that JT was originally from Melbourne, and that he and Kat had met there several years before. Mack was busy checking the entire boat, with Dale in the engine room, doing whatever engineers do.

I called Glen to my cabin after he'd slept off the booze. He tried to sit next to me on the bed, but I made him sit in my office chair. I couldn't be stern if I was hugging him while I lectured.

"I'm really sorry. I know I fucked up. I just had too much to drink, and my anxiety and depression got the better of me. It won't happen again," Glen said contritely.

"You're not seriously going to tell me the devil made you do it, are you?" I asked, hotly. "That stunt could have killed you, Glen. And Dunkin. And you endangered the rest of us, too. I'm not gonna tolerate it."

"What does that mean, exactly? *You're not going to tolerate it?* You're kicking me off the boat?" he asked, incredulously.

"No. Not yet, anyway. For now, you're relieved of duty and confined to your cabin, except for meals and time on deck for fresh air or exercise, and then only when one of us—Alejandro or me—is with you."

He accepted my decisions without comment, but his eyes glazed over. "And, I'm going to strictly ration your alcohol," I added.

"Russ, you know drinking is the only way I can stop remembering. It dulls my senses and."

"Yeah, and it also makes you stupid," I said loudly, cutting him off. Then, in a quieter voice, I said, "Listen. I know you have your demons;

we all do. You've been doing a lot better the past two or three months, but you need professional help. You're a danger to yourself, Glen, and Alejandro and I care too much for you to let you go on like this."

He bowed his head slightly, refusing to make eye contact.

"You can stay aboard until we reach Hawaii. Then, you'll have two options. You can leave of your own accord, with the money you have left, and go wherever you choose. The other option is to do a thirty-day stint in rehab. Without rehab and counseling, you won't be allowed back aboard the *Adelaide*, except as a guest."

I paused a moment to let that sink in before asking, "Do you understand?"

His eyes filled with tears, but he nodded his head. I took a deep breath, relieved to be done with the conversation.

"Come on, let's get you back to your cabin. You should eat something and have a shower, though, before you go back to bed," I told him, then wrapped him in a quick hug when we reach the door to his cabin. "You know how much Alejandro and I love you. This is the only way I know how to help you, li'l buddy."

"All right. I'll do my best. I'm sorry," he answered, then stepped into his cabin and closed the door behind him.

When I returned to my cabin, I found Alejandro there waiting for me.

"How'd it go?"

"About as bad as it could've, I suppose. I'm going to tell the crew to inform us at any time, day or night, if they see Glen anywhere on board without one of us with him." Alejandro nodded, and I could see tears blurring his chocolate-brown eyes. I pulled him into a long embrace.

"We'll get him through this, Alejandro."

CHAPTER 6

Blake Thompson
Waikiki, Hawaii

After dispatching JC in Oklahoma City, I drove to Kansas City and waited three days before flying to Hawaii. I kept an eye on the news broadcasts, but the police had no idea who'd killed JC, although they reported he ingested poison with his food. The story was lost in the headlines of the hotel explosion the very next day.

It'd been a tricky deal, sneaking in the poison. The boss was pleased, and told me to meet Dava in Hawaii. We would keep track of Warren for the remainder of the current *project*.

He also told me I might be released from service soon. I knew he was frustrated with me after the events with Ren in Oklahoma City several months ago, and that's why he forged the photo of me dead from a gunshot wound to the head. He wanted to convince Ren I was gone so he wouldn't suspect I was still active.

It was disconcerting, thinking I might survive this. It'd been twelve years since Anne and I met and we were still in love. I'd almost given up on being with her, though. I seldom had time to spend with her, but she was always appreciative when I could. I've never met anyone like her. I wish I could have brought her with me to Hawaii.

The only time I ever lied to her was about my occupation. There's no way I wanted her to learn of my real activities, mostly illegal. I convinced her I was a United States diplomat and that I couldn't discuss my activities or travel itinerary. She was intrigued by the mystery, but appeared content to leave it at that.

I thrived on the hope I would one day be able to marry Anne, have kids and lead a normal life. Whatever that may be. But Anne was older than I by almost fifteen years and beyond her peak childbearing years. She didn't seem to mind, though, but it made me sad.

I know I'm a cold-blooded bastard. I've killed countless times, ruined the lives of dozens, if not hundreds, more. I've seduced many women—and men—during my employment to advance M's malevolent games. I'm good at it, although not particularly proud of it, like JC had been. If M hadn't forced me into it by threatening Anne's life, I would be a much happier man right now. I think M knew I was reaching my limit and for some reason he was going to let me go.

The irony of that possibility wasn't wasted on me. M was dangling the carrot in front of me as I'd done to so many others over the years. *Do this one last thing, and you'll be released.* The tactic had worked flawlessly so often I couldn't keep count. The victim would play along, only to be killed once they were no longer useful. Even the extremely talented, like JC, met their ends that way. Why did I think it would be different for me? *Because it simply must be.*

～

Warren

I learned not to go to Bacchus Waikiki, one of the few gay bars in the area, in the midafternoon. It was populated by mostly older, local men, and when I entered the room I felt like I was intruding on a private party. It was more comfortable on Friday and Saturday nights.

I liked Hulas better. It attracted more tourists, so I didn't feel out of place and I'd met several interesting guys there. At least I could find a decent hook-up occasionally, to satisfy my needs without entanglements.

Ty became a favorite from Hulas. Darkly handsome, close to my age, without attachments. He said he moved to Hawaii for the surfing; he didn't elaborate, but he didn't match my midwestern idea of what a surfer would look like. He was partial to vodka, which I plied him with liberally.

He was a great distraction from my current situation, and the only guy I invited to my hotel room–*twice*. He was trim with a buzzed haircut, cheerful eyes that telegraphed his smile frequently. In bed, he was a magician; a passionate lover wielding a weapon of *ass* destruction.

I knew he was only temporary, but he was the blissful distraction I needed until the next domino fell in the Malefactor's convoluted catastrophe in the making.

~

Ren

Aboard the Adelaide II

Sydney Harbour

Twilight, bejeweled by the Sydney skyline in the distance, sifted us with a quiet, misty rain. The temperature was cool but comfortable and the bay was calm. Our group sat under the awning on deck for dinner, which was superb. Manny was an excellent chef.

Russ and Alex sat at the head of the table, with Glen beside them. He was happy to see us, I could tell, but hadn't spoken much. He eyed his drink hungrily, and glanced at Russ occasionally, as if to time his sips so as not to be noticed. Russ noticed anyway, but didn't say anything.

Joining us at the table were Mack, JT and Dale; Kat and the new stewardesses were serving drinks and dinner as the courses were prepared.

Aaron and NanC sat next to Terry and me, content to listen as Russ updated us on the refit and the status of the *Adelaide II*. She was seaworthy and ready to sail. The crew understood the *Adelaide II* would be sailing to Hawaii, but without paying customers. This came as a pleasant surprise to Kat's stews, since they were both relatively new to the job and appreciated the time to get some training before their first official charter aboard the *Adelaide II*.

As dinner ended, Alex called for sparkling wine, and when everyone had a glass he asked us to stand, then raised his glass in a toast.

"Here's to the *Adelaide II*, her crew and the smoothest first voyage across the Pacific Ocean." The toast was echoed with *cheers* and *here, here* as everyone raised their glasses and sipped.

So quietly she was almost unheard, NanC said, "And in the memory of your beloved phuro, may his spirit dwell in happier times." I looked at Terry as we sipped again. He was looking at NanC with thanks swimming in his blue eyes. I had no idea what the phrase meant, but I could tell it was heartfelt and genuine. In context, I could only assume she was referring to Beau. My opinion of her softened in that moment.

After a brief silence, Russ said, "Ladies and gentlemen, I hate to put an end to this delightful evening. But I have some business to discuss with Ren in private. NanC and Aaron, your cabins have been prepared and Kat will be happy to show you to them. Your luggage has already been delivered."

"Captain," Mack said, "If you don't need me here, I'll go to the bridge for a while."

"Sure, Mack, that's fine. I'll update you later. I really just want Alejandro, Glen, Terry and Ren to remain."

"Wait, Russ. I'd like Aaron to stay, too," I interjected. Russ raised an eyebrow but he didn't object.

Kat asked, "Would you like me to stay behind and provide refreshments?"

Russ shook his head. "We'll be fine. Keep your radio on, though. If I need you I'll call you." Kat nodded, then instructed her two stews to clear the table.

Russ rose and headed toward the galley. While he was gone, Glen spoke for the first time without being asked a question.

"Ren, if you can find the time, I'd like to speak with you and Terry. Not right now, I mean. But before you leave."

"Certainly, Glen. Not a problem. It's good to see you, by the way. You gave us a scare for a minute," I said gently. Glen just nodded and bowed his head.

"Where's Dunkin?" I asked, trying to keep him engaged.

"Oh. Um, he doesn't like the rain. He's in my cabin. I'll bring him to you later, though. I know he wants to spend some time with you."

"That would be great, Glen. Would you like to stay with us for a visit then? That would be a good time for you to share what's on your mind. We can invite Russ and Alex, too, if you like."

"Sure. I mean, if that's what you want."

Russ returned carrying a tray with a carafe of hot coffee, mugs, cream and sugar and set it on the table.

We helped ourselves, except for Glen, who opted for sparkling water instead.

"Okay," I started. "Who'd like to begin?"

~

Aaron

"I would," I said quickly, glancing in Ren's direction. He held up a hand.

"Just a minute, Aaron. I'd like to tell everyone more about you, aside from the general introductions made when we arrived." I nodded for him to continue.

He explained to the group my background and relationship with Beau.

"I want you to know I have filled him in on everything we know about the Malefactor and *all* the events that have brought us together at this moment. Please consider him part of the family. Answer all his questions honestly, and do not hesitate to say anything in front of him. Do you understand?"

Everyone nodded, then looked at me with renewed interest.

"Well, that was unexpected. Thank you, Ren. I appreciate the honesty and the confidence you have in me."

Looking at each of the others in turn, I continued. "M, as you call the Malefactor, apparently bugged Ren and Terry's house again and overheard our conversation the first night I arrived in Oklahoma City.

"Two days later, he proceeded to blow up the hotel where I was staying, then fired upon Ren and Terry's house with automatic weapons. We're lucky to be alive. I think that may be due to NanC, but that story will have to wait."

"I was wondering why she was here," Russ commented.

"She's a prospective buyer of Ren and Terry's house, who happened to be present when the assault happened. We decided it was too dangerous to leave her there, given M's fondness for destroying anyone this group encounters. Once we're back in the States, I'll arrange for her to be safely hidden and protected until this business is over—if she wishes."

Russ and the others nodded in silence, sipping from their drinks occasionally.

"She's got a great sense of humor, though. The moment the gunfire stopped, she said the event had given her second thoughts about buying the house," Terry added, with a chuckle. "If you get the opportunity, sit and chat with her. She has a particular fondness for cognac, which may encourage her to talk about her past, like it did with me."

"And no, she doesn't know anything about M or our plans," Ren added. "Aaron developed a cover story about terrorists tracking him, who are responsible for the hotel explosion and the assault on the house. We don't want to involve her beyond that."

"I don't think Ren has had time to tell you this," I continued, "and I only mention it in the hopes that it will help me earn your trust. M sent me the video of the events in Beau's basement, forcing Ren to shoot either Terry or his brother, and how Ren resolved the situation. Ren and Terry were present when I watched it. Moments later, they saw the video disappear from every available network source, thanks to a friend.

"I'm committed to finding Beau's killer and, if need be, pull the trigger myself. He *will not* be allowed to continue destroying innocent lives. You have my word."

Shocked silence fell, leaving nothing but the sound of the rain in the background.

"Does anyone have any questions for Aaron? Don't be shy; we're all on the same team, here," Ren said. Surprisingly, Glen tipped his head back to get my attention.

"Go ahead, Glen," I encouraged.

"Mr. Jeffries, if you know about M then you know he's a ruthless killer. He gets his way by threatening the loved ones of the person he's trying to manipulate, and offers huge sums of money. Since he's aware of you now, your family and friends are in danger. I'm surprised you haven't received a threat from him with an ultimatum."

Ren's eyes widened.

"Thank you, Glen. Yes, I'm aware of his methods. I've already taken precautions for my family and friends," I answered.

Glen nodded. "Okay, just keep in mind, if he can't get to the people you care about, he'll target your property and wealth next."

Russ put his arm around Glen and Alex. At six-foot-seven, he had quite a wingspan.

"What do you need from us, Aaron?" Russ asked.

"Not much, actually," I said. "I've read all the journals Glen gave to Ren and reviewed communications from M to Glen and Ren. I have someone working on tracing those IP addresses and anonymous emails now."

"Won't do any good. They're overseas," Glen said, shaking his head sadly.

"Don't underestimate my friends. International tracing is their specialty," I answered with a smile.

"I'd like each of you to tell me exactly what happened from your personal viewpoint. As I said, I've read Glen's journals. Ren and Terry have already shared their experiences. I'd like to hear in your own words what happened. Don't leave out any details, please, even if it seems redundant or superfluous. Russ, would you go first?"

Russ sipped his coffee while he took a moment to consider where to begin. When he finished a few minutes later, I had the broad outline of his involvement, which never directly interacted with the Malefactor.

Alex's rendition was much the same as Russ', although he focused more on their concern for Glen and how they'd come to care for him so much. Glen raised his head, revealing tear-stained cheeks beneath the shadow of floppy, dishwater-blond bangs.

"Ren, I have some information to share that might be of interest, if that's okay with you?" I asked.

"Sure, go ahead."

I turned on my tablet to retrieve my notes and donned my reading glasses.

"Russ, I don't know if Ren told you, but we tracked Warren based on the location of his mobile phone. He's staying at a resort in Waikiki. He's been there since he left Australia." I looked at Russ over the rims of my glasses.

Nodding, he replied, "Yeah, I'm not surprised. I'd love for you to detain him so we can talk to him. I'd like to know exactly what's going through that brain-dead head of his."

"You know he's under M's control now," Ren said. "Whatever he's thinking or doing, I'm sure it's because M has threatened our lives if Warren doesn't comply with his demands. I'm not making excuses for him, but I don't want to condemn him, either. We need more facts."

Russ nodded, but held his tongue.

"We have him under surveillance, which is better than detaining him. I doubt he knows he's being followed, and whatever information we can gather from the surveillance will be more useful than anything he would tell us," I explained.

"So, what's he doing, then?" Terry asked.

"Not much, so far. Mostly hanging out at the hotel or gym, or picking up guys at the local gay bars," I reported.

Ren's eyebrows rose. "That's a surprise, since he's mostly chased women the past few years."

"What's interesting to me is that he's been seeing one guy more than any others, who happens to be an undercover agent working for us." That revelation certainly grabbed their attention.

"Yes, this agent is willing to do just about anything to accomplish his task. He's very good at his job, too, and spotted someone else following Warren; a woman. She probably works for M."

Ren nodded, "That's most likely Dava. She won't be working alone. Take care your agent doesn't get caught in the crossfire."

"We're careful, Ren. And our agent won't do anything to jeopardize our operation, or anything that he didn't want to do. Seducing Warren was his idea, in fact. Here are some surveillance photos, if you're interested," I said, turning the tablet around where they could see.

Ren shrugged, then asked, "What else have you got to share?"

Returning to my notes, I said, "Remember I told you that my friend was able to delete the video and trace its origin to an IP address in Hawaii? We hope to have its physical location soon. Glen, you might be interested in this. The server in Hawaii is one of at least seven tiers of encrypted proxy servers. There may be more."

Glen nodded, "Not surprised. I told you they're probably overseas. Hopeless."

"Not so, my friend. They're not impossible to trace; the process just takes time, especially considering that we must keep our activities hidden from M, our government and the governments of other nations."

"What's next?" Ren asked, suppressing a yawn.

"That's all I have at the moment."

～

Russ

The information provided by Aaron was meager, but I'm sure he was only giving us the highlights. That was fine with me. Ren raised a hand and gestured in my direction.

"Now we have to decide the next step in our plan. From my standpoint, I'm primarily concerned with getting the *Adelaide* safely to Hawaii. It seems that is the focal point for this sordid mess. However, it'll take several weeks for us to cross. I think," my radio squawked then, cutting me off.

"Captain, Captain, Mack."

"Go ahead," I responded.

"Are we expecting company, sir?"

"No, why?"

"There's a boat headed directly toward us from the harbor. No lights, no name visible and no response to hails on the radio. I think we've got trouble coming."

I thumbed the talk button. "I'll be right there," then addressed the others. "Alejandro, get everyone to their cabins and secure the deck, then stay with Glen in our cabin." Thumbing my radio again on the way to the bridge, I barked, "JT, JT, Captain. Get up here and pull the anchor."

"I heard Mack, Captain. I'm already on the way."

"Kat, Kat, Captain. I need you to help Manny secure the kitchen as quickly as possible," I said on the radio. "We might run into some rough water. Then both of you get to your cabins and stay put until I sound the all-clear."

"Understood," came the shaky reply. I didn't have time to explain.

Once on the bridge, I looked aft, watching JT's hand signals to Mack to retract and lock the anchor.

"Okay, we're set. I'm getting us out of here," Mack said. He handed me his binoculars and turned to the engine controls. In moments, we were moving forward and turning out to sea. "How'd you spot the boat without lights? It's raining and dark. I can barely see the railing outside the window."

"It's this little thing called radar. Maybe you've heard of it?"

"Smart ass," I shot back.

"What's the plan, Captain? Do you want me to call the harbor police?" Mack asked.

I shook my head. "Not yet. Let's see what they have in mind. But with no lights and the lack of visible identification, I don't think it's good."

"Agreed."

"Hold your speed down so we don't draw attention to ourselves, but get us beyond the harbor as quickly and safely as possible. Do we have departure clearance?"

"I took care of that last night, Cap. I arranged it for anytime from today through tomorrow, depending on the weather. We shouldn't have any problems."

"Good." I focused the binoculars aft, trained on the boat pursuing us. It was very difficult to see at night with the constant rain, but it was still gaining on us.

"Do we have any weapons on board, Cap?"

"Hmm-mmm. Never thought we'd need them." Then a thought occurred to me. I picked up the intercom phone and dialed Aaron's cabin.

"Yes?"

"This is Russ. Do you have any weapons? We don't, and I'm afraid we might need to protect ourselves."

"Yes. Where should I meet you?"

"Stay put. I'll have Alejandro come to you and bring you to the bridge."

I radioed instructions to Alejandro, then focused on the boat again. It was closer, but not gaining quite as fast.

"Mack, how long before we can safely go to top speed?"

"In about ten minutes, Cap, but that's cutting close. Fifteen would be better."

"Do it in five, then," I instructed.

Without hesitation, he replied, "Aye, Cap."

Alex and Aaron arrived, with Aaron out of breath from the quick trip to the bridge. He was also wearing thin rubber gloves.

"Alejandro, is everyone secure in their cabins?"

"Yes. I checked on NanC, which took a minute. She was shaky and scared with the current situation, but I calmed her down."

"What about Glen? Where is he?"

"He's in our cabin; doing okay. Dunkin's with him."

"Go keep him company, please."

Alejandro nodded and left.

"Captain, I'm moving us to top speed. Seas are calm despite the rain. Should be clear sailing for a while," Mack reported, an undercurrent of urgency in his voice. I nodded, then squawked the radio again.

"Dale, Dale, Captain."

"Go ahead, Captain."

"We're moving to top speed, and I don't know for how long. Will that present any problems?"

"No, Cap. All is well below decks," Dale replied.

"Looks like we're keeping our distance. Maintain speed, Mack."

"Aye."

"Okay, Aaron, show me what you've got," I said, turning toward him. He unzipped a padded nylon case, about one-by-two feet in size and pulled back the top half. I saw what looked like a partially disassembled rifle.

"This is an M4 assault rifle," he said with a grin. He matched the two largest pieces together and attached them with locking pins. "It has a selectable burst fire mode which fires three rounds per squeeze of the trigger." Fully assembled, he pulled the bolt back to test its action.

"I only have three magazines of thirty rounds each, but this should do nicely if we need to protect ourselves against that boat."

"Jeez," Mack said in awe. "How'd the hell did you get that through Customs?"

Aaron smiled. "Let's call it sovereign reciprocity."

"Well, we may soon see exactly how helpful that can be. The boat is accelerating and we can't outrun it," I reported.

Within half an hour, the boat was pacing us on the port side, about a hundred yards away.

"Mack," I started.

"Don't ask, Captain. This type of vessel isn't designed for evasive maneuvers. Too much rockin' and rollin' and we'll be in deep shit," Mack said.

The boat tacked toward us, not on a collision course, but getting close.

The rain had stopped sometime in the last few minutes, which was a blessing.

"Can we go dark?" I asked.

"Shit. I should have thought of that," Mack answered, then squawked his radio. "Dale, kill the lights on and above the main deck." A moment later, darkness surrounded us except for the eerie glow of the instrumentation on the bridge.

"I'm stepping out," Aaron said, loading the M4.

"Hang on, Aaron," Mack said hastily. "You need to go to the railing along the lowest deck. Less sway from our movement than up here," Mack explained.

"Ah, right."

"Don't fire unless we're fired upon first," I instructed. "But if you hear the horn, fire at will."

Aaron nodded and left the bridge.

Mack kept a hand on the wheel while peering into the darkness with his binoculars. "They're getting close."

"Hit 'em with the floodlights. Let's give Aaron some advantage," I ordered.

Two brilliant spotlights, one fore and one aft, lit up at once. Mack managed the controls until the beams flooded the pacing ship. I could clearly see men on deck with guns, and what looked like a bazooka or missile launcher aimed directly at us.

"Sound the horn," I shouted, but he'd seen as much as I and laid on the button. Aaron fired immediately, using the burst mode of the M4. The men on the other boat dove for cover as the bullets raked the side of their boat. I don't think they expected us to be armed.

Aaron ducked below the railing to reload. During those few seconds, the other boat fired, aiming at the spotlights that gave us the advantage. The aft light exploded in a shower of sparks. I could hear gunfire and see light flashes from their weapons as they returned fire.

Aaron fired again, but it only took one three-round burst. The third round was a tracer and I watched its bright red trail as it streaked across the water toward the boat.

He'd apparently hit the galley's propane tank with one of the rounds, and the heat of the tracer round ignited the propane spewing from it. Everyone on deck disappeared in a bright flash when it exploded. The resulting fire was growing quickly and we knew the fuel tanks would explode next.

Mack gently turned the yacht starboard to distance us from the burning boat, still at top speed. When it was evident we were no longer in danger of being harmed by a secondary explosion, Mack asked, "Cap, are we going back to look for survivors?" He looked at me with a squint of curiosity in his eyes. I had the feeling he was prepared to adjust his opinion of me based on my answer. I didn't care.

"Hell, no," I growled. "Reduce speed and continue toward our next port of call."

His eyes twinkled as he gave me a sideways glance. "Aye, Captain. Well done."

Aaron stepped back onto the bridge then. "I hope this doesn't result in an international incident. I have a few years left before I'm eligible to retire, and this could seriously jeopardize my annuity." When I turned toward him to see if he was serious, he gave me a smile and a wink. He was weaponless and naked.

I gestured toward him. "Want to explain that?" I asked.

He looked down at himself and snickered. "The gun, gloves, rounds and my clothes are now on their way to the bottom of the ocean. If we get boarded because of our proximity to the explosion, they won't find any weapons or gunshot residue on any of us."

"Why didn't you mention you had tracer rounds?" Ren asked.

"I, ah, sorta forgot I'd loaded those," he replied sheepishly. "It did the job, though."

He turned to me. "You'll need to repair or replace that flood light they shot out, and check for bullet damage on the port side of the yacht."

I raised a hand. "It'll be done before breakfast."

"Thank you, Aaron. As far as I'm concerned, you're in this up to your perky nipples now, just like the rest of us," Ren said, smiling, and pulled him into a hug. He stiffened in surprise for a moment, then slapped Ren's back in the awkward straight-guy-hug embrace.

I said goodnight to Aaron and picked up the intercom, set to PA. "All clear, everyone. Sorry for the drama. We'll continue to our next port of call from here. We'll meet at breakfast to decide our next move and keep you informed. That is all." When I was finished, I turned toward Mack. I'd felt his glances in my direction since the altercation ended.

"Talk to me, Mack. What's on your mind?"

"I think it's time you clued me in on what's really going on. I didn't sign up for this kind of detail. I'm not saying I plan to leave; not yet, anyways. But I think you owe me an honest explanation, at least. We've known each other a good while, and I've always been straight with you. It's time you did the same."

I nodded in agreement. "All right. Let's get a few miles behind us and give me some time to talk to Ren, but I think he'll agree you and the rest of the crew need to decide whether you want to continue with us."

"Let's keep it between us for now. If I stay, I'm pretty sure I can convince JT, Kat and Dale to stay without giving them much information, especially if we can authorize a financial incentive. I'm not so sure about Manny. Or Kat's stews, for that matter."

"Understood. I'll get back to you in a day or two."

CHAPTER 7

Ren
Aboard the Adelaide II
200 Miles East of
Port Macquarie, Australia

We sailed east to distance ourselves from Sydney, then turned north and paralleled the coastline toward Brisbane. I called a meeting with Terry, Russ, Alex, Aaron and NanC to discuss our options. When everyone was seated around the table on deck and Kat served refreshments, I started.

"Okay, here's the deal. Our next port of call is Brisbane. Terry and I are planning to disembark there and catch a flight to Hawaii. I don't know yet if we'll have to backtrack to Sydney for the international portion of the flight. Terry's going back to Oklahoma, but I plan to stay in Hawaii for a while; at least until the *Adelaide* arrives. What would you like to do?"

NanC spoke first. "What are our choices?"

"I'll arrange for you to fly to Hawaii, then to Oklahoma, if that's your wish, or you can stay aboard *Adelaide* and sail the rest of the way with Russ and the crew. Your decision."

"I think I'll go back to Oklahoma with Terrance. This excitement is too much for me, I'm afraid," she said, her voice quivering. I nodded.

"I'll return to Hawaii and stay with you, Ren, for the present," Aaron said. "We have work we can do there."

"Okay. Naturally, Russ, Alex and Glen will stay aboard the *Adelaide*," I said. "Russ, what about the crew? Who's staying and who's going?"

"Manny and the two stewardesses Kat hired want to fly to Los Angeles now," Russ reported. "Mack, JT and Kat have agreed to stay on indefinitely. Dale is with us until Hawaii and will decide then whether to remain part of the crew."

"Okay, I'll make the arrangements. We'll arrive at Brisbane in about two days, give or take. Make yourselves comfortable until then."

"We'll stay overnight to restock and refuel as needed, then depart at daylight," Russ added.

"Very well. Anyone have any questions?"

No one responded, so I dismissed them. Terry and I went to our cabin. We were there for only a moment when someone tapped at the door.

"Come in," I called, tiredly.

"Uh, hi, guys. Can Dunkin and I come in?" Glen asked.

"Absolutely. Sorry, man, with all the excitement last night I completely forgot that you'd asked to see us. How are you?" I motioned for him to have a seat on the sofa, which he did, casting a longing glance toward the minibar.

"Glen?" I said softly, pulling his attention back to me. "What's on your mind, bud?"

"Oh. I just wanted to apologize for taking the lifeboat. I guess I was afraid M would find me, and." He trailed off. "I want to go back to Oklahoma." I was used to his tendency to abruptly change the subject, but this certainly came as a surprise.

"Really?" Terry and I said in unison. We looked at each other, then back to Glen.

"What brought on that decision?"

"If nothing else, M has proven he can reach me wherever I am. I don't think running away to New Zealand will help. If he's gonna kill me, he's gonna kill me."

Terry sat on the floor so he could pet Dunkin. They were happy to see each other, and it made me smile.

"Besides," Glen continued softly, "I think I've become a burden to Russ and Alex. You know Russ wants me to go into rehab, right?" He looked up at me.

"Yeah, I'm aware. Does that bother you?" I asked.

He shrugged. "Hell, yes. It scares the shit out of me. Not the part about Russ wanting me to go, but you know how I am around strangers. And crowds. I hate crowds. Those rehab places are just too." Tears welled in his eyes. I handed him a box of tissues.

"They're going to leave me in a hospital somewhere and never come back. Russ said if I can't control my drinking, he won't let me stay on the *Adelaide*."

"Okay, here's the deal," I started quietly. "You know Russ and Alex love you very much. All they want is for you to get better. Your drinking will be the death of you, and they can't handle the idea of losing you. Have you thought of that? How much it pains them to see you slowing killing yourself?" He nodded while blowing his nose.

"They have no intention of abandoning you in a rehab center," I continued. "If you make a genuine effort and they see improvement, you know they'll welcome you back with open arms. In a way, they're only protecting themselves from further heartache." I stopped. I felt like I was just reinforcing his preconceived notions.

"But I can't be in a rehab facility like that. I'd be miserable, which would only make me want to drink more."

I sighed; exasperated. Terry looked at me sadly, with an expression that said *what do we do now?* I took a minute to think it over.

"I have an idea, guys. I agree, you should come back to Oklahoma with Terry and me, although I think you should stay on the *Adelaide* at least until you reach Hawaii. Wasn't that the deal with Russ? Then, when all this mess with M is done, you and Dunkin can come live with us." Terry was nodding his head in agreement. Glen turned bloodshot, hopeful eyes toward me.

87

"We'll still find a rehab center, though, a private one where you don't have to be around a crowd of people. If we can't find one, we'll hire a professional to come to our house for private sessions with you —and us—until you're back on track. That way Dunkin can stay, too." Now Glen was nodding, sniffling and wiping his nose.

"What should I tell Russ and Alex?" he asked.

"I'll explain the plan and that you'd rather be in Oklahoma where you have Terry, Dunkin and me to be with while you're going through rehab, rather than being in a facility in Hawaii while they're out sailing charter guests around the islands. Believe me, they'll understand. And they'll be relieved."

We fell silent while he thought it over, Dunkin nestled between his legs at the foot of the sofa. Terry rose to sit on the sofa beside Glen and rubbed his back affectionately.

Finally, Glen looked at me, then at Terry, and said, "Okay."

"Okay," I repeated, "that's settled," and stood to give Glen a hug. He rose into my embrace, but he was sapped of strength and merely stood there, his arms dangling by his sides.

Another knock at the door. I looked at Terry over Glen's shoulder and mouthed, *what now?* "Come in," I called.

Aaron opened the door and stepped in. "Oh, sorry guys, I didn't know you had company. I'll come back later."

"No, no, that's okay. I think Glen was finished, right Glen?" I said. He nodded and left without another word.

Aaron's eyes grew round for a moment, "A man of few words, our Glen."

"Ha," Terry chuckled. "You should have been here the last ten minutes."

"Oh? What's going on?"

"We'll fill you in later," I added. "Did you need something?" I was really hoping to have some quiet time with Terry, with no further interruptions.

Aaron raised his index finger to his lips in a shushing gesture, opened his tablet and let me read his screen, motioning for Terry to come closer and read along.

I have arranged for someone to sweep the boat for bugs when we get to Brisbane. I found this in my room this morning. He held up a small microphone with an electronic transmitter. *It's too small to transmit very far, so there must be a recording device or a boosting radio transmitter hidden on board.*

I unlocked my phone and typed. *OK. Thanks for the heads-up. Do you have any idea who placed them?*

No. It could have been Warren before he left, or any one of the refit or regular crew. And I'm not ruling out NanC.

I scoffed.

I know, he continued. *I doubt it, too, but no one is excluded until they're cleared.* I nodded and Aaron let himself out.

The cabin phone rang. Terry looked at me with arched eyebrows, then answered.

"Hello? Hi, NanC. What's up?" He listened quietly for a moment, then said, "Yeah, I'll meet you at the bar in a few minutes," and ended the call.

"She wants to talk about the house," he said, answering my unspoken question. "I can't believe she's still interested in buying it after what happened. I really think she's just scared and wants company. She said to invite you, too."

I waved a hand. "Nah, you go ahead. I really wanted some alone time with you, but we might as well install a revolving door on our cabin. Anyway, I'd rather stay in here and nap for a while. If you're still there when I wake up, I'll join you."

"I'll see you soon, then. I'm going to check on Glen before meeting her."

When he left, I dimmed the lights and spoke into my phone. "Hey Siri, set a timer for one hour," and laid on the bed.

≈

Terry

Aboard the Adelaide II

When I tapped on Glen's door, there was no answer, so I tried the knob; it was unlocked. Glen lay across the bed with his headphones on, listening to music. Dunkin was stretched out on the floor next to the bed.

"Oh, hey," he said, raising onto one elbow and pulling off his headphones. "What's going on? Did we miss something?"

"No, I just wanted to see how you're doing. I'm going to the bar to meet NanC for drinks, if you'd like to join us," I invited.

His eyes brightened for a moment, then dimmed again.

"No, I'd better not. Not without Russ' permission."

"Want me to ask him? You wouldn't have to have alcohol and we'd enjoy your company. I don't like the idea of you being in here alone."

He shook his head no, put his headphones back on and reclined on his bed again. "I'm not alone. Dunkin's here." I closed the door behind me and headed toward the bar.

When I arrived, NanC was already there, halfway through a cognac with a soda and lime chaser. Her expression lit up when I entered the room. Kat busied herself behind the bar as I headed for a chair beside NanC.

"Terrance, so nice to see you. Do I have you to myself, or will Ren be joining us?"

"Just me, I'm afraid. He may join us later, though. He's napping at the moment."

"Well, his loss is my gain," she said with a smile. I leaned over and gave her a quick peck on the cheek.

"What'll it be, Terry?" Kat asked.

"I'll have a Crown and soda, please, easy on the Crown."

She poured my drink, then excused herself to help Manny in the kitchen. "Holler if you need anything," she said over her shoulder.

"Thanks, Kat," I said, then turned my attention to NanC. "So, we haven't had much time to talk privately since all the excitement started. What's your mood, I wonder?"

"I'm distressed, Terry, to be honest. That's part of what I wanted to talk with you about. That business with the other boat firing on us had me scared out of my wits."

"You didn't have any indication it was coming? I mean, your gift didn't *inform* you?" I'd wondered about that. She'd been pretty good at warning us when something bad was about to happen.

"Not an inkling, Terry. I had no idea what was going on until it happened. As I've told you, it doesn't always step in to save the day. I simply don't know what triggers it." Her brow furrowed in thought as she sipped her cognac, which I noticed was nearly empty. I went behind the bar and poured another drink for her.

"Thank you, kind sir," she said formally. "What can you tell me about all this? It's quite unnerving to be drawn into such intrigue without a clue as to what's happening or why. What have I gotten myself into?" Her eyes were wide and watery as she waited for my reply.

"As much as I would like to, I can't give you any significant details without putting you in further danger. I'm glad you decided to return to Oklahoma with me, although I think the best thing you can do is hightail it back to Arizona as quickly as you can."

"Yes, I have considered that, but I still want to buy the house, despite recent events. Surely this will end soon and the danger will pass."

"I'm surprised you still want to buy the house," I admitted. "I'm glad you do, but I think you should leave Oklahoma City until all this is sorted out. There's no hurry in making the sale, is there?"

She shook her head. "I suppose not," she said with a sigh. "I still have to sell the place in Prescott Valley, and you and Ren need to find a new home, too. Perhaps I'll take your advice and disappear for a while. I have all my luggage with me and I can easily go elsewhere." After a long pause, she added rhetorically, "My, I certainly sound indecisive, don't I? By the way, who's taking care of the house repairs?"

"Ren's straight, Connie, now that the FBI has released the crime scene. It should be finished in a week and a half, or thereabouts," I informed her.

"His *straight?*" she asked, one eyebrow arched in curiosity.

"Oh, sorry. That's sort of an inside term. Have you ever heard the term *fag hag* to describe a straight woman who is best friends with a gay man?" She shook her head. "It's mostly used in a derogatory fashion, which Ren hates, so he uses the term *straight*, which is descriptive without being ugly."

"I see," NanC said softly. "You've never mentioned her before, so I was unaware."

I shrugged. "I've never thought to mention her. She hasn't had any reason to be around when you were, so it never came up," I explained. "She's such a wonderful friend, too."

"What does she do? For a living I mean," she asked.

"She's a private investigator. In fact, she's the reason Ren took up the occupation. He helped her a few times over the years and decided he liked it."

"That's interesting. I wondered what got him started," she replied, trailing off into silence again.

"That clairvoyance of yours evidently left a few gaps in your information," I teased, but she barely smiled.

After a quiet couple of minutes, I pressed. "What's on your mind, NanC? We've settled your travel concerns and the house sale. What else is occupying your thoughts to make you so subdued?"

She chuckled humorlessly and said, "You'll think me silly if I tell you," then she looked at me and took my hand in hers. "I'm worried about you and Ren. I've only known you a brief time, but I've become very attached, especially to you. I don't want anything bad to happen to either of you." Tears welled in her eyes. "Terry, dear, may I be your straight? If you don't already have one, that is," she said hopefully.

I withdrew my hand so I could pull her into an embrace. "Oh, sweet lady. Please don't worry about us. We'll figure out how to resolve this predicament. Ren is very good at what he does. And I would be honored for you to be my straight." When we parted, she pulled a tissue from her sleeve to dab her eyes. I heard a soft clatter as something fell to the floor and looked down.

"Oh, I'll get that," she said hurriedly, but I was already out of my seat and reaching for it.

"No, no, I'll get it." I raised it to eye level to get a closer look. It was a listening device identical to the one Aaron showed Ren and me earlier. She was flustered. "What's this?" I asked.

~

Ren

I was groggy from the nap, but rose anyway when the cabin phone rang.

"Ren," I answered.

"It's Terry. Could you come to the bar immediately? And bring Aaron with you, please," he said and ended the call before I could reply.

A couple of minutes later, Aaron and I stepped into the bar area where Terry and NanC were seated.

"What's up?" I asked. Terry raised his hand so Aaron and I could see the object in it. "Where'd that come from?"

Aaron took it from Terry's palm.

"NanC found it in her cabin earlier today," Terry explained. "It looks like the one Aaron showed us."

"Where did you find it, NanC?" Aaron asked, his tone polite, but guarded.

"It was under the lampshade on the desk lamp. I must have bumped it when I reached up to turn the light on, because it fell onto the desk. What is it?" She asked, puzzled.

Aaron pulled an identical device out of his pocket and held it up. "It's the same as this, which I also found in my cabin under a lampshade," he said, sighing in frustration. "It's a microphone, NanC, the kind someone uses when they want to listen to private conversations."

"My word," she said breathlessly. "Who would put such a thing in my cabin? And why, for God's sake?" Aaron raised a hand to stop the protest.

"Ren, can you get Russ, Mack, Alex and JT in here?"

Ren pulled the crew radio from his hip pocket and squawked it once. "Russ, Russ. Ren."

"Go ahead."

"Please meet us in the bar right away, and bring Mack, Alex and JT."

"Three minutes," came the quick reply.

We waited in silence until the crew arrived.

"Do we need Manny and Kat, too? Or Glen?" Russ asked.

Aaron shook his head. "Not yet. I was going to wait until we arrived in Brisbane, but it looks like circumstances warrant another update now." He handed the two listening devices to Russ and indicated he should pass them to the others to see.

"Those are microphones that were hidden on board. I found one in my cabin this morning, as did NanC. Both were under the shades of the desk lamps. I've arranged for a bug sweep when we arrive in Brisbane, but we should probably do our own search now."

Mack squinted at one of the devices and said, "These aren't powerful enough to broadcast very far. Either someone on board is listening, or there's a booster."

"My thoughts, exactly," Aaron interrupted. "I originally thought there might be a recording device, and there still may be, but whoever planted it would know that if we found it we would be able to get to its recordings and destroy them. No, I think there's a booster radio hidden somewhere on board."

"JT, you and Kat start a search of all guest and crew cabins, and public areas on the boat. Alex, get Dale and the two of you start searching the storage areas and engine room." Russ turned to NanC then, and said, "I'm sorry, but I'm going to ask you to stay in your cabin until the search is done." NanC only nodded, her eyes wide.

Mack raised his hand to get Russ' attention, who nodded for him to continue.

"I'll make sure Manny, Glen and the two stews stay in their cabins until we finish the search. I'll need to stay on the bridge, but will search there, also. That's the most likely place for a radio transmitter."

"Very good," Russ agreed. "Another thing," he added to get everyone's attention before going their separate ways. "Make a note of where you find any more devices."

"Terry, would you escort NanC to her cabin and help her search it as thoroughly as you can?" I asked. Terry nodded and guided NanC by the elbow toward her cabin.

~

Two hours later, Terry, Russ, Alex, Aaron and I met with Mack on the bridge.

"What have we got?" I asked.

"Twenty-seven devices, in all. There are probably more," Russ reported. I looked at Mack expectantly.

"Any luck finding a radio?"

He shook his head in exasperation. "Not a damn bit."

"Any thoughts or suggestions, then?" Aaron asked. No one spoke immediately, so he continued. "One scenario is that the refit crew took the radio with them when they left, leaving the mics. This smacks of an amateur operation, in my opinion. Based on where everyone reported finding these devices, they were all in obvious locations and not very well hidden."

"What if that is just a ploy to make us think it was done by amateurs? Maybe there are other, better hidden, devices, and we're still under surveillance?" Russ offered.

"What if it's one of the other crew members or NanC? They could easily have disposed of the radio while we weren't looking." Mack suggested.

Aaron shrugged. "Anything is possible. It's pointless to speculate now. We'll have to proceed as usual until a professional crew comes through to do a real sweep in Brisbane."

Russ looked at me. "What do you want to do?"

I ran my fingers through my hair and sighed loudly in frustration.

"Business as usual, I suppose. We just need to be careful what we say about M or our plans until we feel sure we're not being monitored. I'm not going to make anyone stay in their cabins. Without proof of guilt, it's callous to confine anyone."

Russ frowned at my comments and averted his eyes, probably thinking about the house arrest he'd placed on Glen. When his eyes returned to mine, I said, "I know what you're thinking, but that's a different problem. Let it be." He nodded. "I need to talk with you about Glen soon."

"Okay," Russ replied.

"Aaron, unless you think there's a reason to keep them, I'd like Russ to toss those mics overboard."

Aaron, shook his head. "They're of no use to us. Toss 'em."

~

Aaron

After everyone dispersed, I found a secluded area on deck toward the back of the boat and sat to message Jerry with the encrypted satellite phone he arranged for me to bring with me.

You awake?

Of course, came the immediate reply.

I never know, with this time difference halfway around the world. I've got much to share with you. Gonna need you to pull some strings for me, if you can.

I'll do my best, Aaron. Bring me up to date and we'll see what our options are.

I spent the next half-hour relaying everything that had happened since the boat attacked us just outside Sydney Harbour.

That bastard is messing with you in the middle of the Tasman Sea, Aaron. This ain't good.

Don't I know it.

Okay, my friend, here's what I suggest.

~

Blake Thompson

Waikiki, Hawaii

Dava and I had rooms at the same hotel as Warren, but in a different tower. We alternated shifts tailing him, but his routine was monotonous. He'd latched on to some poor guy at a gay bar. He should've known better. That's just another death to lay at his feet, once M was done with Warren. Which made me wonder exactly what M had planned for him.

I thought of Anne. I missed her mahogany-brown hair and brown eyes. I pulled my phone from my pocket and sent her a message.

I miss you, lady.

I miss you, too, she replied. *Where are you? Or can you not say?*

Can't say.

Okay. Any idea when I'll get to see you?

Nothing definite, but soon, I hope. It's been too long. You haven't replaced me, I hope.

Not my movie-star-handsome boyfriend! You're not getting rid of me that easily.

That brought a smile to my lips.

Talk to you soon. I love you, Anne.

I love you too, Blake. Can't wait to have you all to myself under the covers.

"True dat," I said to myself, softly.

∽

Aaron

A day and a half later, we reached a point where we would soon have to alter course for a more direct route to Brisbane. I called Ren and Terry's cabin, but there was no answer, so I went on deck. It was a fine, clear day, but the sea was somewhat choppy. I caught Ren in the stairway headed below decks.

"Sorry to stop you Ren, but could I speak with you privately for a moment?" I asked.

"Sure. Let's go to my cabin," he said, leading the way.

"Are you sure we're not being overheard in here?" I wondered aloud.

He shook his head.

I opened my tablet and began typing.

I need you to keep this quiet, and I need you to trust me. Can you do both? He nodded. *OK, I need you to tell Russ to keep us in international waters. We can continue north until we are parallel to Brisbane, but we need to stay far away. Use whatever excuse sounds plausible, but don't take us into Australian waters just yet.*

He mouthed the word, *Why?*

That's where the trust part comes in, Ren. You'll see soon enough. Make sure Russ doesn't tell anyone else; not even Mack, if he can avoid it.

Ren nodded his agreement, so I let myself out.

~

Russ

I was alone on the bridge. It was eerily quiet. The *Adelaide II* was maintaining position on a parallel with Brisbane, per Ren's instructions. I saw flashing lights off the port side and raised my binoculars to get a better look. A very large and fast naval ship was headed our way, floodlights full on, pointing right at us. I glanced at the time; zero-four-hundred.

I picked up the intercom phone and dialed Ren's room.

"You need to get to the bridge, *now*. Bring Aaron with you," I said quickly and hung up.

The frigate slowed as it approached, and a demand blared from a megaphone aimed at us.

"This is the Royal Australian Navy. Heave to and prepare to be boarded. Any attempt to flee will be met with appropriate force."

As it pulled alongside, it dwarfed the yacht in size. I hit the switch to turn on all exterior floodlights.

"JT, JT, Russ."

"Go ahead, Cap."

"We're being boarded. Get up here and help tie the lines."

"Aye, Cap, on the way."

Mack, Ren and Aaron rushed onto the bridge.

"What the fu?" Mack started. I put a hand on his shoulder.

"Maintain position, Mack. I'm going down to greet them. Aaron, I assume this is your doing. You and Ren should come with me," I instructed.

I ushered Ren and Aaron out the door ahead of me and followed them down to the deck. JT had secured the lines. Two Australian sailors stood by the railing of the naval frigate holding assault rifles at parade rest.

Just then, a team of six men in unidentifiable military-style black clothing boarded and walked toward us.

"Aaron Jeffries?" the lead man called, in an American accent.

"Here," Aaron responded, with a lazy salute.

"I'm supposed to say, *Jerry sent me*, whoever that is. I take it you need assistance with a bug infestation."

"Yes, sir, that's a fact. This is Captain Garrett," Aaron introduced us. The team leader removed his black stocking cap when I extended my hand, which he shook firmly. Much shorter than I, buzzed head and commanding eyes, he nodded, then released my hand.

"Sorry, sirs, I'm not at liberty to reveal my identify. Just call me Silvio—don't ask."

"No worries," Aaron said. "We certainly appreciate your help."

"We don't have much time. Assemble everyone on board on the aft deck, except the First Mate, who needs to stay on the bridge." Silvio motioned one of his team to go to the bridge. "Let him know one of my team will be joining him."

I notified Mack, then thumbed the radio to PA and ordered everyone on deck. A few minutes passed while crew and passengers assembled as instructed, looking baffled and scared.

Ren caught my eye and arched his eyebrows. I gave him a thumbs-up to let him know they were friendly.

While the boarding team searched the yacht, Silvio used an electronic wand to scan each person, but only the usual mobile phones, watches and jewelry were noted. However, sixteen more listening devices were found throughout the boat, with the help of their electronics detection gear, but no transmitter or recorder.

Silvio listened to his earpiece, concentrating on what was being said.

"Understood," Silvio said into a microphone on his shoulder. He then turned his radio to a different channel and spoke into the microphone again.

"Boarding team, withdraw. I repeat, boarding team, withdraw."

When the man who went to the bridge was back on deck, Silvio gave a salute to Aaron.

"We never boarded and we never saw you. The Royal Australian Navy has had no contact with this yacht. No official report will be filed. Is that understood?"

Aaron nodded and the boarding team departed.

JT and Alejandro released the tie lines. We stood on deck and watched the navy vessel gracefully depart. Mack shut off the floodlights and the quiet night resumed around us. Surreal.

Aaron called out to the perplexed group, "Okay everyone, the show's over. Go back to bed."

∽

Ren

Aboard the Adelaide II

Approaching Moreton Bay

Brisbane, Australia

The morning dawned brightly in our cabin. We had one full day to go before arriving in Brisbane, and I was determined to spend as much time as possible with Terry. I wasn't sure when we would see each other again, and the next few weeks would be dangerous for both of us.

I had to admit, the master stateroom aboard the *Adelaide II* was luxurious. I could become accustomed to this.

After the interaction with the boarding team a few hours earlier, I was very tired, yet very awake. Terry and I fell into bed, and I'd left instructions with Russ for us not to be disturbed. Terry was still asleep, lying on his stomach, completely buried under the blankets and huddled against me, one arm circled affectionately across my stomach.

I ran a hand under the blankets until I brushed his head, stroking his yellow-blond hair absently. His hand slid below my waistline, then, and tugged me gently. I heard a muffled laugh, then he said,

"Well, I see you're up early—as usual." His head popped up from under the covers revealing a sly grin on his face, his hand still working its magic.

"Mmmm," I sighed, and closed my eyes. "I'll give you thirty minutes to quit that, mister," I told him. "That feels really good, hon."

"Thirty minutes is all I get?" he teased.

"Oh, hell. I'm taking a vacation day. Take all the time you want," I told him as I twisted sideways so I could reach his lips with mine. He flipped his body toward me then so that we lay on our sides facing each other while we kissed deeply and slowly, our bodies touching from nipples to knees.

I could never keep my eyes closed when we kissed; I never wanted to forget his beautiful face or miss an opportunity to commit his gorgeous features to memory. In the early-morning light streaming through the window, his blue eyes were so brilliant they appeared to glow from within.

Our passion for each other fed upon itself. He ducked his head under the blanket, his tongue and lips adding to the sensations plied by his playful hands.

Suddenly, he threw off the blankets and ran his tongue upward from my stomach to my nipples.

"Oh, my God, Terry. Kiss me," I begged, and he buried his tongue in my mouth. Somehow, he slowed time until I couldn't separate this moment from any other time we made love.

He pulled his face away, breathing heavily, our eyes locked on each other. "My turn," he breathed. If there were anything I cherished more than his passion for me, it was my passion for him.

I stared at him with naked lust. He laid on his back with his eyes closed, his arms and legs spread wide while I rubbed, kissed, massaged —worshipped—his body. I tickled him and teased him mercilessly, until he wrapped his arms around me again and pulled me to him, both of us collapsing in laughter.

Time slowed again and we rekindled the passionate kisses until we knew we could hold back no longer, our spirits locked in communion through the windows of our souls.

~

Passionate lovemaking can be exhausting. Invigorating, but exhausting. When I opened my eyes again we were still lying in bed, but it was midafternoon. Terry was asleep once more, and I was afraid that if I moved, even to snuggle closer, I'd wake him.

He was on his side facing away from me, so I rolled up against him and spooned him gently. He didn't stir.

~

Terry

When I awoke in the early evening, Ren was practically attached to me, so tight was his spoon. *Spoonin' leads to forkin'* flew randomly through my mind and I couldn't suppress a chuckle.

I didn't want to wake him, but I needed to pee, so I attempted to slip out from under the blankets.

"Finally awake, eh?" he said with a huge yawn.

"Yeah. I'll be right back," I said as I padded to the bathroom. Before I could finish, he followed me into the bathroom and started the shower.

"Come on, let's shower and get something to eat. I'm starving," he demanded.

Fifteen minutes later, clean and refreshed, we made our entrance in the bar. Everyone was there except Mack, who was no doubt at his usual station on the bridge.

"Sooo," Russ drew out. "I guess you two have had a good romp." His smile was genuine, although he was teasing.

Ren completely ignored the comment, but said, "What time is it? What's to eat? I'm starved."

Kat rose and headed toward the galley. "I'll get some fruit and cookies. Manny is working on dinner, so don't go spoiling your appetites," she admonished. She returned with tropical punch, too, and set a tray on the table by Ren and me.

"Ren? Would now be a good time to talk to Russ and Alex? About that stuff we talked about before?" Glen asked quietly.

Ren looked around the room, then, and said, "Yeah, sure. Now's as good a time as any. Let's take our refreshments out to the sundeck," he suggested.

Once we were settled, Russ said, "So, what's this about?" Alex sat next to Russ, a worried frown perched on his boyish features. With a sigh, Ren explained the plan for Glen to return to Oklahoma to stay with us, once the *Adelaide II* was docked in Hawaii. Neither Russ nor Alex said anything; just nodded their heads in acknowledgement occasionally. However, neither looked happy.

"Glen, are you sure you want to do this?" Alex asked.

Glen nodded slowly. "Yeah, I'm sure. I need help, and Ren and Terry said they'd take me an' Dunkin in for as long as I needed. I want to come back to the *Adelaide* eventually, but you guys know I can't be around a crowd of strangers in a rehab clinic. Especially if you two are working and Ren and Terry are in Oklahoma. I don't have any other family or friends," he trailed off, lowering his head.

"Russ, you told me if I didn't get help, I couldn't come back, so this is all I know to do." He ended with a shrug.

Russ looked as if someone had punched him in the gut. Alex got up and went to Glen, rubbing his shoulders and hugging him from behind. Glen rose and turned toward the hall to his cabin, leaving us in a cold silence as we watched him walk away.

"Fuck," Russ said, slamming his fist on the table when Glen was out of sight. He looked defensively at the rest of us.

"Hey, I don't regret for a minute what I did. Glen put everyone aboard in danger with that stunt." His tone softened. "But I admit, I could have gone about it differently. I intended to talk about this with you two when you arrived in Sydney, but too much shit was going on."

"Don't be so hard on yourself, Russ," I spoke for the first time. "No one here blames you."

"No one except Glen, you mean," he said with an angry look aimed at me.

"Knock it off, Russ," Ren barked. "Don't snap at Terry because you feel bad. Listen, it's not the end of the world. Glen will get the help he needs and he'll have Terry and me for support until he can rejoin you and Alex on the *Adelaide*. Let's leave it at that, okay?"

Alex sat next to Russ again. When he put his arm around Russ' waist, it drained all the anger out of him.

"I apologize, Terry," Russ said. "Ren's right, I have no reason to vent my frustration at you."

"No worries. I know you've been under a lot of stress, and none of it is your doing. At the risk of pissing you off again, I'd like to remind you of something."

I paused for a moment and took a deep breath. "Glen has five years' experience seeing what M can do. He's carrying a lot of guilt inside, and his judgment is clouded. He's not very talkative, but his behavior speaks volumes. He loves you and Alex, and feels responsible for dragging you into this mess."

Russ nodded. Alex closed his eyes and rested his head on Russ' shoulder.

"One last thing, if you don't mind a little advice," I said. Russ looked at me skeptically. "Maybe you and Alex should disappear for a few hours and have a good romp of your own. It'll do wonders for your wellbeing."

JT stepped out and said, "Kat says to come inside; dinner's on the table."

We stood and walked toward the dining room, but Russ said, "Y'all go ahead. I'll join you in a minute."

As Kat set drinks on the table and served dinner, Russ returned with Glen in tow. He motioned for Glen to sit between him and Alex, and when he did, Alex gave him a hug.

"C'mon li'l buddy. Dish up. It's your favorite; kangaroo, popcorn and kiwi fruit casserole," Russ said, which provoked a chuckle from Glen and Alex.

CHAPTER 8

*R*en
Above the Pacific Ocean
En Route to Hawaii

I was proud of Terry. The way he handled Russ' flare-up the day before we left was classic. Terry is such a sunny spirit most of the time, people get the impression he's a pushover, when that is far, far from the truth.

Aaron was asleep beside me. Terry and NanC were across the aisle from us, also asleep. The two stewardesses took the first available flight out of Brisbane, via Sydney, to Los Angeles. Manny resigned upon our arrival in Brisbane and was on the plane with us to Hawaii, having decided it was too dangerous to remain aboard the yacht. I didn't blame him.

Russ, Alex and Glen were a worry for me. Would M leave them alone now that I'd departed? I hoped so. JT, Kat and Dale decided to stay until the *Adelaide II* arrived in Hawaii; perhaps longer. Mack was still an unknown to me. I think Russ worked something out with him, but I didn't delve into it.

I was tired, but restless, so I opened my tablet to review my notes.

Were we any closer to figuring out who the Malefactor is? Or how to combat him? Even halfway around the world, he manipulated us from the moment we set foot on the *Adelaide II*. I couldn't decide if it was a blessing or a curse that we'd had no further communication from him. Failing threats, he usually taunted us in some fashion. Either way, it made me nervous, as if I were waiting for the other shoe to drop.

Aaron was in constant communication with someone, but wouldn't elaborate when I asked if it was Jerry. Silvio, the leader of the boarding team, had said *Jerry sent me*. I hoped Aaron and whomever he was working with were making progress. His contact had some powerful connections to be able to pull off a clandestine operation with the help of a US operative team and the Royal Australian Navy.

I did better working directly against someone I could see, someone whose character I could evaluate and whose moves I could anticipate. This nebulous enemy whom I'd never met, with apparently limitless resources, was proving much more difficult.

Then it occurred to me that maybe M was someone I *could* see, I just hadn't realized it yet. I could rule out Terry, Russ, Alex and Glen without question. I wrote on my tablet a list of everyone I'd met since M resurfaced.

Warren still raised suspicion in my mind, because of his past complicity with the Malefactor. I drew a red flag next to his name. I didn't believe he had the intelligence to mount such a devious, broad assault, but he was certainly malleable in the wrong hands.

Maybe Jacko or the refit crew in Port Adelaide? They certainly had ample opportunity to hide those microphones. The same was true for Mack, Dale, JT, Kat and Manny. Question marks next to their names. And the two stewardesses who fled to Los Angeles; what were their names? Martha was one, I thought. 'M' for Martha, 'M' for Malefactor? I struck a line through her name. Bethany was the other one. I thought if one of them were M, she'd have stayed with the *Adelaide II* to Hawaii if she wanted to keep an inside track on us.

That left two people—Aaron and NanC. I underlined both of their names in bold red. They were the only two who were present almost from the beginning. Was it coincidence that Aaron appeared at our door, announcing he was an old FBI friend of Beau's and eager to catch his killer?

I had no real proof of his friendship with Beau. Maybe I'd been too eager for help to see past a ruse. Should I ask for proof of his friendship with Beau? Photos of them together, perhaps?

NanC was certainly a puzzle. She appeared the same day as Aaron, making a cash offer on the house and claiming to be clairvoyant. Her gift supposedly *informed* her of impending danger, as well as personal information about Terry and me, but had left much danger unreported and some rather large gaps in her knowledge of us.

Was it possible they were working together? Was Aaron the Malefactor, forcing NanC to do his bidding against her will, as was his *modus operandi*?

Aaron certainly brought significant resources to bear, and if he were the Malefactor, he could easily finance NanC's offer to buy our house. But why go to that trouble?

I prided myself on being a good judge of character, which the Malefactor knew after I outmaneuvered Blake. Was M deliberately distancing himself to throw off my perceptions and deductions? He'd certainly succeeded in herding us—which is exactly how it felt, *herding*—toward whatever destiny he had in mind. Anytime we started to relax, he lit another fire under us. I was tired of not being in control.

But neither Aaron nor NanC felt right for the part, so to speak, despite the coincidences and hazy backgrounds. I resolved to talk about all this with Terry when I could get some time alone with him. Not only did I trust his judgment, but it helped me to bounce ideas off him.

~

"Ren. Ren, wake up." Aaron nudged my shoulder.

"What?" I grumped.

"We'll be landing in about two hours. I thought you might want to freshen up and get something to eat."

I slid upright in my seat and stretched my legs. "Yeah, I probably should," I said with a yawn, rubbing my face with both hands.

"Oh," he said with a hint of amusement in his voice, "you might want to close and lock your tablet before you fall asleep next time."

I glared at him as he handed the tablet to me.

"Good observations, I have to admit," he said genially.

"Uh, ever heard of a thing called privacy?" I said harshly, but he only chuckled. Yes, I was cranky from being awakened after too little sleep, but rightfully annoyed that he read my notes without permission.

"Not in this situation, I'm afraid. I need all the information I can get. You're a keen observer, so I took advantage."

"So, you're not pissed you're on my list of likely suspects?" I asked, with a sideways glance.

"Not in the least. I'd be disappointed if you hadn't considered me," he asserted, "but I think you're wasting your time considering NanC."

"Said the man who, a few days ago, said no one was innocent until proven so," I shot back. He chuckled again and we dropped the subject.

Glancing across the aisle, I noticed Terry was gone and NanC was smiling at me.

"He's in the bathroom," she whispered loudly, pointing repeatedly toward the back of the plane. I nodded.

The flight attendants were coming through to take breakfast orders. Good. I was famished.

∼

Russ

Aboard the Adelaide II

En Route to Hawaii

JT and Kat appeared content to let sleeping dogs lie, as it were. Mack was another story. His mood darkened and his demeanor toward me turned hyper-professional since the boarding incident, and he spent most his time alone on the bridge. I've known Mack a long time and I trust him. I decided it was time to give him the background that precipitated these events.

"Mack, Mack. Russ," I said over the radio.

"Go ahead, Captain."

"When will we reach New Caledonia?"

"About a day at present speed, sir."

Damn. I didn't want to wait that long before talking with him. I decided to break my own rule.

Picking up the nearest intercom phone, I dialed our cabin. Glen answered.

"Captain's cabin."

"Put Alejandro on, please."

After a moment of shuffling, Alejandro said, "Hey, what's up?"

"I need you to go by the bar and grab a bottle of Crown and four cups; chasers if you want. Meet me on the bridge, and bring Glen."

"Uh, are you sure that's a good idea?" Alejandro wondered aloud.

"We need to bring Mack in on what's happening to us, and I don't want to wait until we get to Noumea," I explained, then replaced the handset and headed toward the bridge. I was only a moment ahead of Alejandro and Glen.

Mack sat hunched over the computer console and looked surprised when we entered.

"Hey, Captain," he started, then saw the whiskey in Alejandro's hand. "Huh," he grunted. "I take it we're about to have *the* conversation." I nodded. "It's about time, Russ. I was worried," he said, sounding relieved.

Alejandro set the glasses on the small shelf next to the window and poured shots for all of us. Glen hesitated, but the hunger for it overcame his reservations.

"Okay, here's the deal," I said after we knocked them back. "There's a lot you don't know about what's going on. It's going to take some time to fill you in, and I don't want to wait until the next port of call. Are you ready for a very bizarre story?" I poured another round of shots and raised my glass. Alejandro did likewise, although Glen declined. We waited to see what Mack would do.

After a moment, he raised his also, and said, "Cheers."

Over the next hour, I shared everything I could think of with Mack. Glen and Alejandro broke in with additional information or comments to clarify what I said. To give Mack credit, he didn't interrupt, only nodded occasionally. He also went easy on the whiskey, considering he was still piloting a moving vessel.

When I finished, Mack had a thoughtful glint in his eyes, as if he were considering whether to say something. He nodded to himself once and finished the remaining splash of whiskey in his cup before raising his tablet and thumbing it on. He scrolled through several emails before handing me the tablet.

"I received this email about a half-hour after the Australian frigate pulled away the other morning," he said.

I read it silently first, then aloud to Alejandro and Glen.

"Matthew McDonald, Ren has compromised the safety of you and everyone aboard the Adelaide II *by involving you in his efforts to destroy me. He has done so without your knowledge or consent. He has also involved the authorities, which is a gross violation of the conditions I set forth after our prior engagement.*

"I am willing to not only spare your life, but to compensate you significantly if you agree to work for me. If you do not agree, your life is forfeit, along with the lives of everyone you cherish. I'll be in touch. –M"

I looked at each of them in turn after finishing. Glen went pale, his eyes reduced to frightened squints. Alejandro looked concerned for Mack. However, Mack was staring directly at me. When we made eye contact, he spoke.

"You and I have been friends for a long time. You know I don't accept ultimatums from anyone for any reason, but especially when they threaten me or anyone I care for. I don't doubt anything you three have told me today, and this cryptic email only confirms what you've said."

I sighed in relief. "Thank you, Mack."

"I do wish you had clued me in sooner, though. However, I'm not about to let this Barnacle Bill scare me into God knows what—or bribe me, for that matter. I do have some expectations, though," he added.

"Go ahead."

"First, I want to know whatever you know when you know it. My life may hang in the balance and I can't make good decisions without useful and current information." I nodded. "Second, I want you to know that I will do whatever I can to help, for however long it takes. Finally, I'm gonna need a pay raise. Signing on as First Mate did not include hazard pay." He grinned when he finished.

"Consider it done," I agreed, responding to his grin with my own.

Alejandro moved to pour another round of shots. Mack said, "Go easy on mine, mate. I'm still on duty."

Mack raised his glass once more. "Here's to smooth seas, good friends and dead enemies," he toasted.

"Here, here," we echoed.

As Alejandro gathered the cups and Crown and led Glen off the bridge, Mack put a hand on my shoulder to get my attention. I turned to see genuine concern in his eyes.

"There's one more thing you need to consider." I nodded. "Since I received that anonymous email, you can be certain the others remaining aboard did, too. They may not respond the same way I did."

"Yeah," I said with a sigh. "But I don't plan to confide anything to the others, and I'd prefer you didn't, either. Help me keep an eye on them?" He nodded. "You know them better than I do, since you've worked with them before. I trust your judgment."

"Okay. I'd also like to ask that we meet at least once a day to discuss what's going on," he said.

"Deal," I responded and left the bridge. Mack's warning made me wonder if M got to JT and Kat. That might explain their decision to stay aboard.

~

M

Ah, the thrill of the chase. Ren and his group are divided again, and the yacht's crew is in chaos. The FBI grunt and his helpers have failed in their efforts to track me. Dava would soon see to Nanevra C'Doe. I could sense victory within reach.

~

Aaron

Honolulu, Hawaii

We checked into the Hyatt in Waikiki. I reminded Ren that Warren was staying at the Hilton and we didn't want to take the chance that we might run into him.

Terry spent one night, then continued his journey to Oklahoma. NanC also spent a night, but evidently decided to return to her home in Prescott Valley, Arizona, until repairs on Ren and Terry's house were completed. I offered to provide a protection detail for her, but she declined.

I was glad we were splitting up. Even with M's resources, I felt it'd be a lot harder for him to target us if we were separated. I hoped the *Adelaide II* and crew would make the journey across the Pacific without interference, since Ren wasn't on board.

Ren was still concerned for Terry's safety, considering what happened the first time he tangled with M. I assured him a protection detail would be assigned, and he relaxed somewhat.

The room phone rang. "Hello?"

"Hey, it's me," Ren said. "You ready to eat? I need to update you on something."

"Sure. I'll meet you in the lobby in fifteen," I responded and ended the call.

Ren was waiting when I stepped off the elevator and suggested we eat at the sushi bar across the street from the hotel. Being late afternoon, it wasn't crowded, so we had a relatively secluded table to ourselves. Not a fan of sushi, I ordered soup and salad instead. Ren requested two sushi rolls and a ginger salad.

Once the server delivered our drinks, I prompted, "Okay, what's new?"

Ren opened his tablet. "Russ sent me a screen shot of this. It's an email from the Malefactor to Mack, threatening his life if he didn't go to work for M."

"Wow. I hoped they'd be left alone, now that you're not on board," I replied.

"Yeah. Me, too."

"What else?"

Ren sighed. "Russ brought Mack into the fold, so to speak, and shared everything with him. Russ said Mack wouldn't respond to ultimatums and threats, and threw in with us."

"Why is that a problem?" I asked, picking up on Ren's apparent disappointment. He shrugged.

"It's not necessarily a problem, but the more this gets around the more it's gonna get around. I think it's likely that M made similar ultimatums to the others aboard the *Adelaide*, besides Mack. Dale, JT and Kat may not be so quick to side with us. I think we'll lose the element of surprise if too many more people know what we're up against."

"Do you really think we have even a modicum of surprise?" Ren's eyes narrowed before he responded.

"Well, not right now, evidently," he replied, exasperated. "M's been calling the shots since you arrived in Oklahoma City. Every step of the way, he's kept us on the run and out of sorts. I feel like he's toying with us. It's not a good feeling."

"Pity party of one, your table is now ready," I said irritably. Ren's eyes locked with mine in anger. "Listen, Ren, you're not telling me anything I don't know. The important thing is to get out in front of this thing, so let's focus on that, shall we? We don't need to be quarreling with each other."

He sat back in his chair and simmered for a minute. The server arrived with the food. We ate in silence, each occupied with our own thoughts. When we were finished, I ordered two bottles of Asahi with chilled beer mugs.

I guzzled half the beer, then belched loudly. Ren looked around, embarrassed, to see if anyone noticed.

"Pardon me for being so *fucking* rude," I said, also loudly, which had its desired effect. Ren burst into laughter, then guzzled half his beer and followed suit. Our crude behavior drew a look of reproach from the server, so I signaled for the check.

"Come on, then. I've got a surprise for you," I told Ren, after paying for lunch.

"Where are we going?"

"To our suite."

"Huh?"

"Come on. You'll see," I told him.

As we crossed the street and entered the hotel lobby, a rumpled old man in a Hawai'ian print shirt, white shorts and flip-flops staggered in front of Ren, catching him off guard. The man dropped his newspaper when they collided, and Ren nearly dropped his tablet. I reached down, grabbed the newspaper and thrust it toward the old man.

"Nah, I'm done with it. You keep it," he said drunkenly, and stumbled away. I tucked the newspaper under one arm and proceeded to the elevator lobby.

When I pressed the button for the nineteenth floor, Ren's eyebrows arched, but he didn't say anything. We exited the elevator and I looked around. The hallway was deserted. I unfolded the newspaper and withdrew two room keys with magnetic strips, and handed one to Ren. He nodded, finally understanding.

We entered the suite and looked around. There were two separate bedrooms with desks and their own *en suite* bathrooms, and a large living room with a kitchenette. Our belongings were already moved from our old rooms.

"What the," Ren started.

"Relax, it's OK. I thought it'd be a good idea if we stayed together. The room has already been checked for listening devices. We'll change rooms, and possibly hotels, no less often than every three days while we're here. Might as well keep M guessing, right?" I smiled at Ren, who nodded.

"I'll take care of the logistics, but you're paying for the rooms. Got it?" He laughed.

"Yeah. No problem."

"Do you have an alias you'd like to use?"

"Why do I need an alias?"

"Because, if M has his flunkies looking at the reservations and sees our names, he'll not only know which hotel we're in, but which rooms," I explained. Ren stared into space, thinking.

"How about John Stout?"

"Works for me. Okay, we need to get down to business. Hang on a sec," I told him, then called room service. "Send up a couple of six-packs of Asahi, will you? And some coffee," I ordered, then hung up.

"Aren't you worried the room service folks are working for M?" Ren asked.

"Nope. I'll show you why in a few minutes." I answered the knock at the door and let the young man in, asking him to put the beer and coffee on the table. He did so, then popped the lid off a beer and drank.

"Ren, this is Ty. He's with us," I announced. Ren and Ty shook hands and nodded toward each other. "There are others around, but Ty is the one I told you about who's been, uh, *hanging out*, for lack of a better term, with Warren." Ren snickered at my sexual innuendo.

"Hi, Ren. It's good to meet you. Listen, Aaron, I can't stay. As far as the hotel is concerned, I'm a bona fide employee. And I'm on new-hire probation, so I don't want to get fired," Ty said with a grin. "But I'll be around if you need me. You know how to reach me, right?" he asked, rising and walking toward the door, tossing a breath mint into his mouth on the way.

"Yup," I said, and locked the door behind him.

Ren opened a beer for himself and asked, "What other surprises do you have up your sleeve?"

"No surprises, but I do have some information to share."

I joined him at the table and opened my tablet.

"Remember me telling you that M had at least seven tiers of proxy servers?" Ren nodded. "That's been updated. It's more like thirty plus."

Ren whistled. "So, *Jerry*'s made progress with the information you provided," Ren ventured. I neither confirmed nor denied his assumption, which I think irked him, but he didn't pursue it.

"Progress has been made," I stated flatly. "We've traced many of the anonymous emails through the various systems, but they dead-end in Stockholm. We're not giving up. Here's the interesting thing, though. Nineteen of the proxy servers we've penetrated so far are here in Honolulu. This seems very likely to be M's base of operations."

"That would make sense, in a way, since he keeps pushing us in this direction. It started when he sent Warren, otherwise we'd have no reason to be here. But why Honolulu?" he wondered aloud.

"I have no idea. Yet. But I get the feeling we won't get to the bottom of this until the *Adelaide* arrives, and that will be a few weeks. Most of M's efforts seem focused on us as a group, rather than individually," I offered as my assessment. "In the meantime, we'll keep digging."

～

Blake
Waikiki Beach, Hawaii

I was on the phone with Dava when a text from M came through. I ended the call abruptly.

You have my permission to take a week off. Keep your phone on. –M

I returned Dava's call. "Change of plans. You're on your own for a week. If you need help keeping track of Warren, let me know," I told her and ended the call.

Next, I messaged Anne. *Looks like I have a few days off! Are you available?*

I can be, she responded immediately. *When and where?*

Your place Upstate?

What a coincidence! I happen to be here now, she added, with a thumbs-up emoji.

Awesome. I'll send you my flight arrival information when I have it. Can you pick me up in Syracuse?

No problem. Do you know how soon?

Probably not before late tomorrow or early the next day, depending on connections, I told her. *I'll get back to you.*

I can't wait to see you, Blake. Talk to you soon.

~

M

Dava, I'm sending Blake away for a few days. I have a change in your assignment. I need you to go to Phoenix to tie up a dead end. As soon as that's done, go to Oklahoma and keep tabs on Terry until I tell you it's time to kill him.

Blake told me to trail Warren.

I don't give a damn what he told you. This is more important. Warren isn't going anywhere. Do as I say.

Yes, sir.

~

Warren

Waikiki Beach

Ty was getting inside my head. I found myself thinking about him like I used to think about Ren, back in the early days, well before Terry came along. Ren and I were a flash in the pan, whereas Ty and I are more like a slow burn. I hoped I hadn't shortened his life by getting involved with him. M had a way of knowing these things, and wouldn't hesitate to use my relationship with Ty against me. One slip on my part and Ty could die.

Ty messaged earlier and asked me to meet him at Hulas around nine tonight for drinks, which I agreed to do. I glanced at my watch; five-thirty. I went to the closet, grabbed my gym gear and took off, thinking a good workout would do me good and take my mind off things.

~

Terry

Oklahoma City, Oklahoma

Exhaustion was the condition of the day for the last month or so. Today was no different. The long overseas flight from Sydney to Hawaii was tiring enough. With only one night's rest before another long flight to Houston, then to OKC, I was drained. Still, it was good to be home.

I was greeted at baggage claim by two associates of Aaron's, who drove me home. The silent car ride had me on edge. I sat in the back seat and messaged NanC.

I'm back in OKC. Have you made it home yet?

Arrived in Phoenix a few hours ago, but I'm spending a couple of nights with friends in Goodyear. I could use a distraction.

I understand! I hope you know not to talk about what's been going on.

Don't worry, Terrance. The last thing I want to do is relive the events of the past few days by blabbing to friends. No, I plan to tell them all about my soon-to-be new home in Oklahoma City. How are the repairs coming?

I haven't arrived home yet, I explained. *On the way there now, accompanied by two very serious associates of Aaron's. I'll text you tomorrow. I'm planning on a long, hot shower, an early dinner, then bed. I already miss Ren.*

I bet you do. When you're settled at home, you should call him and let him know.

Thank you for the relationship advice, Momma Nan, I teased.

TTYL, Terry.

To be truthful, I missed NanC, too. I sincerely hoped M would leave her alone.

~

The house was dark when I arrived at the deep end of dusk. My FBI escort waited while I unloaded my luggage.

The agent in the passenger seat rolled down his window and called out to me.

"We'll be in the area, Mr. Franklin. Do you still have the phone Mr.

Jeffries provided?" I nodded. "Okay. If you have any problems or need help for any reason, dial nine-one-one on *that* phone—not your house phone. Your call will be routed to me automatically." I nodded again, and they drove away.

I let myself in the front door so I wouldn't have to carry the luggage around to the back. I noticed the realtor lockbox was gone; so was the For-Sale sign. There was a note on the kitchen counter by the coffee pot. *I'll be by daily to sweep the house for surveillance devices, until you tell me to stop. –YKW*

I snickered. YKW? *You Know Who*, no doubt, a.k.a. *Bill Murray.*

On the back of his note was another. *YKW is an odd duck. CW.* That had to be Connie Watson, Ren's straight. I smiled, and decided to give her a quick call to let her know I was back.

"Subtle Investigations, Connie speaking," she answered, distractedly.

"Hi, Connie. It's Terry. Just wanted to let you know I'm back at the house. Is there anything I need to know about concerning the repairs?"

"Hey, Terry. Nope, everything is going well. You'll see in the morning when you look around. Everything okay with you? How's Ren?"

"I'm exhausted, but doing well. Ren is staying in Hawaii for a while. I'm sure he'd love to hear from you, though," I told her.

"I'll check in with him in a couple of days. I've got a nasty adultery case going right now," she said.

"Be sure to tell Ren that when you talk to him. He loves those," I said, laughing.

"Don't I know it," she said, laughing in response. "He gets bored so easily."

"Trust me, he is far from bored right now. Okay, I just wanted to let you know I'm home. Let's get together soon and catch up." She agreed, and ended the call.

After I unpacked and started laundry, I thawed some fruit salad from a bag in the freezer to have for dinner with some chamomile tea.

I showered and crawled into bed, lying on Ren's side so I could smell him on the pillow.

All is well at the Gifford-Franklin manse, I messaged Ren.

Good to hear, my love. Are you in bed?

Yup. Ready for a good night's sleep, but without you next to me I doubt I'll get it.

Aw, he answered. *Are you pouting?*

Maybe, I admitted.

G'nite, Terry. Call me tomorrow and let me know how the repairs look. Not too early, though—time change, and all that.

OK. I love you, Ren.

Love you more.

CHAPTER 9

Russ
Aboard the Adelaide II
Suva Harbour, Fiji

Our original plan was to make our next port of call at Noumea, New Caledonia, but Mack convinced me otherwise. A large storm was rotating far north of us, but headed our way. Mack suggested we bypass Noumea and sail on to Suva at maximum speed, where we'd take shelter from the storm in Suva Harbour. It would be a race between us and mother nature, but he thought we'd be safer there. The facilities in Fiji were better, and he felt the harbor was more protected.

Also, Mack had a friend who worked at a local yacht club; someone who might be able to secure a berth or dock space for us at the marina. Slowing to navigate Suva Harbour, we finally arrived at the marina just hours before the storm hit. It'd taken us over six days to make the journey. I was relieved for the *Adelaide II* to be safely anchored.

The harbor was crowded with other boats also seeking shelter from the storm, but there was a party atmosphere between the marina and the looming clouds above. Once the boat was securely docked, Mack called me on the radio.

"Captain, Captain. Mack."

"Go ahead."

"Request permission for Olivia to come aboard, sir."

This was his friend at the yacht club? "Permission granted."

"Thank you, Cap. Are you available to meet us in the main bar in about thirty minutes?"

"Yeah. See you then."

"Everyone else is welcome, too," he added. I squawked the radio in reply.

JT and Kat requested permission to dine ashore, which I granted. That left Dale, Alejandro, Glen and me to join Mack and Olivia. I asked Alejandro to bring Glen and prepare a snack tray of fruit and sandwiches, while I ducked into our cabin to shower and change clothes.

When I arrived at the bar, everyone was present except Mack and Olivia, but they weren't far behind me. When they arrived, Olivia was drying her medium-length brown hair with a towel. In the tropics, only tourists bothered with umbrellas.

"Hello, everyone," she said with a broad smile, revealing lovely white teeth and laugh dimples. "I'm Olivia." Mack stepped around her then, to make introductions.

"Olivia," he said, starting with me, "this is my friend Russ, uh, Captain Garrett, I should say," and she extended her hand.

"Please, call me Russ. I don't stand on formality most of the time," I returned her smile.

"Pleased to meet you, Russ. It's good you don't stand on too many things, or you'd be seven feet tall," she giggled.

"Next to Russ is Alex, Russ' partner, and at least for now, our chef," Mack continued. "That's Glen, our permanent resident, on the other side of Alex. And finally, you know that little redheaded firepot at the end, Dale."

"Stop skulking behind everyone, you ol' drunken sailor, and come give me a hug," Olivia cajoled. Dale rushed forward and into her arms.

"Such a delight to see you again, dear Olivia. You pop up in the most unexpected places," Dale said, punctuating his remarks with kisses on each of Olivia's cheeks.

"I could say the same about you, ginger," she replied, mussing his hair. Everyone laughed except Glen.

"Alex, Glen, it's a pleasure to meet you," she continued, still smiling.

Glen blushed, but didn't say anything. Alejandro pushed Dale aside.

"Hey, if hugs are being dished out, then I want one," Alejandro asserted, smiling at Olivia. Dale jumped between them.

"Well, if you insist, you spicy little jalapeño. Com'ere," Dale puckered his lips, closed his eyes and stretched his arms wide, but Alejandro ducked under them and into Olivia's arms. "Aww. Missed again," Dale pretended sorrow, snapping his fingers. "Always late to the party, I am."

Looking at Mack, Olivia said, "I see he hasn't changed a whit."

"And that surprises you?" Mack laughed.

"Not in the least, and I wouldn't have it any other way."

"Now that introductions are over, why don't we have a seat at the bar? Alejandro has refreshments ready, and if I know my li'l jalapeño, that probably includes some kind of tropical knockout cocktail," I said.

While we settled, I smiled to myself and felt the tension flow out of me. I'd forgotten how good it felt to laugh.

Olivia looked to be an Islander; dark skin, wide smile, open and friendly eyes and an infectious laugh. She could be from any of the Pacific Isles, but I couldn't detect any kind of accent. My curiosity got the better of me.

"Where are you from, Olivia, if you don't mind me asking."

"Not at all. Do you know where Pago Pago is, in American Samoa?" She asked.

I nodded. "Certainly. It's on our route to Hawaii," I readily acknowledged.

"Well, I'm from nowhere *near* there," she responded, deadpan serious. Alejandro guffawed, and I glared at Mack.

"Someone's been coaching the players, I see," I accused, my face flushed.

"Sorry, Cap. Hard not to yank your chain now and then," Mack said, dipping his head to hide a smile. I laughed, taking the teasing in stride.

Olivia continued, "I'm originally from Hilo on the Big Island, but I spend most of my time here in Suva nowadays," she explained.

"Ah," was all I could muster in response.

Alejandro set a platter of shot glasses on the bar. "Okay, I've got a boost to get everyone started. It's a shot, so that means no sipping," he ordered sternly, wagging his finger in our general direction.

"What's in it?" Mack wanted to know.

"I'll tell you after we've had the first round," Alejandro smiled mischievously.

I already knew what was coming. Everyone took a glass, except Glen; I handed his to him.

"To smooth seas, a stiff mast and a steady blow," I toasted.

In a loud whisper, Alejandro shared, "That's what he says every night when we go to bed."

Olivia's eyes widened in mock surprise as she chuckled.

"Or something like that," I added lamely. We clinked the shot glasses and drank.

Several people exclaimed at once. *Wow,* or *oh my God!* Mack even coughed quietly.

"Tell 'em what's in it, Alejandro," I said.

"I call it an afterburner. Half Bacardi 151 and half peppermint schnapps, straight from the freezer," he explained. "Who wants another round? Get 'em while you can," he added, "151 is scarce nowadays." Only Glen raised his hand for another.

"Russ said you might have a tropical bombshell, or something?" Olivia prompted. "I'll have one of those." Mack and Dale called for the same. I waved him off.

"Not for me, Alejandro. I'll have a Crown and Seven, double-tall, please."

Glen's signal for another shot having been ignored, he didn't make a request, but I held up two fingers, so Alejandro would know to make another like mine for him. Alejandro nodded. At least Glen wasn't drinking straight from the vodka or whiskey bottle, and I was encouraged by his effort to curb his intake. He might make it beyond Hawaii after all.

"Tropical bombshells coming up. Actually, it's called Reah's Rum Drink," Alejandro said, and retrieved a large pitcher from a fridge under the bar. He poured for Olivia first and let her taste it.

"OOOh, yes," she cooed. "This is much more to my liking. I can taste the coconut rum. What else is in it?"

"Peach nectar, orange and pineapple juice and Champagne or sparkling wine, plus the garnish, of course," Alejandro relayed. "Not too sweet?" She shook her head while sipping through a thin straw. Alejandro poured for the others and himself, then fixed Glen's and my drinks.

"Why do you call this Reah's Rum Drink?" Dale asked.

Alejandro shrugged. "I read it in a book and it sounded good, so I decided to try it," he explained.

Dale and Olivia had apparently known each other and worked together off and on for many years. They kept us entertained with stories that often resulted in side-splitting laughter from everyone. Their humor and stories fed on each other and appeared to be bottomless.

After an hour, Alejandro excused himself to start dinner in the galley, taking Glen with him.

I noticed Glen hadn't taken his eyes off Olivia the entire time he was there, until she caught him staring, then he'd either duck his head or turn away. I pondered that he might be smitten with her. If so, I could certainly understand; she was sunshine and laughter in human form—a delight to be around. It was the first time I'd seen Glen exhibit even a hint of interest in anyone.

When they left, Olivia remarked, "That fellow, Glen. He's a quiet one, eh? What's his story?" She looked at me with questioning eyes over the rim of her drink while munching on a cube of melon from a toothpick.

An uncomfortable silence fell, with no one quite sure what to say. Mack and Dale looked at me, apparently leaving it to me to provide an answer. I moved around to the bar and poured myself another drink. My radio beeped. Saved by the bell.

"Captain, Captain, JT."

"Go ahead."

"Kat and I have finished dinner and would like to speak with you privately, if you have a minute."

That was a surprise. I hadn't expected to hear from them until tomorrow.

"Very well. I'll meet you in my cabin," I replied. I returned to the group. "Sorry, folks, I've got to step away for a few minutes."

"Everything copacetic, Cap?" Mack asked.

"Carry on carrying on," I replied. "I'll be back shortly. If you can't pour your own drinks while I'm gone, give a shout to Alejandro and he'll take care of you."

"Are you kiddin' me, Cap?" Dale said, incredulously, moving behind the bar. "I've been pouring my own liquor since I was seven. Leave 'em in my experienced hands."

I laughed. "You've got a six-year head start on me, Dale. You're in charge of the booze, then," I said over my shoulder as I departed.

I stopped by the galley on the way. "Alejandro, I'm meeting JT and Kat in our cabin for a brief huddle. All is good. Check in at the bar in five minutes if I haven't told you I'm back, okay?"

"Ten-four, Admiral," he replied.

I entered Alejandro's and my cabin and left the door open. A few minutes later, JT knocked at the door.

"Come in," I invited, gesturing for them to sit on the bed while I sat at my desk. Even the captain's cabin was cramped compared to the guest cabins. "I'm surprised to hear from you. What's going on?"

"Well, Kat and I were thinking about leaving. We've decided not to, though. We still plan to go with you to Hawaii, and after that, too, if you're agreeable."

He was nervous, and I felt like there was more to the story than he was telling me. "What's going on? This isn't like you two."

JT paused to think how to answer.

"It's kinda hard to explain. All that business with the gunboat attack, then the boarding incident," he said, pausing.

"JT, just tell him what happened. It isn't right and he should know," Kat prodded.

JT fidgeted with his phone for a minute, his head bowed. Then he sighed heavily and his posture straightened so he could look me squarely in the eye. "There's this bloke, I don't know who, but he says if we don't work for him and report all activities we observe and conversations we overhear aboard the *Adelaide*, he'll kill us."

JT's face was flooded with panic as he continued, "Kat's pregnant. We just found out days ago. And now some wacko is threatening my whole family." He ducked his head again before resuming eye contact. "I was gonna go along at first, 'cause there was some significant cash involved. Then Kit Kat brought me to my senses," he said, looking at her with gratitude. "She reminded me that this isn't me. I wouldn't be the father I'd want my children to have."

Quietly, then, Kat asked, "What do we do, Russ? How do we make this right?"

"Huh," I breathed. "Mack, Mack. Russ," I said on the radio. "Come to my cabin, please."

Moments later, he stepped into the cabin and stood with his hands on his hips, looking from them to me and back again.

"Hey, JT, Kat. What's going on? I thought you were out for the evening," Mack said.

"They were, but came back to talk with me. Mack, as we feared might happen, the Malefactor has contacted JT and Kat. He's threatening their families' lives if they don't work for him," I explained.

"Did you get an anonymous email signed by M?" Mack asked.

They nodded. "But that's not all, Mack. While we were ashore for dinner tonight, we were, uh, approached by a man who said his name was M. He said we hadn't responded to his email, so he was there personally to *secure our commitment*, is how he put it," JT reported.

The conversation fell into a lull while we considered what to do.

"All right," I sighed. "For now, tell him you'll do it. Then report whatever you see and hear, just as you were instructed. Now that we know, we can work this to our advantage—if you two go along."

They agreed immediately.

"Good," I continued. "We'll do our best to keep you from harm, but you need to understand how wide and deep this goes. Mack, you have my permission to tell them everything they need to know."

"Give me a couple of minutes to fill them in. Later, we can decide what we want them to report to mislead the Malefactor," Mack suggested.

"JT, Kat—thank you for coming forward with this. Okay, make it quick, then join us in the bar. Mack has a guest on board," I instructed and left them in my cabin.

When I rejoined the group, Glen was setting the table and Alejandro was bringing out large platters of food.

"What's for dinner, Alejandro?" I asked. "It smells wonderful."

"Roasted couscous with fresh cherry tomatoes, roasted asparagus and pan-seared New York strip steak seasoned with smoked paprika, topped with romesco sauce," he replied. "And lime gelato for dessert." He paused to smile up at me and tiptoed for a quick smooch. I obliged, losing myself for a delicious moment in his chocolate-brown eyes.

"Excuse me, everyone," Alejandro called loudly to get their attention at the bar. "Dinner is served. Bring your drinks with you, please." As we settled, Mack returned with JT and Kat in tow.

Alejandro gestured toward two empty chairs. "Are you joining us? There's plenty for everyone," he invited.

"No, but thank you. JT and I ate already. It looks delicious, though," Kat answered.

"How about a rum drink, then, and you can join the conversation while we eat," Alejandro suggested. Only JT accepted, with Kat asking for sparkling water. They sat while Alejandro poured their drinks and Mack introduced them to Olivia.

Mack sat to the right of Olivia, while Glen took a seat on her left.

Considering that he usually sat with Alejandro and me, I thought that was remarkable.

"All right, dig in folks. Don't let it get cold," Alejandro encouraged.

The clatter of utensils on plates and the lull in conversation while everyone began eating reminded me of holiday meals when I was a kid, surrounded by siblings, cousins and adults. It was a pleasant, nostalgic moment.

～

I scooted my chair away so I could lean back and stretch my legs under the table. The meal was winding down. Olivia was still the center of attention. She kept everyone entertained with stories of good times, or funny memories of tough times, working with Dale and Mack. I hadn't laughed so much in years.

Alejandro leaned against my side and rubbed my belly affectionately with his right hand. I ran my fingers through his hair, then rested my arm across his shoulder.

"Alejandro, Glen, that was a wonderful dinner," I said, which was immediately echoed by all who'd eaten.

"Thanks, everyone. Tips are gratefully accepted, but as I used to say when I was a go-go dancer in Puerto Vallarta, please just throw soft money," he answered with a laugh. I pinched his ear playfully.

Changing the subject, I said, "Olivia, while I'm thanking people, I'd like to thank you for arranging the *Adelaide*'s dock space in the marina. That couldn't have been easy, with so many boats looking for a place to weather the storm."

She merely tilted her head in acknowledgement and raised her glass to me.

"Do I owe a docking fee, or is there something else I can do to repay you?"

She glanced up at Mack, then, but didn't answer.

"Uh, well, the thing is, Russ, I sorta offered her passage to Hawaii in exchange for the favor," Mack said. His left hand went under the table, as did her right. I suspected they were holding hands discreetly.

I didn't respond immediately. My only hesitation was that she'd be exposed to danger from the Malefactor, should he learn we'd taken on a passenger, especially one who was a friend of the crew.

"She's due a visit home and has the time off. We have plenty of room, with the guest cabins being available. If I've overstepped, I apologize. I'd be happy to pay for her fare," he added quietly. I think he interpreted my silence as disapproval.

I shook my head and raised a hand. "No, no, that's not necessary. She's welcome to sail with us, but you'll need to brief her on our, mmm, circumstances," I explained. "If she's still game, then I'm fine with it."

She looked up at Mack again, eyebrows arched. Mack nodded in agreement.

"*Intrigue*," she whispered loudly. "I love it."

"If you will excuse us, I think we should have this conversation in private," Mack stated and stood. Olivia followed and as they walked away they were holding hands. Glen noticed; his crestfallen expression saddened me.

"Hey, Glen," I said, to draw his attention away from the departing couple, "would you help Alejandro clear the table and clean the galley?" He nodded, stood and walked toward the bar first.

"Glen," I said, my voice stern with warning. He returned to the table and started collecting dishes. Alejandro sighed and rose to help, but leaned down to whisper in my ear first.

"He hasn't spoken a word all evening, but he's been careful with his drinking. Don't be too harsh with him, okay? Besides, did you see the way he was looking at Olivia?" I nodded with a heavy sigh.

"I'll help in the galley," Kat offered, rising from her seat, and I thanked her with a smile.

Dale and JT returned to the bar, so I joined them. Dale prepared another Crown and Seven for me.

"Thanks," I said. My phone vibrated in my pocket. A text from Ren.

Terry asked me to tell you this. NanC says giving the pretty lady passage to Hawaii is a good idea. WTF?

Yeah, Olivia, a friend of Mack's. We're docked in Fiji waiting out a storm.

She arranged dock space for us at the marina. How the hell did she know about Olivia?

How do you think? came the sarcastic reply. *She's clairvoyant, remember?*

Right. I believe that about as much as you do.

What else is going on? Ren asked.

Not much, except that JT and Kat have been solicited by the Malefactor. They fessed up and we're figuring out how to turn it to our advantage.

Dale and JT had stopped talking and were staring at me.

"What?" I asked.

"Nothing," Dale said. "JT just asked you what's going on with Glen, but your head musta been in the third dimension."

"Oh, sorry. I was messaging Ren. But nothing's going on with Glen. He's just more quiet than usual. You know how he is around groups." We stopped talking when Glen walked by on the way to the galley with another load of dishes.

Mack and Olivia returned then, with Olivia's exuberance considerably reduced. It appeared she hadn't taken Mack's revelations well. Mack raised his eyebrows and sighed as they seated themselves at the bar.

"She still wants to sail with us," he said.

My phone vibrated again.

How long will you be in Fiji? Ren wanted to know.

A couple of days, at least. We're hunkered down under a pretty severe storm. Why?

Aaron said he can arrange to have the Adelaide *swept for surveillance devices while you're there, discreetly, of course. He's also going to have them provide a pistol and ammunition. You can keep it locked in the safe in your cabin if you like, but we think you need to have something on board, just in case. You'll need to devise a reason to get everyone but you and Alex ashore, though.*

I like that suggestion, I told him. *I'll see what I can arrange and get back with you.*

K. Make it soon, though.

I looked up to find everyone looking at me again.

"Well, we got NanC's blessing to bring Olivia along," I told Mack sarcastically.

"Don't tell me,"

"Yup. Evidently she has a *good feeling* about it."

"What are you two talking about?" Olivia asked. "And who's Nancy? Why do I need her blessing? I thought Russ and his partner owned the *Adelaide*."

"Russ and his *business* partner, Ren," Mack clarified for her. "Not Alex, his life partner. You'll probably meet Ren when we get to Hawaii. Anyway, it isn't important. Russ was just being facetious."

Mack pulled me aside then, and spoke quietly.

"Russ, would it be okay for Olivia and me to sleep in the master suite while we're in port? We won't trash the place. She's never experienced that kind of luxury. Once we're under way, we'll move to my quarters."

I patted him on the shoulder and said, "Sure, go ahead."

Alejandro appeared then, carrying another platter full of glasses and a pitcher. "I have something extra special for you, as an after-dinner drink. I call it a Russian Roulette." He poured for Olivia first, then the rest of us.

"I think I like this better than the rum drink," Olivia observed. "Is it a White Russian?"

Alejandro shook his head. "Almost. All the ingredients of a White Russian, plus a jigger of Bailey's Irish Cream," he explained. "With all those types of alcohol, it's a game of Russian Roulette as to which one will knock you off your barstool."

～

The weather delayed us longer than expected, causing us to stay docked in Suva for three nights. I was glad, though, because it gave me time to get everyone off the yacht while Aaron's cohorts could sweep the *Adelaide II* for bugs. Good news there; none found. That gave us free rein to bait M with fake reports from JT and Kat.

The morning of the fourth day dawned calm, bright and clear; a cheerful contrast to the constant rain and overcast skies of the previous three days. Suva Harbour was thick with departing vessels.

A leisurely three days passed, sailing northwest from Fiji. We were currently midway between Wallis Island and American Samoa, with at least ten days sailing still ahead of us. The weather forecast was decent.

JT and Kat kept to themselves when not on duty, usually sunbathing and reading, or listening to music. Glen avoided everyone, especially Mack and Olivia, which concerned me and puzzled them. I didn't share with them my thoughts about Glen's attraction to Olivia. That would only chum the water.

The crew was content with the daily routine, and I was thankful to have a respite from M's sinister schemes.

Terry reported, via Ren, that the repairs were completed on their house. It, too, was scanned for surveillance electronics every day, but so far nothing had been found. Aaron insisted they continue for the foreseeable future.

Ren said he and Aaron were making progress tracing M's communications, but didn't elaborate. I think he was worried about our messages being intercepted.

All in all, I felt like our situation was improving, but the moment I arrived at that conclusion, I reached to knock on wood; I certainly didn't want to jinx us.

∿

Ren

Honolulu, Hawaii

Aaron rented a car for the morning. We were currently parked a half-mile from a palatial home in Turtle Bay. Aaron had kept silent about the home and the reason we were there, alternating between observing the estate through binoculars and making notes on his tablet.

"Is this M's home? Are the servers located here? This place has more security than the White House," I observed, trying to drag the information out of him.

"I think so, I believe so and I agree," he responded, answering me sequentially. He pulled the binoculars away from his face and put them in the back seat. He started the car and headed north to Kuilima Drive, then turned northwest.

"We'll talk over lunch. What sounds good, bar food, local cuisine or Asian?"

"I'm fine with something local," I answered. He glanced at his tablet.

"Okay, let's try Roy's Beach House. It gets decent ratings," he said.

"You're awfully perky today. You must have researched the area before we left. What gives?"

He smiled at me, saying, "As I said, we'll talk over lunch. I'm starved."

A few minutes later, we pulled into the parking lot at two o'clock. We missed most of the lunch crowd, so it was quiet.

We sat outside on the deck with a beautiful ocean view, under a wide umbrella. Roy's lunch menu was limited, but varied. While scanning the selections, we asked the server to bring us his favorite local brew. He delivered two schooners of Pai Mahiai, which he explained was a Belgian style ale produced by a local brewery in Honolulu.

I ordered the blackened ahi appetizer and the Kobe beef burger. Aaron requested two appetizers for his meal, shrimp cocktail and baby back ribs. When the server left, I raised my glass to Aaron, who did likewise.

"Okay, let's hear what you've deduced," I urged. The beer was good, but I was anxious to hear what Aaron was keeping from me and apparently enjoying it.

"Right, right. Well, you were correct. That luxury estate back there is what I suspect is the Malefactor's home. According to county records, it is owned by Malcolm Dekker, who has lived there for more than forty years."

"What? It looks new," I protested.

Nodding, Aaron agreed, "Yeah. But when his family bought the property in the early sixties, there was little more than a beach hut. When Dekker inherited it from his grandfather, he was already worth millions. Gradually, he built a home and kept adding to it. It's more than a luxury home, now; it's a fortress."

"Malcolm Dekker. M—Malcolm, M—Malefactor. That piece sure seems to fit," I mused.

The server arrived with two more beers, my appetizer and Aaron's shrimp cocktail.

"What else do you know about the place," I asked, and slid a big bite of blackened ahi tuna onto my fork.

"As I said, it's a virtual fortress. It has four power generators and two backup generators, with a stockpile of fuel that could power the whole estate for a year, if need be. The low boundary wall is deceiving; electrified across the top, pressure sensors in the ground for thirty feet on either side and full audio and video surveillance every twenty feet."

I released a long, low whistle. "Jeez, this guy is not only wealthy beyond imagining, but more paranoid than Glen," I commented.

"That's not all," Aaron continued. "The wall borders the estate on three sides, with the only open areas being the beach and a guarded front entrance. Even the entrance has a steel gate that can be closed in seconds. Access from the beach is unobstructed, but not unprotected. Just inside his property line, there are signs warning beachgoers about buried power lines, vicious dogs and armed guards."

Aaron paused to drink from his schooner and eat a few pieces of shrimp.

"Of all that, do you know what I find the most peculiar?" I shook my head at his question. "Twenty feet on the public side of his property line along the beach, he's got two manned stations offering free ice water and fruit to anyone who happens to come along. *And food and water for their pets.*"

"That's a façade. Those stations are likely manned by trained guards as a front line of defense should anyone venture too close."

"Yeah, you're probably right. No one would be the wiser, would they? And it would give the perception of a good-natured wealthy homeowner trying to make nice with the beachgoers." He ate another shrimp, discarding the tail in his empty beer glass. "Oh, I didn't mention the helipad, with room for not one but *two* helicopters."

"How many members on his service and security staffs, do you know?"

"Nope."

"Do you have any photos of Mr. Dekker?"

"Yeah, a few, but they're several years old. I'll show you when we get back to the hotel."

The server returned with the rest of our food, so we turned the conversation to other things. We had decisions to make.

CHAPTER 10

$\mathcal{B}$lake
Honolulu Airport

I'd just collected my luggage and messaged Dava to pick me up outside baggage claim when my phone chimed. It was M.

Did you enjoy yourself in Cazenovia?

In fact, I did. I wasn't surprised he knew where I'd gone.

Shut up; I don't care.

Exasperated, I took a deep breath before replying. *Instructions, sir?*

I have Dava working on a new assignment, temporarily. Keep an eye on Warren. I'll be tasking him soon and I don't want him trying to sneak off. Also, I don't want to take any chances he'll recognize you, so I want you to go to the Hyatt Regency. Call in a back-up team if you need help.

I waited a moment but there was nothing further, so I made my way outside.

The young Lyft driver to the hotel was flirty and overly chatty until she looked at me in the rearview mirror and saw the look of irritation on my face. She stopped talking and turned up the radio volume.

I settled deeper into my darkening mood. The boss sure had a way of ruining a good afterglow. I thought of Anne, then, and how relaxing it'd been to spend time with her.

Whenever I visited her, instead of going to her home by Cazenovia Lake, we stayed at the Brae Loch Inn. The Scottish manor was built in the early eighteen-hundreds and had a wonderful, welcoming atmosphere. Truly an inn, the Brae Loch had a dozen rooms, an excellent restaurant and a full bar. Anne still chuckled girlishly at the waiters, who wore crisp white shirts and traditional kilts.

"I should start wearing a kilt if it's gonna get you all worked up like this," I teased her.

The first two days we never left the inn, spending our time lounging in the room, dining in the restaurant or sitting at the bar. We occasionally strolled through the small gift shop. It delighted me to see her savor every experience.

I was jarred out of my reverie by the driver announcing we'd arrived at the hotel. She hopped out to retrieve my luggage from the trunk and handed it to a bellhop.

"Welcome back to the Hyatt Regency, Mr. Thompson." Looking up, I recognized the young man.

"Oh, hi James. Thanks. Would you take these to my suite, then bring me the key? I'll be in the lounge."

"My pleasure, sir," he replied.

When I turned to tip the driver, she was staring at me lovingly with big, brown puppy eyes. I handed her twenty dollars and forced a smile as I thanked her and turned away.

I stopped at the ATM in the lobby before proceeding to the dimly lit lounge, where I found an open seat at the far end of the bar. Mason was tending, as usual. Apparently, he'd seen me enter the hotel, because he brought my usual drink over immediately and placed it before me.

~

Aaron

"Russ estimates they'll arrive in about five days," Ren reported, laying his phone on the table. I nodded.

"Good. I have a suggestion about that, if you're agreeable," I said, taking a pull on my Long Island tea.

"Sure. Whatcha got?"

"Where did you say their stowaway is from? Hilo?" I asked. Ren grinned at my description of their extra passenger.

"Yeah, Hilo. Why?"

"I want to avoid complications, if possible. No bugs were found on the *Adelaide* in Fiji, and she's been at sea since then. I think it's safe to say she's unmonitored—except for JT and Kat." Ren nodded in agreement. "We've changed hotels and hotel rooms intermittently with no recognizable pattern, so I think we are also unmonitored," I continued.

"Yeah, yeah. So, what's your suggestion?" he said impatiently.

"I think Russ should drop her in Hilo before proceeding here. If M doesn't know about her yet, then perhaps she can escape his attention."

Ren thought it over for a few seconds. "Yeah, that would be prudent. For that matter, he could set Dale, JT and Kat ashore at the same time. That would just leave Mack, Russ, Alex and Glen aboard."

I agreed with him.

"Okay. I'll message Russ with the idea when we get back to the room. Since Olivia's presence may have been reported to M, Russ should make an effort to protect her. In my opinion, he should never have agreed to give her passage."

I glanced at Ren when he suddenly stopped speaking. He looked as if he'd seen a ghost. I followed his line of sight to see a tall, handsome man enter the lounge and sit at the bar.

"You've got to be kidding me," Ren said in a shocked whisper. He picked up his phone and quickly scanned his photos, then handed the phone to me. I looked at the photo and again at the man who just entered; yep, the same guy.

"Who is it?" I asked quietly. The lounge was dim, and no doubt the man's vision hadn't adjusted yet. Ren thumbed through a few more photos to show me another.

"It's Blake Thompson; M's front man. Remember this photo?" He turned it so I could see. *Oh, hell.* I nodded after seeing the image of Blake Thompson with a gunshot to the temple, slumped over the steering wheel of a car. Ren had shown it to me the night we met at my hotel in Oklahoma City.

Ren continued. "I thought he was dead, killed by the Malefactor because I outwitted him."

"Well, I won't state the obvious," I said in sympathy, then reconsidered. "Okay, yes I will. How do you know *he* isn't the Malefactor?" Ren just shook his head slowly from side to side.

"Because you said M was elderly and living in that estate on Turtle Bay?" he jabbed.

A bellhop strode purposefully into the lounge then, stopped and looked around. When he spotted Blake at the bar, he approached from the side, causing Blake to turn away from us to speak to him. The bellhop handed Blake something, and Blake fished a tip out of his wallet.

"Come on," I said. "This is our chance to get out of here without being seen." We stood quietly. Ren threw forty bucks on the table and we walked out the door casually, as if nothing were amiss.

"Don't look back," I instructed Ren, in a tense whisper. He nodded once, and maintained a steady stride. Once out of the lounge, we made an immediate right toward the elevator lobby, cutting off any chance Blake might see us.

~

Ren

We were the only passengers on the elevator, except for a hotel employee who exited on the fourth floor, while we continued to the twelfth. My mind reeled. My thoughts jumped from one random possibility to another so quickly, I couldn't organize them coherently.

"Calm down, Ren," Aaron said smoothly.

"No, no, this is too much. We've got to get out of this hotel," I demanded.

"I don't think that's a good idea."

"Why the hell not?" I blasted. "If Blake sees me, he'll shoot me on sight and to hell with the consequences," I said angrily.

"I highly doubt that," Aaron said. His tone was calm and even, unlike mine, which was drenched in panic.

The elevator door opened and Aaron led me by the elbow along the hall. It felt like a very long hall, indeed. He slid the plastic key in the lock and pushed me through.

"Do you need something to calm your nerves?" he asked. "You sound like you're about to have a come-apart."

I shook my head. "I've already had a couple of drinks and I don't want to cloud my thinking. Now tell me why we shouldn't leave the hotel," I barked.

He brought us both bottles of water from the minifridge, and said, "Come on, let's sit and discuss it."

I took a few deep breaths, then sat at the small table by the window.

"I agree, you need to keep out of sight," Aaron started, sitting across from me, "but we should stay here for now. He doesn't know me, does he, or what I look like? I can keep an eye on him, or pull in a few favors to get help if I need it."

"Aaron, do you not recall that the Malefactor knows of your existence? He blew off the top of your hotel, for cryin' out loud, trying to kill you. What makes you think he doesn't know exactly what you look like? M could easily have sent him photos."

"Yeah, good point," he conceded. After a quiet couple of minutes in thought, he excused himself, saying "I'll be right back," and slipped through the adjoining door into his room.

I fidgeted and sipped on the water, which failed to quench the seething anger I felt inside. Aaron was gone a full half-hour, which in my current state of mind felt like half a day, and I was getting more irritable. I was startled by the loud knock at the door.

I walked over and squinted through the peephole. "Who is it? What do you want?" A stooped, elderly man with a hotel jacket stood there, holding a package.

"Sorry to bother you Mr. Stout. I have a package for you from a Mister," he glanced down at the package, "uh, Townsend. I'll need you to sign for it, sir."

"What?" That was Aaron's alias. I pulled my head away from the door and looked toward the adjoining door to his room. Looking through the peephole again, I said, "Put the package on the floor and step back, please." When he'd done so, I slowly opened the door and bent over to pick up the package.

"My apologies again, Mr. Gifford. Please take four steps backwards into the room, and continue to face me," the old man said, using my real name. He punctuated his instructions with forward jabs of his right hand, which was now holding a small pistol aimed at my chest. "And don't call out to your colleague, as that would only complicate matters."

Holding the package like a basketball between my two hands and ready to pass, I stepped back, slowly. The man followed me into the room with a rickety gait and let the door shut softly behind him. He glared at me with dark, pinpoint pupils.

I was boiling inside. "I'm surprised you could summon enough bravery to face me in person, you shriveled fucking coward," I cursed. "After all, it's more your style to have someone do your dirty work for you, isn't it M? Or should I call you *Malcolm Dekker?*" I spewed the name, hatred flaring white hot inside me.

~

Terry
Oklahoma City, Oklahoma

I was worried about NanC. I'd called and messaged her several times over the past few days, but she never responded. I remembered she said she was spending time with friends in Goodyear, a suburb of Phoenix, but that was a week or more ago and I thought she'd be home in Prescott Valley by now.

My only communication from her was a request to relay a message to Ren and Russ; *giving the pretty lady passage to Hawaii is a good idea*. I passed the message on to Ren. I could almost hear the skepticism saturating his one-word response—*fine*.

If I didn't hear from her by tomorrow evening, I decided I would give her number to Aaron and see if he could trace her location with it. I had no other contact information for her and no other way to locate her.

The repairs to the house were done, and I was very pleased. Connie did a great job supervising while we were away.

Brandi found a beautiful house for us in north Quail Creek, nestled in the crook of the golf course, on Oak Hollow Road. I'd asked her to search in the Belle Isle West neighborhood, a lovely area just west of North Pennsylvania Avenue, between NW Expressway and NW 63rd Street. She said she hadn't found anything she thought I'd like, but would keep looking. I was hopeful I'd have something selected before Ren returned home.

~

Warren

Waikiki Beach, Hawaii

Ty had become a regular fixture in my bed, and I found myself feeling more and more attached to him. He never invited me to his place, saying he was too embarrassed for me to see it, cramped and unkempt as it was. Also, it wasn't close to Waikiki and I was afraid to stray that far, for fear of sparking M's anger.

Ty'd spent the last two nights with me. When I awoke, he was in the shower, so I decided to join him. He finished before I did and stepped out to towel off. A few minutes later I did the same, then brushed my teeth.

"Warren?" I heard him call from the bedroom.

I ducked my head out, with my toothbrush still stuck in my mouth and raised my eyebrows at him.

"Your phone keeps going off. Sounds as though someone is anxious to reach you."

"Nnn-kay," I mumbled unhappily. There was only one person that could be. I finished in the bathroom and went to the nightstand to get my phone.

You've had your fun, now you've got work to do. Ditch the boy-toy and end it. You won't be seeing him again. If he's still there in an hour, well, you know what can happen–M.

Dressed, Ty slid up behind me and flung his arms around my middle. "Anything urgent?" he asked, his voice muffled by his mouth being buried between my shoulder blades.

Damn it.

"No, no, it's all good. What are you up to today?" I asked casually, putting my phone back on the nightstand.

"Oh hell, man, I've *got* to do some laundry and run some errands. If there's any daylight left, I might head out to the beach for a while. You wanna meet me there later?"

I turned in his arms and put mine around his waist, dipping both hands into his back pockets so I could get a firm grip on his bubble butt. He planted a lingering, passionate kiss on my greedy lips.

"Mmm, I'd love to. Text me when you're on the way and where you'll be," I said when we parted. I was still naked from the shower, and now aroused, thanks to his soft lips on mine.

Looking down at his handiwork, he said, "I know I've worn you out the past couple of days, but I can still take care of *that* for you, before I leave." He grinned, which made his eyes twinkle.

"Ah, no. I'll take a raincheck, if that's okay," I deflected. He shrugged agreeably.

"All right, hon. Text ya later," he said, then pecked me on the cheek again and let himself out.

I stood where he left me, dejectedly staring at the space he'd occupied just a moment before. When my eyes started to sting, I forced myself to move. I dressed, packed my bags and sat on the bed until another text arrived from M.

Move to the Sheraton. Now.

I picked up my things and walked out the door, closing it and an idyllic few weeks with Ty behind me.

~

Ren

I was about to launch the package directly at Dekker's face, but he raised the pistol and pointed it at my head.

"I wouldn't do that if I were you," he growled. "Take the lid off the box and look inside, Mr. Gifford."

"Fuck you. I'm not playing these stupid games for your amusement."

"Shut up and do it," he shouted.

I lowered the package and he followed suit, lowering his gun slightly. I pulled the loose lid from the box and looked inside. There was only a handwritten note. I reached in and picked it up, dropping the box on the floor, and read it.

It's me—Aaron

When I looked up again, the old man's posture had straightened and he looked three inches taller. He unexpectedly tossed the gun to me, which I fumbled to catch without dropping; it was plastic.

"What the hell?" I muttered.

"It's me, like the note said." When he spoke in his usual voice, I finally caught on. He pulled off a white wig, fake bushy eyebrows, then peeled away fake skin from his cheeks, neck and hands.

"I can't take the contacts out until I wash this stuff off my hands," he complained. I was amazed at the transformation.

"You son of a bitch," I exclaimed in admiration.

"You know, for someone who prides himself on his observation skills, you're kinda worthless at spotting a disguise, especially when it's standing right in front of you," he commented. "It's amazing what some makeup and spirit gum will do."

I tossed the toy gun back to him, shaking my head.

"I need a drink," I said, and moved to the suite's wet bar.

"Make me one while I yank these contacts. I'll be right back," and he disappeared into his room again. He was back moments later and I handed his drink to him.

"So, you still think I can't keep an eye on Blake without being noticed?" he taunted.

"You win, Aaron. That was brilliant," I complimented. "You're an asshole, but a brilliant asshole," I added.

"I can't refute the first assessment nor deny the second, my friend," he agreed.

"So, you're going to tell me the FBI gives training to its agents in disguises?" I prodded.

He shook his head, with a smile. "Not for my particular line of work now, but it was occasionally useful in my early career. I picked up the talent in high school and college, doing community theater. I discovered I had a knack for it." He shrugged. "I've got this little kit I carry with me, with the barest of essentials to change my appearance. The rest is posture, wardrobe and acting."

I could only shake my head.

Aaron's phone rang. He glanced at the screen and answered it quickly.

He lifted his glass to take a drink, but was interrupted by his phone. He pulled it out of his pocket and looked at the screen, frowning, then answered.

"Jerry? I thought you were going to stick to text communications," Aaron said with concern heavy in his voice. He listened for a moment, then started pacing, still silent. Finally, he spoke. "I can't return just yet. Can you handle it for me? Uh-huh. No, even if I left now, it'd take me half a day to get there; I'm still in Hawaii. Yes. Yes. Okay. Do what you can."

He looked at me, and for the first time I saw real fear in his eyes. Beads of sweat were forming on his forehead. I could hear the urgency in Jerry's voice, but not make out the words, and I was getting concerned for Aaron.

"Thanks," he concluded and ended the call.

"So that's the infamous Jerry, eh?" I said, trying to lighten his mood. I failed.

"Ren, I know it's probably just a distraction to pull me away from this, but."

I waited a moment for him to continue, but he'd stalled.

"But?" I prodded.

"The Malefactor, I assume, has kidnapped my wife," he stated flatly, then collapsed shakily onto the sofa.

"Oh, my God, Aaron," I exclaimed. "What are you going to do? You should leave immediately."

He leaned forward, planted his elbows on his knees and rested his chin on his fists. He slowly shook his head.

"No. I'm not leaving." His phone chimed and he opened an email. "Jerry just forwarded the anonymous email he received about Sophia," he said, and proceeded to read the message aloud.

"I don't know who you are, but I will find out soon. As you can see, I have reverse-tracked your tracing software. I am not without resources of my own.

"Meanwhile, I do know who Mr. Jeffries is and what he's doing to help Ren. You've managed to block his email address and phone numbers from me, so I'm forced to communicate through this backdoor method.

"Please inform Mr. Jeffries that I am enjoying the company of his lovely wife, Sophia. I must say, she seems reluctant to be civil and refuses conversation. No matter. I don't really need her cooperation; simply having her here is leverage enough.

"She is comfortable and safe—for the moment—but that could change at any time, depending on how her husband reacts to her disappearance. I am demanding no ransom, merely asking politely for him, and you, for that matter, to withdraw all assistance from Ren. I'll be in touch. —M"

"Jerry's trying to trace the source of the email, but it goes right back to those tiers of proxy servers all over the world, including the estate at Turtle Beach. He's still working on breaking through," Aaron concluded.

We sat in silence. I thought of how I could continue without Aaron's help while Aaron was rereading the email.

I picked up my phone and said, "OK, we need to get you a flight home immediately."

"Not gonna happen," he interrupted. His voice was low and tight, filling with anger.

"Aaron, think about this for a minute. This is your wife we're talking about. If you can get her safely released simply by dropping your investigation, then that's what you must do."

He shook his head firmly. "No. Remember me telling you that we have to get out in front instead of being manipulated every step of the way? That applies to me as well as you," he explained. "I think he's crazy and would have no qualms killing her, except that she's the wife of an FBI agent. The pressure I could bring to bear in an official capacity would be more than he can handle.

"I'm staying right here until we break this. And I do not think it's a coincidence that this happened so soon after we staked out Dekker's estate in Turtle Bay. We're getting close, and I think he's panicking. We'll see how he reacts to being the one manipulated for a change."

"You think he'll bring her here, don't you?"

He shrugged. "I think it is very likely. If I run back to Virginia and she's here, it turns into a cat-and-mouse game. I think that's exactly what he wants; to goad us into another rushed decision."

"Do you know whether Dekker is at his estate?"

"No, not certain yet. I haven't had the resources to put a twenty-four-hour surveillance team there, yet. But there's only one helicopter there now, which leads me to believe he's away and the second 'copter is parked wherever he'll land to bring him back here."

I thought about his logic, and felt like he'd made reasonable assumptions. I settled into the idea of him staying with me, and to be honest, I was relieved.

"Then I suggest you ask Jerry to start tracking charter and private flights to all airports in Hawaii. I doubt he'd take a commercial flight, even using an alternate identity."

Aaron nodded and picked up his phone again. Another thought occurred to me.

"Do you think Jerry and his family are in danger?"

"Again, I have no idea. In the email, M made it sound as if he didn't know who Jerry is, but that could easily be a lie," he said, while typing a message to Jerry. "I'll mention it to him so he can take precautions, just in case."

Aaron looked exhausted, so I wasn't surprised when he excused himself to go to his room and nap. I decided I would use the time to call Terry.

"Hey, how are you, handsome?"

I moved to the bed and laid across it, my feet dangling over the side, and closed my eyes.

"I'm good. Tired, but good. It helps to hear your voice. I miss you, baby."

"Same, here. Any progress on the case?" he wanted to know.

"Yeah, some, but I don't want to talk about it right now. I'd rather hear about what you're up to and how the house hunt is going."

I could hear the enthusiasm in his voice as he told me about the house in north Quail Creek Brandi was taking him to see.

"Do you want me to send you the photos?"

"Nah, that's okay. I trust your judgment. I don't really care where we live as long as you're by my side."

"You're depressed. What's going on?" he asked, compassion in his voice.

I sighed. "M has kidnapped Aaron's wife, Sophia," I replied.

"Damn. When did that happen?"

"We just found out, so we're not exactly sure, but we think it was probably a few hours after we found M's home. At least, what we think is his home. There's an estate on Turtle Bay. All the communications we get from M go through the servers at that location, at some point. And get this; the estate is owned by Malcolm Dekker," I explained.

"So, all this time, we thought he was signing M for Malefactor, but it was for Malcolm?"

"It seems that way."

"Is Aaron going home?"

"No, he's staying," I said, and relayed Aaron's decision process. "There's more. Aaron and I were in the hotel lounge having a drink and discussing the surveillance we'd done at Dekker's estate, when Blake Thompson walked in and sat at the bar."

"I thought he was dead."

"Yeah, so did I. Evidently that photo of him with the head wound was faked."

After a moment's silence, Terry said, "I'm coming back to Hawaii. There's too much going on and I want to be there with you."

"No," I said quickly and too loudly. I took a deep breath before continuing. "No, I think you need to stay home. It's too easy for M to attack us when we're all together. The *Adelaide* will be here in a few days. Warren and Blake are here, at M's bidding. Probably Dava, too. We know where M lives and we're working out a plan to get access to his servers. Aaron thinks he'll know when M returns to the estate. It'll be one less thing for me to worry about if you're at home with the protection detail Aaron arranged."

"So, you won't worry about me being here alone?" Terry teased.

"I *will* worry, just not as much as if you were here." My serious tone was unaffected by his lighter one. "You're the most important person in my life, Terry, and while M is active, I will worry wherever you are."

"Okay, I didn't mean to make light of your concern. I understand, and feel the same about you. That's why I want to be there; to be at your side no matter what happens." His conciliatory attitude now made me feel bad for sounding as if I were chastising him.

"It'll be over soon, I hope. Then, I want nothing more than to wrap myself in your arms in our new home and put this miserable experience behind us," I said softly. He sighed.

"Have you heard from NanC?" I asked, changing the subject.

"No, and that's a worry. It's been days since I've heard from her. Do you think Aaron would mind running her mobile number to see if he can track where she is?"

"I doubt he'll mind. Text it to me and I'll give it to him."

"Okay, hon. Talk with you soon. I love you."

"Love you, too. 'Bye."

CHAPTER 11

Russ
Aboard the Adelaide II
800 Nautical Miles Southwest of Hawaii

Alejandro and I warned the others not to come to the sundeck unless they were okay with nudity. We stretched out on our towels for the first time since leaving Australia to soak up some sun. An hour or so later, Dale and Olivia arrived, bringing ice-cold beer and sandwiches. I wasn't surprised that JT and Kat stayed away; Mack was on duty and tucked away on the bridge.

Dale brought a boombox and was playing some classic Moody Blues, but not so loudly that it interfered with conversation.

"Captain, Captain. Mack."

I picked up the radio. "Go ahead."

"I need you on the bridge for a moment. And could you bring Alex with you?"

"On the way."

When we stepped into the air-conditioned comfort of the bridge, Mack was glaring at Glen in consternation. He glanced at us briefly, but didn't seem surprised that both of us were nude.

"Glen? What are you doing on the bridge?" Alejandro asked.

151

"Well, that's sort of the problem," Mack said dryly, with another quick look in our direction. He stood, leaning against the computer console with his arms crossed tightly over his chest.

"Okay, what is it?" I pressed.

"Care to fill them in, Glen?" Mack asked.

Glen's forehead was bunched in angry lines, while he faced off with Mack. His arms hung tensely at his sides, fists clenched.

After a long, fuming moment, Glen looked at Mack and accused, "You and Olivia are a couple, aren't you?"

"Glen, buddy, stop," Alejandro tried to intercede.

Mack responded, his voice low and calm, while maintaining eye contact with Glen. "It's okay, Alex. I got this. Not that it's any of your business, Glen, but no, we're not. More like friends with benefits. She's free to do whatever and be with whoever she wants. If you're interested in her, let her know, then respect her decision, good or bad."

Glen's face was flushed and his brow was furrowed. I could see conflicting emotions scrambling across his face, fear and rejection prominent among them.

His shoulders sagged, then, and his head fell forward. His anger vanished as quickly as it had risen.

"I'm sorry, Mack. I shouldn't have said anything. You're right, it's none of my business," he apologized. Quickly, as if embarrassed, he rushed past Alejandro and me and left the bridge.

A long moment passed while the tension dissipated.

"What the hell?" I asked.

"I don't know, Cap. He barged in here like he was ready to go a few rounds, then just stood there, staring at me. That's when I called you," Mack explained.

"I should have warned you, Mack. I noticed Glen's, ah, interest, in Olivia several times. I never thought he'd act on it, though. He's never shown interest in anyone before. Did you smell alcohol on his breath?"

"Hmm, no. I don't think he's been drinking."

"I think it was very patient and very generous of you, Mack, the way you handled it," Alejandro interjected, and stepped around me to give him a hug. "Thank you."

Mack tensed awkwardly. "Uh, Russ, would you please tell your naked, gay boyfriend he's hugging a straight guy? Seriously, his dick is touching my leg. Did I mention he's naked? And gay?" But he patted Alejandro on the back affectionately before stepping back.

Alejandro and I laughed as we left the bridge. "Come on, Alejandro, let's go to the cabin and clean up," I suggested.

"I think we should get *dirtier* first, so we don't have to clean up twice," he countered.

"You've convinced me, but only because I want to conserve our fresh water supply."

"Sure, you do," he teased, laughing.

~

M

Let them plot and plan all they wanted. It would do no good. After I found where Ren and his FBI flunky were staying, I sent Blake there knowing Ren would eventually spot him. It was fortuitous that it'd happened within minutes of Blake's arrival. Ren's reaction was classic and completely anticipated; instant shock with an instinct to flee.

I had four staff members on the payroll there; James and Mason, both of whom knew Blake. James had turned into a good recruiter, approaching Will and Jack on my behalf, whom I hired just to keep track of Ren. Blake was unaware of these extra agents—so far.

When Ren and Jeffries hightailed it out of the lounge while Blake was distracted, Jack was already standing in the elevator lobby and boarded the elevator with them long enough to see which floor they selected, then exited well before then. Yes, it was simple to gather the information I needed, once I had the manpower in place.

Sophia Jeffries adamantly refused to speak to me, even in simple conversation. I threw in a few questions to lead her into thinking I was trying to discover her husband's location, but that was a ruse; her input was worthless. However, her presence in the bunker under my office was invaluable.

JT and Kat were keeping me updated on the *Adelaide II's* activities and whereabouts, so I didn't need Mack or Dale. That was just as well, since they never responded to my emails. Well, Mack never responded. Dale always sent the same response; *FUCK YOU!*

I toyed with them anyway, sending threatening emails and dropping hints to show I knew what was going on. They were about three days away from Hilo, where they were taking Olivia. I couldn't care less about her, but I enjoyed taunting the others with threats against her life.

Inside of a week, every one of them would be dead. The crew of the *Adelaide II* would die at the hands of Warren. Of course, Ren would be last so he could witness the deaths of everyone he cared about, then I planned to kill him myself. I would cherish looking him in the eyes while I did it.

After she finished her assignment in Arizona, I sent Dava, unbeknownst to Blake, to Oklahoma City to kill Terry when I signaled the appropriate time.

Blake would stay put to tie up the loose ends; Warren and his boy-toy, the various agents I'd hired, JT, Kat and eventually Aaron Jeffries. I was seriously considering releasing Blake from service, afterwards. He's been loyal to me from the beginning, despite being coerced at first.

The satisfaction of concluding this project would be enormous.

Jeffries and his cohort, whoever he was, had succeeded in finding my family estate in Turtle Bay. I should've moved those computer servers elsewhere years ago, but no one with the right talents to find them had ever come along. The main server was still untouched —so far.

Oh, and that frumpy little Gypsy Terry was so fond of. I'd already ensured her disappearance. It would be fun to throw that in Terry's face when the time came. No, he'd never hear from Nanevra C'Doe again. The thought made me smile.

~

Ren

I gave NanC's phone number to Aaron at Terry's request and explained that she'd fallen out of contact. He nodded, showing his concern, also. In less than an hour he reported that her phone was still in Goodyear, Arizona, and probably at a hotel on North Dysart Road, just north of I-10.

That made sense, because Terry said she was going to visit friends there for a few days before returning to her home in Prescott Valley. But, Aaron said, according to cell tower records, her phone had not moved in days. He arranged for a regional agent in the area to go to the hotel to check it out and expected a report soon. I dreaded the news, whatever it may be.

While we waited, Aaron donned his disguise to observe Blake, but he appeared idle. I suggested he was waiting for the *Adelaide II* to appear. Aaron countered that Blake was waiting for *me* to appear, so we decided to test his theory. Aaron arranged for us to move to the sixteenth floor, well away from the room we'd had for a couple of days.

Aaron reported that Blake was again in the lounge, sitting at a table in a dim corner where he could see everyone who entered or exited. He told me to go to the bar, order a drink, and take it with me to the room, and he would observe Blake's reaction to seeing me.

I approached the bar without looking around the room, ordered a Crown and soda with lime, paid in cash and turned to leave. I knew Aaron was disguised as a hotel employee, standing just outside the lounge. When I passed him, headed to the elevator, he fell into step a few feet behind me. Blake was a few feet farther back, following me, apparently unaware of Aaron.

I pushed the elevator call button and waited. When it arrived I, stepped onto the elevator and tapped the button for the twelfth floor. Out of the corner of my eye, I noticed Blake and Aaron also enter the elevator.

"What floor, guys?" I asked. Aaron kept silent.

"Twelve is good, thanks," Blake said. I turned to look at him, smiled, then pretended shock when I recognized his face. He was grinning ear to ear.

"Surprised to see me, Ren?"

"Uh, yeah. You could say that. You're supposed to be dead."

He threw his head back and laughed; I faked irritation. "Evidently you didn't outsmart me quite as well as you thought," he said smugly.

"Fuck off, Blake," I cursed.

"Oh, Ren. Don't be a sore loser," he taunted.

The elevator slowed and stopped at the twelfth floor and I stepped out, followed by Blake. Aaron held the door with a hand and stuck his foot out, tripping Blake unexpectedly. Blake fell forward toward me, but I quickly sidestepped and he landed hard on the floor. I flung my drink in his face and hurried back into the elevator while Aaron pressed the close button.

"Oh, Blake, I hope you're not sore," I mocked as the doors slid closed. He reached desperately to put a hand in the gap of the door but was too late and we were on our way back to the lobby. Aaron pressed a button and stopped us on the third floor, where we exited, then called another elevator to take us up to the sixteenth floor.

After going to our room, we stayed put. Later, Aaron received an email from the agent in Phoenix about NanC, and shared it with me. I sighed and called Terry. It was late afternoon in Oklahoma.

"Hey, gorgeous," he said brightly when he answered.

"I've got some sad news about NanC," I said softly, but bluntly.

"Okay," he replied slowly and waited for me to continue.

"Aaron managed to track her location based on her phone; she was still in Goodyear. He sent an agent to the hotel where she was staying and they got a manager to let them into her room." I paused.

"Go ahead, Ren. I'm okay."

"Hon, she was dead, still in her street clothes. There will be an autopsy, but it looks like she died of natural causes, several days ago," I told him. "Her phone was still on the nightstand, plugged into the charger, and all her luggage was still there. Do you know who she was visiting in Goodyear?"

"Wow. I can't believe it. Uh, no, she never told me the names of who she was visiting, just that they were friends. Maybe someone can go through the contacts in her phone and look for people with addresses in Goodyear," he suggested. I was surprised he was taking it so well.

"I'll relay that suggestion to Aaron, but I'm sure his associates have already thought of that. Are you sure you're okay, hon?" I asked.

"Yeah, I'm okay," he sighed. "I was prepared for the worst, as it was unusual for her not to stay in touch, especially since we were still working on the house sale."

"I guess you'll have to ask Brandi to put it back on the market," I said lamely.

"I'll take care of it. I'll be interested in knowing the results of NanC's autopsy. With M wreaking havoc, I wouldn't put it past him to have had her killed and make it look like natural causes." Changing the subject, he asked, "How are things going there?"

I gave him a quick rundown. "The *Adelaide* will be here in a couple of days. Aaron and I confronted Blake, just to let him know we were aware of his presence. I think he has a couple of bruises to his elbows and his ego. Russ said they're feeding false information to M, via JT and Kat. They're taking precautions, though, in such a way as to irritate M."

"You know that will just provoke him," he reminded.

"Yeah, but they're at sea and I'm not, so Russ is calling the shots."

"So, what's next on your agenda?"

"Aaron is working on a plan of attack. We're taking the fight to M, right in his own home. I don't want to say any more than that over the phone," I explained, "even though these are supposed to be secure."

"All right. Please be careful. Thanks for letting me know about NanC. Call me tomorrow, will you?" he asked, his voice quavering slightly.

"Of course, sweetheart. Talk to you then. I love you."

"Love you, too. 'Bye."

～

Blake

I was furious.

Boss, Ren spotted me. I think he already knew I was here, I messaged.

I am aware.

Was I a decoy, a lure or a warning? I asked, still fuming.

All three. Don't do anything to him. I'm working on an end to this project and I don't want you interfering by improvising.

OK, boss. *But I know what floor he's on at the hotel.*

No, you don't.

Where's Dava, then? She's not answering my messages.

None of your business. Now leave me alone. I'm busy.

I was used to his short temper, but I've never known M to get so personally involved in his projects. He always left that up to me or another team leader. *What's the crazy bastard up to,* I wondered. Maybe this is why he's dangling that full-release carrot in front of me.

~

Russ

Aboard the Adelaide II

When we rounded the eastern-most point of the Big Island, I arranged for a shuttle to meet us about four miles east, offshore of Hilo Bay, supposedly to pick up Olivia when we arrived and transport her to shore. Then we'd continue to the Ala Wai Boat Harbor near Waikiki. That's what we told JT to report to M and he went below to do so.

As we approached the coastline near Hawai'ian Park Paradise, a hushed swirl of activity began.

Mack slowed the *Adelaide II* to a crawl, announcing over the PA that we were slowing to avoid sandbars in the shallow water and warned everyone to be prepared for sudden turns or stops. Alejandro and I readied the lifeboat, rounded up Dale, Glen and Olivia and hustled them aboard. Dunkin wanted to go with Glen, but we kept him aboard.

Glen was at the controls of the lifeboat, waiting for my signal. Alex released the tether line and Mack increased speed and turned eastward. "Okay, folks, we're turning out to sea for a couple of miles to get out of the shallows. Should be good in a few minutes," he announced over the PA.

When we were a half-mile from the lifeboat, Mack aimed a floodlight at them and flashed it twice. Glen started the engine and steered it toward shore.

Mack steered us northwest again, in the general direction of Hilo and made another announcement over the PA system. "All right, everyone. We have clear sailing now and will be in Hilo Bay in about three hours. That is all."

We kept our real plan from JT and Kat, just in case they were tempted to report it to M instead of the story we'd planted.

My radio squawked twice; Alejandro's signal that Kat had left the cabin and was headed to the main galley. Quickly, I switched my radio back to the usual frequency and said, "Attention crew, attention crew, this is Russ. We're not docking in Hilo Bay, so there's no need for dock prep. A shuttle will meet us beyond the shallows to take Olivia ashore in about three and a half hours, then we'll continue on our way. Mack and I will handle the transfer, so the rest of you can relax for a while. Russ out."

I waited a moment, then thumbed the radio again, "Alejandro and Kat, Alejandro and Kat. Russ."

"Go ahead," Alejandro replied.

"Yes, Cap?" Kat said.

"I'm in the mood for a prime rib dinner. You think you two could hustle up enough for all of us?"

"Ten-four, Cap. I'm all over it," Kat replied.

"Ditto, Admiral," Alejandro said, laughing.

"Knock that shit off, Alejandro," I grumped.

"Sorry, Russ," Alejandro said apologetically.

"All right, that's better. Listen, I'd like to have the meal before we send Olivia ashore, if you two can get it done in time," I added.

"No worries, Russ," Kat replied. "You think maybe Glen could help us in the galley?"

"Nope. He snuck into the bar this morning and nicked a bottle of whiskey. He's passed out in his cabin," I lied.

"Damn. I wondered why Dunkin was roaming the crew quarters. I tried to let him into Glen's cabin, but it was locked. Okay then, I guess Alex and I can manage."

"Maybe JT can help," I suggested.

"Ha," Kat said. "He can't cook to save his life, but maybe he can boil water and prep some veggies for us. I'll draft him, Russ."

"I heard that," JT joined the conversation.

"Carry on carrying on," I replied.

Two and a half hours later, we reached our rendezvous spot with the shuttle. Mack slowed to a stop and we dropped anchor.

Alejandro, JT and Kat were putting the finishing touches on dinner. I ducked my head in the galley doorway. "How's it coming?" I asked.

"All is good, Adm—uh, Russ," Alejandro started. Kat grinned. JT sat at a small table nearby, apparently bored with nothing to do.

"Okay, good. Dale is manning the bar while lusting after Olivia," I lied again. "JT, would you help me with something in my cabin?"

"Sure, Cap. Whatever you need."

"Excellent. Let's go. We'll see you at the table in a few minutes," I said to Alejandro and Kat, and gestured to indicate JT should precede me to crew quarters. When we arrived at the cabin door, he stepped aside so I could open it, then I motioned for him to go in. I followed and closed the door behind me.

Mack was sitting in my office chair, waiting for us, holding a pistol pointed in JT's general area. JT took half a step back, and said, "Aye, Mack. Wot's going on," panic in his voice.

"What's the last thing you reported to M?" I asked.

"Just wot you told me to, Cap. That we're sending Olivia ashore at Hilo, then going on to Ala Wai."

"Good. We're going to your cabin now and you're going to give me all the electronics you have; phone, tablet, iPod, wind-up watch, flashlight or beta VHS player—I don't care what it is."

"Uh, Cap, beta and VHS are different," JT started.

"Never mind that," I said, cutting him off. "Then we're going on deck and sit at the dinner table until Alejandro and Kat start serving food. You'll take Kat's phone and whatever electronics she has on her. Understood?"

JT nodded quickly, "Yes, sir, I understand. But why?"

"We're just taking some extra precautions, JT. Nothing for you to worry about."

I led the way out of the cabin followed by JT, with Mack behind him. We collected everything electronic from their cabin in a pillowcase and headed up the stairs to the aft deck, bypassing the galley, and sat at the dinner table.

I squawked the radio and said, "Alejandro, Alejandro. Russ."

"Go ahead," he replied immediately.

"The table is set, whenever you're ready."

"On the way."

A moment later Alejandro and Kat came through with trays of food. Kat looked at JT, seeing the worried look in his eyes, then looked around the rest of the table.

"Where is everybody?" she asked, setting her tray with salads for eight people on the table, where there were settings for only five.

"JT," I said, nodding toward Kat.

"Kit Kat, give me your phone, please."

"Why?"

"Don't argue, hon. Just give it to me," he repeated. She fished it out of a pocket and handed it over. "What else have you got?" he asked.

"Nothing. Everything else is in the cabin. What's going on, JT? Russ? You guys are scaring me."

JT sighed and shook his head. "Just leave it for now," he said, putting her phone in the pillowcase under the table along with the other electronics.

I stood then, and said, "Come on, everyone," and led them to the railing.

JT lifted the pillowcase, tipped the open end down and dumped the contents into the water. We watched as everything sank out of sight.

It was quiet for a moment, then Alejandro said brightly, "Okay. Let's eat. Who wants a drink?"

We returned to the table and resumed our seats. Alejandro was the only one with sunny spirits. As he and Kat set the food in the center of the table, I told them we'd set Dale, Olivia and Glen ashore many hours ago, at an undisclosed location. I didn't want M to know where they were, and wasn't taking a chance that either of them might report the change to him.

"As I said, we're just taking extra precautions to protect as many people as we can. I'm sorry if you feel as if we don't trust you," I explained.

"You could have accomplished that without pointing a gun at me," JT grumped.

Mack grinned. "It wasn't loaded." JT was still miffed, but his shoulders relaxed when Kat pulled him into a hug.

I raised my glass. "Here's to a quick end of bad times and renewed trust among friends."

There was a round of *cheers* and *here, here*. The mood lightened considerably. "Okay, let's eat. I'm starved."

After the meal, I told JT and Kat to pack their belongings.

"Where are we going?" Kat asked.

"I really did arrange for a shuttle to meet us here, but not to transport Olivia. I'm sending you two ashore before we move on. There's no reason why you should stay aboard while we sail into more dangerous waters. If you've already been paid by M, I suggest you take the money and run. Go back to Melbourne, or wherever, but do it immediately."

Half an hour later we said goodbye to JT and Kat as they boarded the shuttle. When it was a quarter-mile away, I told Mack to set course for Waikiki.

CHAPTER 12

My frustration with Dava was stretching me to the breaking point. I sent a crew to ensure she'd completed her assignment in Arizona, but they found several mistakes —mistakes that could put this project in serious jeopardy. She'd apparently been too anxious to return to Oklahoma City and her *whim du jour*. It was too late to do anything about it now. However, her employment—and her life—would end soon. I simply won't tolerate incompetence.

She thought I was unaware of her romantic entanglements in Oklahoma City. But what she didn't know was that the object of her affection worked for *me*. This would be a fun little diversion.

Ren

"Okay, let me know when you're docked. We'll come aboard and bring everyone up to date." I set the phone on the table.

"That was Russ, I assume," Aaron said.

I nodded. "It's just him, Alex and Mack aboard the yacht now. Dale

163

and Glen are taking an air taxi and will be here in an hour or so, but the *Adelaide* won't arrive for several hours."

"What about JT and Kat?"

"Russ sent them ashore in Hilo. It sounds as though they parted on good terms. Kat is pregnant; they found out in Fiji. Russ thought they'd probably go back to Melbourne to be close to JT's family until the baby is born."

Aaron nodded and returned his attention to his tablet.

"Have you devised a plan? I'm restless being stuck in the hotel room." He probably thought I was whining.

He closed his tablet, stood and said, "Let's go, then. I think we'll be okay if we stay together. Let's head to the pub. We can have a few beers and wait for everyone else to arrive."

"Thank God," I breathed. "I'll text Dale and Glen and tell them where to meet us," I said while grabbing my phone.

I wanted to walk to the pub, since it was less than three miles away and I could use the exercise, but Aaron advised against it. He said that would make us easy targets, so we ordered a Lyft ride instead.

The pub was mostly empty, being midafternoon. We sat at a table and ordered beer and nachos. Aaron brought his tablet so he could keep working and had already resumed glaring at it, deep in thought.

"Care to share your thinking?" I asked. I was still bored, but at least we had a change of scenery. He sighed, annoyed by the interruption, but leaned back and crossed his arms.

"Okay, what's our objective? Gain access to Dekker's estate, right? Hunt him down and decide how to deal with him. If he's in his bunker and refuses to come out, we force our way in. I'm not sure how we do that without an FBI tactical team or a tank. Do you have any suggestions?" he asked. "He's got a fully armed security force inside those walls."

"Let me think about that for a minute," I said, as the beer and nachos were delivered.

While he waited, his phone rang.

"Hey, Billy. Any progress?" He listened for a couple of minutes, said thanks and ended the call.

"Who's Billy?" I asked.

"He's the guy who found NanC in Arizona. Bad news. The only contacts she had in her phone were your realtor and Terry."

"Damn, that's odd. I need to call Terry. He's not gonna like that," I told him.

When I finished telling Terry, he said, "Dammit, Ren. Listen. I want to go to Phoenix, claim the body and arrange for a proper burial for her."

"I understand, sweetheart, but I don't think it's a good idea. I feel better with you at home and the security detail looking after you."

Aaron's phone rang again. "Billy? Yeah, go ahead. I'm listening." I told Terry to hang on; I wanted to relay any information Aaron might be getting. When he ended the call, he asked me to put Terry on speakerphone.

"Terry, I'm gonna put you on speakerphone. Aaron wants to conference," I told him. I put the speaker on and set the phone on the table between us.

"Terry, it's Aaron. I just heard from my associate Bill again. He'd like you to get there right away so you can identify the body. He's unable to locate any living relatives."

I had to change mental gears. I'd been arguing against Terry going, but now even Aaron was pushing for him to go.

"Billy will take care of your flights. He said to tell you to check the departure times for the first nonstop flight on Southwest Airlines from OKC to Phoenix tomorrow morning. I'll give him your contact information and he'll text you with the boarding information. When you arrive at Sky Harbor, he'll meet you at the gate."

I could hear the relief in Terry's voice. "Oh, thank God. I thought it was going to be a battle with you two, trying to make me stay here. Okay, I'll be at the airport well before that flight in the morning."

"There's one more thing, Terry," Aaron added. "Your security detail is going with you. As long as Ren doesn't mind compensating them for their time and paying their expenses." He looked at me expectantly.

"Uh, no, of course not. If they're willing to go, I want them to," I agreed. "Just promise me you'll be careful, hon," I said.

"I will, I promise. Thanks for all your help, Aaron. 'Bye."

I tapped the phone to end the call and looked at Aaron. Neither of us spoke for a moment, while we drank beer and finished the nachos.

Finally, I asked, "So why the rush to get Terry to Arizona?"

He washed down the last bite of nachos with a long pull on his beer, then sat back and opened his mouth.

"Don't you dare belch like you did the other day," I demanded harshly. He looked appropriately chastised.

"First, and I didn't want to tell Terry this, but she's been dead for several days and the body is decomposing. The sooner we can positively identify her—or not, the better it'll be. Identification has to be done in person, and since she has no living relatives they can find, Terry is the best option. Second," he paused and shrugged. "I like the idea of messing with M, to be honest."

"I don't follow," I admitted.

"You realize, don't you, that M probably has someone in Oklahoma City watching every move Terry makes? When Terry suddenly departs for Arizona, they'll be scrambling to catch up."

"But if they killed NanC, M would know Terry would go to her. That makes me think he's walking into a trap," I surmised.

"And that's why I wanted his security detail to go with him. But here's the thing. I don't think the body in that hotel room is NanC, and we just need Terry to confirm it."

"Why in the world would you think it wasn't NanC?" I asked, incredulously.

"Mainly because the clothing on the corpse was cut. It was split in the back, the arms forced into the sleeves, then the sides were tucked under the body. That means someone put the dress on the body after death. And think about this. Why would NanC have gone to bed with her clothes on, anyway?"

I understood his reasoning. "So, you not only think the body isn't NanC, you think she's alive somewhere and M has gone to unusual lengths to make us think she's dead. Again, why? To use her against us later?"

"That I don't know. I haven't thought that far ahead. For now, I just want Terry to confirm it isn't NanC. That may help us figure out our next move."

I nodded, turning the possibilities over in my mind. I wished I'd been able to see the body and the room.

"Okay, that's taken care of for now. Can we please get back to my brilliant plan to mount an assault on Dekker's fortress?"

I leaned back and looked at him curiously before I spoke. "Answer me this, Aaron. How can you be so indifferent to Sophia's circumstances? Aren't you worried about her? Don't you care what happens to her? If I were worried about Terry's possible fate, I'd be totally worthless."

My questions refocused his attention, as if he'd failed to consider all the possibilities.

His expression hardened, then, and his eyes glazed over for a moment, before connecting with mine again.

"Indifferent?" he shot back. "Don't presume to know anything about my wife or our relationship," he said sharply.

I regretted my comments, thinking I may have pushed him into facing a reality he wasn't prepared for.

∾

Aaron

I disliked where Ren was going with this conversation. I was doing my best to compartmentalize my emotions, separating them from my analysis of the problem at hand. I seriously believed even the Malefactor would hesitate before murdering an FBI employee's spouse. I also knew Sophia understood that.

She was my soulmate and it gouged my heart to know she was being held against her will and in danger. But I knew she wouldn't want me to abandon my self-appointed assignment to attempt to rescue her. No, she'd wait it out, knowing I'd find her eventually.

If M harmed her in any way—my resolve to rid the world of his evil presence hardened inside me.

Ren regarded me with an appraising expression, no doubt curious how I would respond to his prodding. I decided to shut him down on that front.

"So, are you going to answer my question or not?" I asked bluntly. He blinked.

"What question, again?"

"Do you have any suggestions how to enter M's fortress?" I repeated, exasperated.

"As a matter of fact, I do," he said, with a twinkle in his eye. I motioned impatiently for him to continue.

"I think you're making this a lot more complicated that necessary, at least at the first," Ren said. "Here's what I think. The information we have, with Jerry's support somehow, could easily lead one to the conclusion that M was involved in terrorist activities. I mean, don't your agencies work together, or share information?"

I nodded. "We do. Especially if the CIA gets wind of a terrorist plot in the US, they relay the information to Homeland Security and the FBI to investigate."

"So, why not find a sympathetic federal judge, present the evidence and get a warrant for Malcolm Dekker's arrest under suspicion of terrorism? Or at the least, detain him for questioning? You're a persuasive man, Aaron. I don't think it would take much to obtain a warrant. Then we just walk up to the gate, present it to the guards and see what happens."

I thought about it for a minute, but I couldn't find anything wrong with the plan. After all, Dekker already knew we'd scoped out the estate. He'd either be there or not, whether we knocked on the door with a warrant or lobbed grenades at it. If the first method failed, we had the second option to fall back on.

"Come on," Ren cajoled. "Dekker won't think we'd settle for such a dull approach, considering all he's done to us. No, he'd expect us to roll in with guns ablazin'." I stopped him with a hand raised in surrender, smiling.

"You know what, Ren? That's brilliant. I have to admire your thinking. You're an asshole at times, but a brilliant asshole," I laughed and raised my beer in solute.

Ren laughed, too, and raised his glass.

"What the hell is this, then? Some kind of damned mutual admiration society?" a booming voice accused.

Looking up, we saw Dale approaching, talking loudly from twenty feet away, with Glen a few steps behind.

"Oh my effin' God," Ren exclaimed, jumping to his feet. Glen ducked around Dale and ran into Ren's arms. "I'm so glad to see you guys," he said, hugging Glen, then slapping Dale on the back.

"You, too, Ren," Glen said, then nodded toward me. "Hi, Aaron."

~

Terry

Goodyear, Arizona

When I arrived at Sky Harbor Airport, security detail in tow, I was greeted at the lounge gate by a thin man in a black suit who introduced himself as Bill Dawson. "But call me Billy," he said amiably as we shook hands. With only carry-on bags, we left the airport immediately and made the short drive to Goodyear.

Contrary to typical FBI agent behavior, in my limited experience, Billy was gregarious and friendly as we headed to the hotel, although respectful of my feelings about NanC.

"It's good that you arrived as quickly as you did, Mr. Franklin. Ms. C'Doe appears to have passed several days ago and the room has started to smell. Pardon my directness, sir," he added apologetically.

I nodded. "It's been several days since I've heard from her, which isn't normal. I've been worried about her."

"Transportation is on standby to remove her from the premises, but I asked them to wait until you could see her and identify the body."

I nodded, again. Tears threatened.

When we pulled into the hotel parking lot, he drove around to a side entrance, parked and led me inside to NanC's room. A man stood by the door and handed me a mask. "You may want to wear this while you're inside, sir," he suggested.

Billy and I entered the room, leaving the security detail in the hall. The air conditioning was on maximum and the room was surprisingly frigid, which I assumed was meant to slow the decomposition process. The stench was overpowering.

I looked around the room. NanC's bag was on the luggage rack, with clothing partially strewn about, as though she'd been interrupted while unpacking. Her phone was on the nightstand, right where I'd been told it was found. Toiletries were set out on the bathroom vanity. Shoes were primly set at the side of the bed, ready for her to step into when she rose. A sheet covered her small form on the bed. I stepped forward, Billy by my side.

"Mr. Franklin, we need you to positively identify Ms. C'Doe, if you can. I know this is difficult and that you were close. I'm sorry." He reached over and gently pulled the sheet down to about her waistline, revealing the same red pantsuit she'd worn when we parted ways on the way home.

My eyes blurred then, and I felt my stomach heave as I scanned upward to her bloated face. I turned away and stumbled from the room. Out in the hallway once more, I tossed the mask aside and fell to my knees, doing my best not to vomit—and failing. When I finished, I rolled sideways onto my butt and leaned against the wall, still gagging. Billy handed me a cold bottle of water. "Here, drink some of this," he suggested. I drank.

Then Billy nodded to the attendants, indicating it was okay for them to remove NanC's body. He grasped my elbow and steadied me as I returned to my feet.

"Billy," I gasped between breaths.

"Yes, sir?"

"Billy," I repeated, locking my gaze with his. "That's not Nanevra C'Doe. She looks very much like the NanC I know, and no doubt resembles the photo on NanC's passport, but she isn't NanC."

Billy's demeanor then reverted to what I'd experienced with the security detail; cold, detached and professional. He immediately dialed a number on his phone.

"Please tell the coroner's office there has been a complication. We need them to expedite the autopsy. I'll explain later. Also, send the crime scene crew out here immediately." He ended the call and turned to me.

"Mr. Franklin, we need to talk. In deference to Mr. Jeffries, I'd rather not take you to the office. Where are you staying while here?"

I shrugged. "I only brought an overnight bag in case I ended up staying, but planned to return home late tonight. I don't have a hotel reservation," I explained. "I can't stay at this hotel, though," I muttered.

Billy stared at me for a moment, then approached my security detail to confer. I was beyond caring what they discussed. The woman in that room was not NanC. So, where was she? Why did she leave her belongings behind? I was confused and needed to talk to Ren. When I raised my phone to make the call, Billy stopped me.

"No calls just yet, Mr. Franklin."

"I need to talk to my husband and Aaron Jeffries," I said, continuing to dial. He jerked the phone from my hand then.

"We're taking you to a safe house. We'll be able to talk privately there and ensure your safety, too. Come with me," he said, leading me back to the car. Numbly, I followed, with the two agents on my heels.

The entire situation felt surreal and I couldn't concentrate on what I'd just seen. As we entered the car, I turned to the security team in the back seat and said, "Considering that you've been looking after me for days since I arrived in Oklahoma and have come to protect me on this trip, don't you think I should know your names?"

They turned stone cold faces toward each other, then back to me. In unison, they removed their impenetrable black sunglasses. The one on the left said, "Abbott." The one on the right said, "Costello." They replaced their sunglasses and sat in silence. Absurdly, I started to laugh as Billy drove us out of the hotel parking lot.

"He's in shock," Billy said, looking at the agents in the rearview mirror.

Evidently, I was the only one who found humor in the situation.

"Face forward and buckle your seatbelt, please, Mr. Franklin," Billy coaxed, which only made me laugh that much harder.

We drove the better part of an hour before pulling into the driveway of a nondescript home in a quiet neighborhood. The garage door opened and we glided inside. Another FBI clone stood waiting, and invited us into the house.

"Billy, I'd like my phone back, please. I won't make any calls, but while we're talking, I need to make flight reservations."

"Very well. I'll trust you on that, for now. Do you still plan to return to Oklahoma this evening?"

I shook my head as he handed the phone to me. "No. I'm making reservations to get me to Hawaii as quickly as possible. And I would prefer you didn't tell Aaron, by the way. He and Ren will just try to talk me out of coming."

"Interesting," Billy said. "I didn't know that's where he was. There must be something really serious going on," he baited, but I refused to bite.

A few minutes later, another agent entered the house and placed NanC's bag on the coffee table, removing her phone and everything else he managed to stuff in there.

"Mr. Franklin," Billy said, trying to get my attention. The smell wafting out of the bag was too much for me, and I ran to bathroom, retching along the way. When I returned a few minutes later, the bag had been removed, and only NanC's phone, passport and purse remained on the table.

"My apologies, Mr. Franklin. I should have asked the agent to leave the bag outside to air out."

"That's okay. And do me a favor, please. Call me Terry."

"Very well, Terry. We need to discuss a few things."

I nodded. "Surely there's a cold beer in this place? Or bottled water? Anything will do." I went to the kitchen to see what I could find. The fridge was loaded with beer and a few essentials for making sandwiches. I grabbed bottles for everyone and carried them back to the sofa.

Abbott and Costello had completely let themselves go. One had removed his jacket while the other had loosened his tie. Both still wore their sunglasses, which made me snicker. Surprisingly, both accepted the beers I offered them, as did Billy. The other agent had disappeared while I was in the bathroom.

I sat next to Billy and said, "Is it okay with you if I work on my flights while you ask whatever questions you have?" He nodded. "Okay, then. Shoot."

"When's the last time you had contact with Ms. C'Doe?" Billy started.

"I don't remember exactly, but my call log should have that information." I thumbed through the entries to find the right one, showing it to Billy. He nodded.

"Yeah, that matches the information in her phone. What was the nature of your relationship?"

"Billy, you make it sound like the dead woman in the hotel is NanC. It isn't. I'd appreciate it if you'd stop referring to her in the past tense. I'd rather you asked questions that would help us figure out who has NanC now or where she's gone. How'd they substitute that poor woman in the hotel? And why, for God's sake? If someone has gone to all that trouble to make us think NanC was dead, then she must still be alive somewhere, and probably being held against her will."

I stopped to catch my breath before continuing. "To answer your question, the nature of our relationship is that we are friends. We met a few weeks ago when she came to see the house Ren and I put on the market and made an offer to buy it. We fell into a quick friendship that surpassed that of just a potential homebuyer and seller."

Billy listened without interruption, sipping his beer occasionally. "What else do you know about her, Terry?"

That had me stumped. "Uh, not much, actually. She lives in Prescott Valley. She said she was visiting friends in Oklahoma City, but I never met them or even knew their names. She claims she is, uh."

"Yes?" Billy prompted.

"Well, now it sounds ridiculous, but she says she is clairvoyant."

"Hmmm," Billy responded. "So I've heard, from Aaron." He leaned back and sipped his beer before continuing. "I've received a significant amount of information from Aaron. And your security detail here needed to know a few basic things about your, uh, situation, when they were assigned to you."

"Like?" It was my curiosity aroused this time.

"I'll leave that to Aaron to share, when you talk with him."

We sat in silence for a few minutes and I was caught completely off guard when Abbott spoke.

"Will you need us to go with you to Hawaii, Mr. Franklin?" He slid his sunglasses down his nose and arched his eyebrows at me.

"I hadn't thought that far ahead, to be honest," I admitted, sitting back in my chair. "I know Ren would feel better about my safety if you were with me. Hell, I'd feel better about it, too. So yeah, I guess I would like you to come. All expenses paid, of course."

"All right. I'll arrange tickets and priority boarding for the three of you while you go with Abbott and Costello to get clothes, toiletries and suitcases."

"Are you coming, too?" I asked.

Billy drained what was left of his beer before answering, setting the empty bottle on the coffee table. "No. I don't know much about Aaron; we've only met a couple of times. I do know he's way up the ladder at FBI headquarters and that he's involved in some serious shit. We have a mutual friend in another agency who's been, helping, let's say, with Aaron's assignment. I'm aware that Aaron's wife has been kidnapped and her whereabouts are unknown. We stick together, Terry. If my friend says Aaron needs help, then he'll get it."

"I understand he has his hands full in Hawaii," he continued. "So, let's not waste any more time. You three get the stuff you need for extended travel and I'll make the arrangements. I'll be here to help behind the scenes, if I can."

CHAPTER 13

*R*uss
Mamala Bay
One Mile South of Ala Wai Boat Harbor

"Mack, Mack. Russ."

"Go ahead, Cap."

"Why are we stationary?"

"Waiting on our reserved dock space to become available. It may be a few hours, or possibly tomorrow. The yacht occupying it is apparently having engine repairs and can't be moved, and we're not allowed to drop anchor here."

"Damn. Okay, I'm gonna call Ren and see if they want to take a shuttle to get to us."

"Sounds good. Mack out."

"Alejandro, Alejandro. Russ."

"Go ahead, Admiral," he replied, with a snicker.

"Where are you?"

"Our cabin, sir. Care to *dock* in here while we have some time?"

"As tempting as that sounds, it'll have to wait. I'll be there in a minute." Alejandro was sprawled on the bed when I arrived, but stood to greet me with a kiss and a hug.

"Looks like it may be several hours before we can dock. I'm thinking of having everyone shuttle to us and we can have dinner on board. Do we have enough supplies?"

Alejandro nodded. "Yeah, that was the plan all along, except that we'd be docked in the marina. We'll only have seven to feed, so that'll be no problem. If we get them to shuttle here, Glen can help in the galley while you entertain everyone else."

"Okay. I'll call Ren," I said, and pulled my phone off the belt clip.

"Hey, Russ," Ren answered. "Are you already docked?"

"Nah, we've hit a snag. Our dock space is still occupied. They don't have many that will accommodate a boat the size of the *Adelaide*, so we'll have to wait," I explained. I could hear him conferring with Aaron, then he spoke to me again.

"I've put you on speaker. What do you suggest?"

"Alejandro and I were thinking the four of you could take a shuttle to the *Adelaide*. We can move farther out where we can drop anchor and stay offshore for the night. Maybe our space will be cleared in the morning."

"Hi, Russ, this is Aaron. Glad you made it here safely."

"Thanks, Aaron. We're glad, too."

"I think it's a great idea for us to come to you. I feel like we're sitting ducks when we're on dry land. Ren and I need to talk to everyone about some plans we're making, which we'll do when we get there. How do we do that, by the way?"

"I'll arrange for a shuttle to pick you up. Where are you?" I asked.

"At the pub next to the marina. How long, do you think?" Ren answered.

"Less than an hour. If it's going to be longer, I'll contact you. Stay put. Someone will come and find you."

"See you soon," Ren replied, and ended the call.

Alejandro stood patiently, waiting for me to finish the shuttle arrangements. As I ended the call, he pulled his shirt over his head.

"Mack, Mack. Russ," I hailed on the radio.

Alejandro untied the string on his board shorts, which then loosely fell around his ankles. His eyes gleamed, and his teeth shown brilliantly white between smiling, sensuous lips.

"Yes, sir?"

"Uh. Mmm. Ren and the others will be arriving via shuttle in the next hour or so. Keep a lookout, will you?"

Alejandro turned away from me, but looked at me over his shoulder as he lightly spanked his firm butt cheeks, then turned to face me again. He was as aroused as I.

"You sound distracted, Cap. Everything okay?" Mack asked.

"Yeah, yeah, no worries. Something's just come up I need to take care of. Let me know when the shuttle is within sight, okay?"

"Will do."

Alejandro took me by the hand and led me to the bed. I couldn't think of a better way to pass the time.

~

Two hours later, a reunion of sorts was underway. Ren, Aaron, Glen and Dale arrived in less than an hour. Mack took the *Adelaide II* to a safe location where we could drop anchor. Glen was helping Alejandro in the galley; the rest of us were at the bar, with Dale tending.

"How'd it go with JT and Kat?" Ren asked.

"Not bad, actually," I replied. "As far as I know, they're headed back to Melbourne to be close to JT's family until Kat has the baby."

"So, if you and Mack were agreeable to keeping them on, they wouldn't be able to for quite a while, right? Her being pregnant, then needing time off with the baby, and so on." Aaron added.

"Depends," Mack replied. "If they lived in Hawaii and we kept our charters around the islands, JT could still work without being away from Kat and the baby that much." He looked at me. "Russ would have to be okay with it, though."

I nodded, but didn't add to the comment. Instead, I turned to Ren and asked, "What else is new?"

Ren and Aaron exchanged a long glance, as if deciding who should respond. Ren dove in, then, ticking off his comments on his fingers as he went.

"NanC is dead. Or maybe not. We'll know soon. Aaron's wife, Sophia, has been kidnapped by the Malefactor. Blake Thompson is alive. We know where M lives, we think." He paused, then and looked at Aaron. "What else? Did I forget something?"

"Yeah, a couple of things. Warren has moved to a different hotel, and we still don't know what M has in mind for him. We're working on a plan to confront the Malefactor. Oh, and Terry will be here—with his security team—tomorrow afternoon," Aaron said, flatly. The look on Ren's face was priceless.

"What the hell, Aaron?" he exclaimed. "You know I didn't want him here."

"Wasn't my choice. He told Billy he was coming whether we wanted him to or not. Billy expedited the arrangements and his security team offered to come, too. It won't hurt to have a couple more agents on our side," Aaron explained.

Ren pulled his phone from a pocket to call Terry.

"Won't do any good," Aaron continued. "Even if you're able to reach him, he'll have to land in Honolulu before you could send him home again. Somehow, I don't think even you can force him to do that."

"Who are Billy and Blake?" Mack interrupted, confused.

Distractedly, Ren answered. "Blake works for M; we thought he was dead. Billy is an associate of Aaron's who helped Terry in Arizona, when we thought we found NanC dead in a hotel there."

Dale, who'd ben uncharacteristically quiet, finally spoke. "I wonder if I made the right choice throwing in with you guys. I don't know nearly as much as the rest of you about what's happening, but it sure seems like some serious shit is going down." He turned to Mack, then, and asked, "Have you heard from Olivia? Did she make it home?"

Mack nodded. "She messaged when she got there, but I haven't spoken with her."

"Too bad she couldn't join us for dinner," Dale added. "She's one hell of a woman."

Mack glanced at Ren and said, "Yeah—no. It's probably best if she stays as far from us as possible, right now." Ren nodded in agreement.

My radio squawked. "Russ, this is Alex."

"Go ahead," I responded.

"Glen is on his way to set the table and I'll bring out the food shortly. Y'all want to eat on deck or in the dining room?"

"On deck. The weather is gorgeous," I told him. "Make sure you have clothes on, Alejandro. We're in mixed company."

"Ten-four, Admiral," he answered with a laugh.

Dale lifted his radio then. "Belay that order, you little habanero. It's clothing optional on this boat," he teased.

"Not for you, Dale. Unless you're alone in the engine room, exchanging hummers with those precious engines of yours," I deadpanned. Everyone burst into laughter, and Dale's face flushed.

"Good one, Cap. Very good," he complimented, raising his glass.

~

Ren

I was torn between emotions. On one hand, I was pissed at Aaron for dropping the news about Terry's arrival the way he did. On the other, I felt guilty for being glad and relieved he was coming.

Once Glen set the table, we moved on deck. Alex had prepared a meal with a mushroom theme. Homemade cream of mushroom soup, a small wedge salad with bleu cheese crumbles and sautéed chicken strips with peppers and mushrooms, followed by roasted prime rib and whole grilled portabella mushrooms.

Conversation was generally light, with everyone filling everyone else in on events since we were together last.

I pushed my plate away, finally, feeling like I was about to burst. Glen appeared with fresh coffee, which I accepted, although I declined the key lime pie Alex brought out for dessert.

"What's the agenda for tomorrow, then?" Russ asked. "You and Aaron have a plan to confront the Malefactor?" I nodded, but Aaron jumped in to explain.

"First thing in the morning, I'm going to the First Circuit Court to get a warrant to detain and question Malcolm Dekker, who we think is the Malefactor. He owns a huge estate on Turtle Bay. If I'm successful getting the warrant, Ren and I plan to simply approach the gate and present the warrant to the guards." He shrugged. "We'll see what happens."

"Do you think he's there? What about your wife, is she there, too?" Russ continued.

"I don't know, to both questions. But we have to start somewhere."

"While he's blowing smoke up the federal judge's skirt for the warrant, I plan to pick up Terry at the airport," I announced. "Anyone want to join me?"

Glen immediately raised his hand.

"Humph," Aaron grunted. "That won't work. His flight doesn't arrive until early afternoon. You and I need to be banging M's knockers against the drawbridge by then."

"All right. I guess. Dammit." I reluctantly agreed.

"Pity party of one, your," Aaron started.

"Shut up, Aaron. That's getting old," I barked in return.

Aaron nodded and grinned.

"It's getting late, gents. If you're going back tonight, I need to call for the shuttle, unless you want to stay aboard and go back first thing in the morning," Russ informed us.

"I need to go tonight, guys," Aaron said. "I've got to prepare some documents for the judge, and that'll take a few hours."

"Alrighty, then," Russ said, standing. "I'll arrange the shuttle. Mack, would you move the boat back to where we were when they boarded?" Mack nodded and made his way to the bridge.

~

Terry
Above the Pacific Ocean
En Route to Honolulu, Hawaii
I looked to my left, then to my right. Abbott and Costello were

seated on either side of me. Their presence was a comfort, but they insisted on maintaining their enigmatic façades. When we were in the departure lounge in Houston waiting to board the flight, I called them out.

"So, Abbott and Costello are your real names?"

Abbott nodded *yes* while Costello shook his head *no*. Jeez.

"Who's on first?" I asked, my irritation with them apparent. Neither responded, although I'd swear Costello's mask split for just a second when the corner of his mouth twitched. I returned to reading on my tablet.

After takeoff, I tried using the plane's wi-fi to text Ren, but it didn't work while flying over the ocean. I'm sure Aaron had told him by now that I was on the way. It's the last thing he wanted, but I refused to stay away. Whatever happened, we'd face it together, just like before.

Connie was such a dear. I'd called her from Houston to let her know I was headed back to Hawaii and didn't know when I would be home again. She said she'd keep an eye on the place and let *YKW* in to check for bugs, as needed. The poor woman was so busy, she could hardly find time to breathe, much less play caretaker of our house.

Damn. My thoughts were flitting around as randomly as one of NanC's run-on outbursts when we first met.

"Mr. Franklin," Abbott said quietly to get my attention. "You're fidgeting, sir. Can I get you something to calm your nerves? A dozen sedatives? A jug of wine? A gallon of whiskey, perhaps?"

Was that sarcasm I detected?

"Uh, no, thanks. I'm fine," I answered, completely surprised by the mere fact that he spoke. "And dammit, stop calling me *sir* and *Mr. Franklin*. Call me Terry. I've *told* you that."

Costello leaned forward then, and shook his finger at Abbott. "Bad, Abbott. *Bad*," he admonished.

"Oh, hell," I said, unable to stop a snicker. "Bad Abbott?"

It was Abbott's turn to lean forward and stare at his partner. "Don't you need to go to the loo, Costello?"

Looking from one to the other, I was completely tongue-tied for a moment. "You guys are jacking with me, aren't you? *Bad* Abbott and

Loo Costello? Give me a break," I finally managed. I snickered again, then burst into laughter. These guys were a riot. They reached across me and knuckle-bumped each other in a *mission accomplished* gesture. I just shook my head and closed my eyes.

~

Aaron

When I stepped off the elevator, I almost collided with Blake Thompson. I kept walking. He whirled and fell into step beside me.

"Well, Mr. Jeffries. Where are you off to in such a hurry, I wonder?" he needled.

I stopped suddenly, facing him, pretending I was about to speak, then looked past him and waved. "Ren, over here," I called. When Blake turned to look, I wound up the tightest swing I could muster and slammed my fist hard into the left side of his face. I wound up for another swing, but it wasn't necessary. He collapsed in a heap like a puppet whose strings had been cut.

My fist hurt like hell. I flexed my hand to work the pain out of my knuckles and turned away. Hotel security was rushing toward me. I'd already put my ID badge on the outside suit coat pocket, so I just pointed to it when they approached and said, "Aaron Jeffries, FBI. Hold that man until the police get here. I'll be back in twenty minutes."

I hurried out the exit, looking once over my shoulder. Blake was sitting up and rubbing his head, but not looking in my direction. The security guards were bent over him, asking him questions. Within seconds, I was inside a waiting taxi and on the way to the district court. *Damn. I'm too old for this shit*, I thought, trying to catch my breath.

~

M

Warren, go to the Ala Wai Boat Harbor. Buy some strong binoculars on the way, then stay out of sight and wait for my instructions.

I turned my attention to Dava.

Where are you?

In Oklahoma City, waiting on your signal to kill Terry.

You idiot! Terry went to Phoenix after you botched the job and is now on his way to Hawaii. It's too late to catch up now. Stay put until I tell you differently.

She's useless. Couldn't think her way out of a paper bag, and certainly couldn't think for herself. Even though she'd failed in Phoenix, I felt I'd gained enough time anyway to misdirect Ren.

I needed people like Blake, who knew what I wanted before I knew it myself. People who could anticipate my needs.

As if he knew I was thinking about him, he messaged me.

Boss. I got decked. That FBI fucker hit me with a sucker punch and knocked me out cold in the middle of the hotel lobby. I have no idea where he or Ren have gone. Instructions?

Anger bubbled up inside me until I thought I'd burst a blood vessel.

Just wait. I'll be in touch.

I slammed the phone down on the desk—hard. Am I surrounded by idiots? Even Blake was getting lazy—again.

～

Aaron

Dekker Family Estate

Turtle Bay, Oahu, Hawaii

"Seriously, this couldn't have waited until we picked up Terry?"

I shook his head. "Hmm-mmm. I didn't want to take a chance that M might get wind of the warrant before we could get here to serve it," I told him as we pulled into the drive by the gate at Dekker's fortress. "Besides, I asked Ty to meet them at the airport. He'll make sure Terry and the security team get to the marina safely so they can take a shuttle to the *Adelaide*."

"I thought Ty was keeping track of Warren," he accused.

I shrugged. "We know where Warren is. He's unlikely to stray far from the hotel in the brief time Ty will be gone," I assured him. "Come on. Let's see who's home."

We left the vehicle. I had my FBI identification and the warrant in one hand, held high above my head.

As we approached the gate, a guard picked up a megaphone and spoke to us. "Stop on your side of the double white lines, gentlemen. Keep your hands above your heads."

We did as he instructed. He descended the short flight of steps from the guard tower and approached us, stopping at another white line a foot away from ours.

"My name is Aaron Jeffries, with the Federal Bureau of Investigation. I have a warrant for the detention and interrogation of Malcolm Dekker," I said with a flourish of the documents in my hand.

The guard reached toward me. I handed him my identification and the warrant. He studied both for several seconds, handed them back and said, "Very well, sir. Wait here while I announce your presence. You can relax, now, sirs," indicating Ren and I could lower our arms.

"I'll need to make a brief phone call, Mr. Jeffries, then I'll show you inside." He caught my gaze, waiting for me to confirm I understood. I nodded.

He returned to the guard tower. I could see through the heavily tinted glass that he held a phone to his ear.

~

M

The land line rang; a rare enough occurrence that it worried me.

"What is it?" I answered heatedly.

"This is security at the front gate. We've got an FBI agent by the name of Aaron Jeffries here with a warrant to interrogate Malcolm on suspicion of terrorism. He says he just wants to talk."

"Do not, under any circumstances, let that man inside the gate, do you hear me?" I screamed into the phone.

"I hear you. But this is a courtesy call, to let you know the situation. He has a legal warrant signed by a federal judge. I will not refuse entry. I'm sorry; I just can't do that."

"You're not sorry, but you will be," I growled, slamming the handset into the cradle.

~

Aaron

Two minutes later, the guard returned.

"Gentlemen, unfortunately, I've been instructed to deny you entry." He gave me a measured look and dipped his head. "However, I have refused to follow those instructions," he said, as he again looked me squarely in the eye. "Your credentials are valid and you have a legally executed warrant."

A long pause ensued, when neither Ren nor I knew exactly what would happen next, as the guard continued to scan us with a seasoned eye for spotting deceit.

He stepped back then, two steps, placing his fists on his hips. "Are either of you armed?"

"I am," I admitted. I gestured toward my feet. "May I?" He nodded, holding a hand up behind him, as if to ward off any hotshot defenders who might be tempted to shoot.

"What's your name?" I asked the guard as I bent over to retrieve my pistol from the holster around my ankle, handing it to him.

"Well, now. I guess that's only fair, seein' as how I know who you are. My name is Dekker," he threw out, as if he were throwing down his gauntlet in challenge. He squinted at both of us then, gauging our reactions. Ren and I both paused unintentionally, staring at the guard.

"Well, I know you're not the Malcolm Dekker we're here to see," Ren said angrily, jumping into the gaping silence. "You're not old enough. So, you're who? Grandson? Adopted? Bastard child of a long-forgotten mistress? Illegitimate product of an incestuous affair with his mother or one of your sisters or cousins?"

"Ren," I said sharply. "Tread carefully, here."

Surprisingly, the guard laughed good-naturedly. "Nah, he's good.

And nailed it on his third guess, near enough. The geezer fucked my mom just once, after catching her cleaning the guest quarters after hours. He's still a horny ol' dude, but we keep him secluded now. Essentially locked up. At his age, he can't do much harm anymore. Can't mess with the help or pay off his sins like he used to. Nowadays, he's stuck watching porn or fifties TV—if there's a difference," he laughed. Returning to a more serious tone he added, "My name is Jackson Dekker, after my grandfather."

"At least he takes care of his own," he continued. "Mom is head of housekeeping, and I run the security team. But you know what? When you guys appeared was the first time the boss ever openly ordered me to violate the law." His face hardened, then, and he shook his head.

"Ain't gonna do it. I don't wanna end up like him. I'd like nothing more than to pack up Momma and disappear. She needs to retire now, and enjoy her twilight years with nothing haunting her or bearing down on her."

A heavy silence fell, then, as Dekker ran out of steam. His demeanor conveyed regret for sharing more than he thought was prudent.

I extended my hand to give him my pistol, but he gestured toward the car.

"Please put it in your vehicle, Mr. Jeffries." I did so. "Follow me, then," he said, turning toward the secondary interior gate.

"These guys are okay, men. Let 'em pass," he called out. He turned back to us and said, "I hope you're not disappointed, gentlemen. Malcolm isn't as, uh, *interesting* as he used to be. But keep yourselves out of reach or he'll scratch your eyes out if he has one of his hissy fits —which he undoubtedly will."

My curiosity grew with every step inside the estate.

~

Jerry White
CIA Headquarters
Langley, Virginia

I almost missed the timid chime on the computer, it was so quiet. I pushed the paperwork I was studying aside and leaned toward the computer monitor. Another of the Malefactor's proxy servers had been breached.

Wait.

I looked closer, then scanned the last several breaches. This wasn't a breach of *another* server. It was the *last* server. I now had the bastard's base of operations—and it wasn't on Oahu. *Damn. It's in our own back yard.* I went to work attacking his firewall.

∾

M

An alarm sounded on the computer, startling me. I don't know who the bastard is or how he managed it, but he just breached my firewall; I never thought it could happen. He knows where I am and has no doubt sent that information to the FBI fucker helping Ren.

Blake. I need you to get a charter flight immediately to Dulles in DC—as quickly as possible. Leave now. Take a puddle jumper to the Luray Caverns Airport. Get to the Stalactite Café and text me when you arrive. This is urgent. Spare no expense. GO NOW.

∾

Blake

What the hell? I stared at the text message on my phone. Why would he send me to Virginia? Now, of all times? This whole damn thing felt like it was about to crumble, just like it did last time, in Beau's basement. I messaged Anne.

I love you, Anne. How are you?

Huh? I'm good. I wasn't expecting to hear from you. Are you okay?

Yes, my love. I'm good. I just wanted to tell you I love you. I hope to see you soon.

I love you, too, Blake. You're scaring me.

Don't worry. It's all good. I'll explain soon.

CHAPTER 14

*R*en
Dekker Family Estate
Turtle Bay, Oahu, Hawaii

Aaron and I sat in a sumptuous library, with hand-carved, floor-to-ceiling shelves on every wall and along pleasing aisles throughout the room, almost like a maze. Heavy, comfortable furniture was scattered around the room, with indirect lighting warming every nook.

Jackson led us into the grand, yet dimly lit room, gesturing for us to sit in two high, wing-backed chairs facing a mahogany desk. "Malcolm will be here momentarily," he said, then retreated the way we came.

Upon his exit, I heard a door to my right open. I turned in that direction. A middle-aged nurse wearing hospital scrubs backed into the room, pulling a wheelchair with her. She slowly turned and pushed the chair to the other side of the desk. I couldn't help but notice her unusually large breasts.

The chair, occupied by Malcolm Dekker, I presumed, fit perfectly under the desk, as if it were made especially for a wheelchair occupant. The elderly man in the chair looked at each of us with rapidly blinking eyes, trying desperately to focus on our faces. His breathing was labored, even with the oxygen tube tucked under his nose and over both ears.

After setting the brakes on the chair, the nurse stepped back a couple of paces behind Dekker and stood with her arms crossed judgmentally, glaring at Aaron and me as if we were grim reapers hovering over Dekker with scythes of death.

Dekker's eyes finally found mine and locked on tight. "So. You're the bastard who's been dogging my family," he grunted.

I looked at Aaron, nonplussed.

"Mr. Dekker, we'd like to ask you a few questions, please," Aaron interjected.

"Who the fuck are you?" Dekker demanded.

"Sorry, sir. My name is Aaron Jeffries, with the FBI. Jackson said he would announce us. We've been investigating a series of domestic and international threats to our national security. Many of the communiques we've intercepted have been relayed through computers at this location. What can you tell me about that?"

"Not a goddamned thing," he answered testily. "Look at me. You think I give a *shit* about national security when I struggle every *damn* second to suck a breath of air into my lungs?" He panted heavily, as if to prove his point.

"Very well, sir. Where have you traveled in the last year?" Aaron continued. Dekker grunted a laugh then, which launched him into a coughing fit. The nurse rushed to his side to pat him comfortingly on the shoulder.

"Don't touch me, dammit," Dekker barked. She backed away quickly. Dekker returned his gaze to Aaron. "Where have I traveled in the last year? Ha. I haven't left this damned prison, if you must know, for more than a decade. Nurse Bigtitty here can testify to that," he asserted, pointing behind him with a thumb. Nurse Bigtitty wasn't amused, but evidently felt compelled to offer her own opinion.

"You listen to this man," she chided us. "He's elderly, terminally ill and abandoned by his family. He's got no reason to lie. I've been his nurse for over ten years, and he's never left this house." She reeled herself in, then, when Dekker shot her a withering look over his shoulder.

"Hush, woman," he grumbled.

Aaron fell silent, at first, I thought due to the double assault from Dekker and his nurse. I glanced at him and saw he was reading a message on his phone. This didn't look good. He looked at me, then, and shook his head. When he stood, I followed suit.

"Mr. Dekker, you have my apologies. I have apparently made an error in judgement as to your involvement. I will do my best to ensure you're not bothered again. However, I must ask. Does your son have access to your wealth and resources? Is it possible he might have subverted your life's work toward his own malevolent desires?"

Dekker smiled then; a tight-lipped, secretive and evil smile. He knew something he wasn't telling. He began to chuckle, then to cough uncontrollably. Nurse Bigtitty yanked the nasal cannula off his face and replaced it with a full mask and cranked up the oxygen to help him breathe.

"You work for the government?" she asked, astounded, glaring at Aaron. "Just goes to prove education ain't what it used to be." She released the brakes on the wheelchair, whirled Dekker around and stomped toward the door with determined strides. "Do your research, G-man," she called over her shoulder. "Mr. Dekker only has one son, and he's the one who let you in here. He ain't the one you gotta worry about," she shouted, which triggered a solid backhanded thwack from Dekker over his shoulder that landed squarely on her left breast.

"You listen to me, you old geezer," she said loudly as they crossed the threshold to the next room. "You hit me again and I'm gonna hold a pillow on your face until I put you outa my misery." The door closed softly behind them.

~

Glen
 Aboard the Adelaide II
 Mamala Bay, Waikiki, Hawaii

I hated the stillness that weighed upon us aboard the *Adelaide II*. Not that we were still, exactly, but it felt like doom hovered above, causing us to unconsciously crouch beneath it. I had a feeling things were going to get much worse, and soon.

The *Adelaide II* was holding station a half-mile offshore, with the bow pointed toward the beach. I lay on the sundeck, naked. I thought of Olivia, then, and touched myself, but arousal eluded me.

Russ and Alex were with me, asleep, also soaking up the sun. Their usual banter and affectionate teasing had been absent for a change. Russ, in particular, was keyed up, and that worried me.

Early evening was rapidly approaching and we hadn't heard from Aaron, Ren, Terry—*anybody*. I desperately wanted a drink. I raised my head and looked around. Dunkin was snoozing in the shade, his tongue lolling sleepily from his mouth. I stood and headed toward the bar. No one would notice if I had a couple of swigs, right?

Wrong.

"Glen, Glen. Mack," squawked my radio. I looked up to the bridge as I grabbed the radio.

"Uh, hello?"

"Glen, you should wake Russ and Alex. Ren and Aaron will be here in a few minutes. Ren says Terry and his team will be here in a couple of hours, and we need to start dinner soon."

"Okay, Mack. Will do," I replied.

~

Ren

As the shuttle approached the *Adelaide II*, I saw Glen standing, almost jumping up and down, on the sundeck, nude, waving at us. I shook my head, smiling, wondering what the shuttle crew must think of Glen.

Glen roused Alex and Russ, who wrapped themselves in towels and quickly disappeared below decks. Never the modest one, Glen tossed us the tie line and we transferred to the *Adelaide II*.

I was anxious to see Terry. I *needed* to see him—to hold him in my arms. He'd gone through a horrible experience with NanC's purported death, and I knew he was still distraught. He refused to believe she was dead, since the body discovered in Goodyear was not hers. With no means to communicate with her, he held onto the meager hope she was still alive. Held captive by the Malefactor, no doubt, but at least alive. My dour misgivings ran deeper, to a darker hue.

"Ren," Aaron said quietly.

"What?" I replied irritably.

"You were awfully quiet on the way back. Tell me your thoughts about our visit to Dekker's estate," he requested.

"You, first," I countered. He sighed heavily.

"Fair enough. I thought that Jackson Dekker turned out to be a decent guy, considering the twisted family he was so unfortunate to be born into. He carries a lot of resentment, but has managed not to let it ruin him."

Just then, his phone rang, which he answered immediately.

"Jerry? What have you got? Okay, wait. Ren's here. Let me put you on speaker." He did so and set it on the table between us.

"Hello, Ren. It's nice to meet you, finally, but we don't have time for a proper introduction. Aaron, I finally penetrated M's firewall. You're not going to believe this. It's right here, in Virginia, near the Luray Caverns. I can give you the GPS coordinates, but you'll have to engage your FBI group to do the follow-up."

"That's outstanding, Jerry. Yeah, text them to me so I don't write them down wrong. Is there anything else?"

"Not right now."

"Okay. You've been amazingly helpful, Jerry. I've got to get off the phone and make arrangements to get to Virginia."

"Don't waste any time. The moment I crashed his proxy servers and breached the firewall, he was alerted. Whatever he has up his sleeve, he'll unleash it very soon."

"Understood. I'll be in touch. Thanks again, Jerry. Bye."

While he tapped rapidly on his tablet, Aaron asked me to ask Russ to send for a shuttle, then suggested I get my luggage. When I arrived on the aft deck, Aaron was waiting for me before boarding the shuttle. We'd only been aboard the *Adelaide II* for a couple of hours, and now had to leave again. Damn.

When we arrived at the shuttle dock, a black SUV waited for us; Aaron's handiwork, no doubt. We loaded our bags in the back and slid into the back seat. Aaron was unusually quiet since the phone call with Jerry.

"What's on your mind, Aaron? Are you thinking Sophia might be in the building with M's servers?" I asked quietly.

"There's an excellent chance of it, in my opinion. It's not that far from our home."

"So, are we mounting an assault or a rescue?"

"I'll talk to the tactical team leader once we're airborne. She'll know better how to proceed. She'll probably scout the location long before we get there," he explained.

The driver turned off on a side road before we were even close to the airport.

"Where are we going, Aaron? I thought we were catching a flight to DC," I said.

"We are, but not a commercial flight. I called in another huge favor and managed to get us on a military flight at Hickam Field. We'll fly nonstop to Joint Base Andrews."

I nodded, feeling very lucky to have Aaron on our side, with all his connections.

"Damn, that reminds me. I heard from Ty while you were getting your bags. One of his associates has kept an eye on Blake Thompson for us. He left for the airport a couple of hours ago. I'll give you one guess where he's headed."

"Virginia, no doubt." He nodded. "I guess that confirms we're on the right track."

"Yup," he agreed. "Ty also picked up Terry and his security team and is taking them to the shuttle dock."

"Do you think Blake will get to DC before us?" I asked.

"He'll have to take a commercial flight or a charter. Either way, military planes get airspace priority. The only problem is, we're flying to Joint Base Andrews, while Blake is flying to Dulles. Dulles is significantly closer to Luray. A shuttle plane can get us to the Luray Caverns Airport, though. I just have to figure out where to get one."

"Are shuttle planes not allowed to land at Andrews?" I asked. He shook his head.

"Not unless it's a flight emergency."

"Surely you can arrange for an exception, considering the circumstances," I suggested.

"I'm working on it, Ren. I'm working on it."

Once we cleared security, we were met by an escort vehicle which led us to the plane. We took our bags from the back of the SUV and waved at the driver, who then followed the escort vehicle back to the security gate.

We made our way up the mobile stairs and were greeted at the door by the pilot.

"Good afternoon, gentlemen, please take a seat of your choice and buckle up. We will depart in five minutes. Once we're airborne you can help yourselves to food and beverages. Sorry, no flight attendants to take care of you," he said, smiling.

"I understand you're in a hurry. Once we're at cruising altitude, I'll punch it a bit. We should land at Andrews in about eight hours. Meanwhile, if you have any questions during the flight, pick up any phone. It'll ring the flight deck and either the co-pilot or I will answer."

"Will we have phone and wi-fi service during the flight?" I asked.

"Yes, sir. I'll sound a tone when we've reached thirty-five-thousand feet and that'll be your signal that it's okay to use both."

The pilot turned toward the flight deck.

~

Terry
Honolulu, Hawaii

Ty met us at the gate and introduced himself. If he hadn't shown me his FBI credentials, I never would have believed he was an agent.

He wore board shorts and a snug T-shirt that complimented his sparkling eyes and engaging smile.

"You must be Terry. Hi, I'm Ty," he said, extending his hand, which I shook, but he held it longer than was customary.

"And this is your security detail?" Ty asked, looking over my shoulder.

"Yes. Ty, meet Bad and Loo. Bad and Loo, Ty," I introduced. They shook hands. "Those are nicknames—don't ask," I added.

My phone rang. Ren. "I need to get this, guys," I said.

"Can you walk and talk at the same time?" Ty teased. I nodded. "Good. Let's go. You can talk along the way."

I answered the phone and walked a few feet behind Ty, with Bad and Loo behind me.

"Hi, sweetheart. How are you? Where are you?"

"Hey," he replied, sighing. "I'm good, I guess, considering I won't get to see you for a while."

"Really? Why not? I thought this guy, Ty, was taking me to you," Terry wondered aloud.

"If I'd been there, I would have met you at the airport myself. Aaron and I are on a plane headed to Joint Base Andrews, outside Washington DC," he explained. I could tell he wasn't happy about it. "It's a long story, hon. Aaron and I need to think out some strategy, so I'll tell you later. Have you made it to the *Adelaide* yet? I bet they were happy to see you."

"No, I just arrived. The flight was delayed. We had to circle wide around a storm."

"Ah. That explains why I didn't hear from you earlier. I thought your plane landed hours ago. Well, I feel better now. Anytime I don't hear from you when I'm expecting it, I worry something's happened." I could hear the relief in his voice.

"That was a good diversion. You almost made me stop thinking about why you're going to Washington DC. If you don't want to go into the long story, give me the short version in fifty words or less," I suggested.

"You'll just worry," he argued.

"No more than worrying about what you're not telling me."

He sighed in resignation. "Okay, the condensed version then. Aaron and I visited Dekker's estate in Turtle Bay earlier today and confronted Malcolm Dekker. He's old, Terry. Very old, frail, and terminally ill. A feisty cuss, for sure, but not capable of doing all the things we attribute to the Malefactor. Shortly after, Aaron's friend in the CIA contacted us and said he'd broken through the last of M's proxy servers and was attacking the firewall—in Luray, Virginia. So that's where we're headed. We hope Sophia is there, too, and that we'll be able to rescue her as well as apprehend M."

"Damn," I breathed. "That's the condensed version? I can't wait to hear the full story," I told him. "So, if Malcolm isn't the Malefactor, who is?" I pressed.

"Ah, well. That's part of the longer version. I'll tell you about it later, okay? Say hi to everyone for me when you get to the boat. We left in a hurry and I didn't get to say bye to anyone except Russ."

"I will. I love you, Ren."

"I love you, too, and I miss you so much. Talk to you soon. Bye."

∾

Warren

Ala Wai Boat Harbor

The phone beeped.

OK, Warren. It's your turn in the spotlight. Are you at the harbor?

Nearby, yes.

Good. Walk southwest along Holomoana Street, past Lagoon Beach. Go as far as you can until you are standing by the western-most row of boat slips. Text me when you're there.

I finished my beer, paid, and asked the bartender where Holomoana Street was. He looked at me as if I had three nostrils.

"Seriously? Step out the front door, turn right and walk about twenty feet."

"And then?"

He just shook his head in disgust and turned away, muttering "fucking tourists." While his back was turned, I grabbed the cash I'd left for a tip and stuffed it back in my pocket. Bastard.

I stepped out and turned right, looking around to get my bearings. Sure enough, there was Holomoana Street. I took off at a comfortable pace along the side of the road, anxious for this to be over.

~

Terry

We'd almost reached the shuttle dock when I thought I saw Warren, of all people, standing on the curb looking lost.

In the driver's seat, Ty exclaimed, "Holy shit. I don't believe it."

"What?" I asked, craning my neck around to get a better look at the guy I thought was Warren.

"Uh, nothing. I just saw a guy back there that I know."

"Warren Millpond?" I suggested. Ty's head spun toward me so fast I half expected his neck to snap.

"You know Warren?" Ty asked.

"Well, yeah. He used to be a good friend, before he took up with— some unsavory people."

"That's putting it mildly," he said wryly, and pulled the vehicle to the side of the road. "Come on, guys, we're gonna see what he's up to."

Warren was a couple of blocks ahead of us, but never looked around. It's a good thing, too; he'd recognize Ty and me.

Bad and Loo were right behind me, clearly not dressed for the climate. Those black suits looked hot and uncomfortable, while I was wearing shorts and a T-shirt. Ty was dressed Hawaiian style. As a group, I'm sure we stood out like four drag queens at a Westboro Baptist Church revival.

Warren slowed, evidently looking for a specific place or path. Ty motioned for us to slow, too, and made a shushing gesture for us to stay quiet. Then he stopped and whispered to Bad and Loo.

"You guys armed?"

They looked at each other before Loo slid his sunglasses down his nose and gave Ty a withering look. Ty nodded. "Okay, cross the street and pace us from there."

"Listen," Ty continued, "I've been tailing this guy for weeks and he's completely oblivious. Had no clue he was being followed. But I also discovered someone else following him, too, sometimes a man, sometimes a woman. I haven't seen either of them for a couple of days, but that doesn't mean they're not here somewhere. Be careful, and keep your eyes open."

~

Russ

All this intrigue was getting on my last nerve. I took a couple of hours after Ren and Aaron left to spend alone with Alejandro, and that helped a lot. Now, it was quiet with only Dale, Mack, Glen, Alejandro and me aboard the *Adelaide II*. Dunkin was around somewhere, probably napping in whatever shade he could find.

I was surprised Terry and his security detail still hadn't arrived, as it was now late afternoon. Alejandro took Glen to the galley with him to start dinner. I had no idea what he was planning, but I was starved.

Dale was in the engine room or his cabin, choosing to have some alone time. Mack was at his usual perch on the bridge. He asked for the night off and was planning to take the shuttle Terry arrived on back to shore. I suspected he had plans to see Olivia. Since her departure, Glen managed to pull himself out of his puppy-dog attraction to her. I still felt sad for him, though.

I decided to do my rounds and make sure everything was ship shape for visitors.

~

Warren

A fire-breathing dragon had taken up residence in my belly. I was so nervous, it was making me nauseous. I sat on the rocks bordering the sea barrier at the western-most pier, as M had instructed. I pulled the binoculars from the satchel and scanned the bay. All those yachts looked alike to me, but after a couple minutes of searching, I spotted the *Adelaide II* about a half-mile away. I wished I was still aboard and had never fallen under M's malevolent fist.

I pulled the phone from my pocket and texted M.

I'm here. I can see the Adelaide *in the bay.*

Excellent! Can you see who is aboard?

I see a shadow in the wheelhouse, which is probably Mack or Russ. No, scratch that. Russ is on deck. I'd recognize that lanky form anywhere. Mack must be on the bridge. If anyone else is on board, they're either below decks or on the opposite side of the boat where I can't see them.

Send the following text to the number saved in the phone. Send it now. RIP —M

What the hell is that supposed to mean? I asked.

Just do it, Warren, and I'll tell those agents following you to set you free.

I whirled around and saw Ty a few yards away, with Terry at his side. Across the street, two men were running toward me, and they were armed.

Quickly, I typed in the text and sent it to the number saved in the phone.

OK, it's done. Now call off the dogs!

I'm so glad, Warren! You've done wonderfully well. And I want you to know that you're the one who pushed the button.

What the fuck are you talking about?

~

Glen

Aboard the Adelaide II

My feelings were hurt that Ren hadn't come to say goodbye before he left, but Russ said they'd been in a hurry. Something about catching up to the Malefactor, with very little time left.

Russ went to do his rounds. No one was in sight, so I sneaked to the bar and grabbed the whiskey, put it to my lips and guzzled about a quarter of the bottle.

"Glen," Alex yelled from the galley. Startled, I turned so fast I almost dropped the bottle. I thought he'd caught me drinking.

"What?" I yelled back.

"Go to storage and get a case of tomato sauce, fresh melons and strawberries. I'm out in here," he instructed.

"Uh, uh, okay. I'm going."

I headed to the storage unit below where we kept the nonperishable items. Boxes and boxes of canned goods and dry goods were stored there, in nice alphabetical order. I liked it when things were orderly.

I heard something beeping in one of the bins. I pulled several boxes out of the way until I found the source and ripped open the cardboard box.

~

Terry

Ty motioned for me to move behind him, which I did. He produced a small handgun from somewhere and had it leveled at Warren.

"Ty? What are you doing here?" Warren asked. "Is that you, Terry?" I peeked over Ty's shoulder to see a troubled expression on his face. "What's going on?"

"Drop the phone and the satchel. Do it now. I won't ask you again," Ty ordered, still slowly approaching Warren. Abbott and Costello were now on either side of us, their weapons also drawn and pointing at Warren.

"Drop everything. Do it now," Abbott shouted at Warren, who looked confused and as if he were about to be sick. He looked at the phone, shaking his head.

"Terry, I think I've done a really bad thing. Where's Ren? Please tell me he isn't aboard the *Adelaide*," Warren pleaded, tears filling his eyes.

"What bad thing have you done, Warren?" Ty said in a calm tone, trying to soothe Warren.

Warren flailed his arms, still refusing to drop the phone. He brushed tears from his eyes so he could see and started tapping the numbers. All three agents fired. Warren collapsed on the rocks, dead before his head hit the stone beneath him with a sickening thud.

～

Glen

A gray LCD display was counting down and just passed forty seconds, thirty-nine. Wires disappeared deeper into the box.

Panic flooded my mind. All I could think of was to get everyone off the yacht. I ran up the stairs shouting at the top of my lungs, "Abandon ship, abandon ship." I ran through the galley but Alex wasn't there. I ran to the bar and dining room after, still screaming.

Out on deck, I still couldn't see anyone. Then I remembered the sun deck and ran forward as fast as I could. "Abandon ship, everybody abandon ship," I shouted repeatedly.

"Russ, Alex you've got to get off the yacht," I screamed hysterically. Their heads popped up from where they were sitting on the sun deck, then they stood. I never slowed. I ran as fast as I could and grabbed them to drag them to the railing.

"Glen, what the hell is going on?" Russ demanded, pulling me to a halt.

"Go," I shouted. Russ is taller and heavier than I am, but I somehow got him and Alex over my shoulders in a fireman's carry and leapt over the railing. Before we hit the water, the *Adelaide II* exploded, blowing us farther away.

CHAPTER 15

Ren
Above the USA
En route to Washington DC

Aaron ended the call and turned to me. "Okay, it's all taken care of." He leaned forward and put his face in his hands, rubbing his eyes gently. He was beyond tired. We both were. "Let me get some cold water and I'll fill you in."

I nodded and said, "I'll take one, since you're up." He handed a bottle to me and resumed his seat.

"All right. The tactical team has already scouted the coordinates Jerry gave us. It's a small coffee shop near the Luray Caverns called the Stalactite Café. It's sitting on a section of land that's been undergoing urban renewal for years. There used to be entrances into the caverns in the area, but they were all plugged years ago. That section of the caverns isn't open to the public anymore. Too dangerous." He paused to take a long drink of water.

"So, here's what the Tactical Team Leader thinks. The café is probably a simple front, covering a secret entrance to part of the cave. There are all kinds of power lines and such leading into a conduit tunnel behind the café—too much for a simple café to need."

"And somewhere inside the café is a door to a tunnel or elevator that leads to a secluded section of the caverns," I surmised.

Aaron nodded. "That's what the TTL thinks. We've detained everyone who works there for questioning and replaced them with our own people; cooks, servers—hell, even the customers are our people."

"So we sit back and wait for the Malefactor, Blake and whoever else to show up and then what?" I asked.

"I don't know. It'll be out of my hands at that point. The TTL will have to evaluate the situation. She knows Sophia is likely being held prisoner there, and for that matter, so might NanC."

"You really think NanC is a prisoner?"

"I doubt it," he said, shrugging. "Although I have to consider the possibility. I think it's much more likely that she's an accomplice. Whether voluntarily or by coercion, I have no idea. It would be just like him to drag an innocent elderly woman into his service."

I nodded, not liking the direction this conversation was leading. "Well, he's never taken prisoners that we know of, so that supports your argument."

"He did with Terry and his brother, when you first tangled with him," Aaron pointed out.

"No," I shook my head emphatically, "that wasn't M, that was Hanson. He was the one who wanted to kill his own children because they're gay. M just gave him the means to do so," I explained. "Hanson was merely a *project*."

"Ah, that's right. But, he kidnapped Sophia," he reminded me.

"Well, there is that," I conceded. "There's also the effort he expended to conceal NanC's disappearance. Why go to the trouble to find and kill a lookalike in Phoenix and dress her like NanC? How likely was it, do you think, that anyone who knew what NanC looked like would ever see that body?"

Aaron nodded. "Yes, but, surprisingly, that's where he made a mistake."

"How so?"

"He should have destroyed NanC's phone so we couldn't locate her. We'd have had no idea where she was. That mistake let us find her, and subsequently become suspicious because her clothing had been cut and the body poorly dressed. That's why I insisted on sending Terry to identify the body."

"So, you think M is still using NanC, otherwise he would have really killed her in Arizona instead of a substitute," I added, continuing his reasoning.

"Exactly. And remember, Billy said when he did the background check on NanC's address, she didn't own a home in Prescott Valley, or elsewhere. I think all of that was forged by M to divert suspicion away from NanC."

"This means that besides Blake Thompson, Sophia and the Malefactor, we may have NanC there, either as an unwilling accomplice or a prisoner," I nodded, mulling over our discussion.

"I hate to say it, but of those two options I hope it's the latter. It will break Terry's heart if it turns out NanC was a willing accomplice in all this. Hell. M probably knows how close Terry and NanC became, and may be holding her to use against him somehow, to get to me."

"What scares me about all this is that we still don't know who the real Malefactor is, although I'd bet a year's salary it's Malcolm Dekker's illegitimate son, Jackson."

"That's contrary to your earlier evaluation of him. Either way, I think we'll have the answer very soon. The real Malefactor will either be in that cave or the last set of servers Jerry breached will have his identity."

Aaron's phone rang again. He looked at me with a *what now* expression and answered the call. "Hi, Abbott."

~

Terry

Waikiki, Oahu, Hawaii

I couldn't catch my breath. I stood there panting, staring down at Warren's body, trying to understand what just happened.

"Are you okay?" Ty asked.

"What kind of stupid question is that? No, I'm not okay," I shouted. "Why did you shoot him?"

Just then we heard a huge explosion offshore and whirled to see one of the yachts annihilated in a rapid chain of at least three blasts. They were so powerful, we felt the pressure wave wash over us.

"To prevent that from happening," Ty answered in the sudden calm. "Damn. We're too late."

When the smoke dispersed, the wreckage was horrible to behold. The yacht was rapidly sinking, with its bow jutting above the surface.

Curiosity seekers on other yachts were already powering toward the sinking vessel, while a Coast Guard helicopter approached from the Honolulu Search and Rescue Center.

Ty turned to me, then, and asked, "Do you know who was aboard that yacht, Terry? I know Ren and Aaron have already left for the mainland. Who's left?"

It took a moment for his meaning to sink in.

"What are you saying? That was the *Adelaide*? How can that be?"

Abbott and Costello were both on their phones. Abbott signaled to get Ty's attention. "Can you take Terry to a hotel somewhere?"

"Huh-uh. I've got to take him to the field office," Ty responded. Abbott spoke into his phone again, and a few seconds later Ty's phone rang.

"This is Ty," he answered and listened for a moment. "Yes, sir," he responded and ended the call.

"Come on, Terry. The cops are on the way and we need to get you away from here." He gripped my arm forcefully and pulled me away, leaving my security detail standing by Warren's body.

"Wait. We have to find out who was aboard. I need to know if they survived," I protested, trying to pull away from Ty.

"Listen, Terry. I'll tell you right now, that blast was strong enough to kill everyone aboard. Just be thankful Ren wasn't there. Now, let's go before the cops get here. Aaron says you may still be in danger."

Ty forced me forward again, almost at a run, until we were back inside his vehicle and driving away.

"Now tell me who you think was aboard," Ty demanded.

"Russ and Alex, for sure, and probably Mack, the First Mate. Also, Glen would be there; he doesn't stray far from Russ and Alex. That would only leave Dale, the engineer."

"No visitors or charter guests?" Ty pressed.

"No," I shook my head. "Uh, wait. Oh, my God. Dunkin." I slid down in my seat.

Ty reached over and gripped my shoulder firmly. "Stay with me, Terry. Who's Duncan?"

"Sort of the ship's mascot. He's our dog, a Norwegian Dunker. There's no telling where he was on board."

"Well, as I said, just be grateful Ren wasn't aboard. This could have been a lot worse. Once I get you settled, I'll see what I can find out from Aaron. We'll let your security team deal with things here."

"I'm okay, Ty. Thanks. Where are you taking me," I asked, amazed by the ever-expanding debris cloud that circled above this never-ending cyclone.

"Where have you stayed before? The Hilton's nice." I nodded absently. "Okay, that's where we'll go. It's not far."

"You really think everyone aboard was killed?" I wondered aloud.

"I don't know, man, I don't know. I guess it would depend on where they were on the yacht when it exploded. I wouldn't hold out much hope, though. I know that's hard to hear, Terry, and I'm sorry. But it's better to be prepared for the worst."

All I could do was nod. I thought that if NanC had returned with me to Oklahoma instead of going to Phoenix, she'd be with me today. Maybe she would have known about the explosion and could've warned us. I still refused to believe she was dead.

Ty parked me at the bar with a whisky and soda while he took care of getting my room and a connecting suite for Abbott and Costello, and turned over the luggage to a bellhop. Then he returned to the bar and ordered a drink for himself.

"Have you tried calling Ren?" Ty asked.

"No. He's on a plane to DC."

"Uh, yeah. A military plane, Terry. Full cellular and wi-fi service, even over the ocean. Try calling him," Ty suggested.

"Well, shit. Why didn't you tell me that before?" I grumped.

"Bring your drink. We'll go to your room so you have some privacy to talk."

I nodded again, and walked along quietly as he directed me toward the elevator lobby.

∽

"Do you know Ty?" I asked Ren, when I finally had him on the phone.

"Yeah. I met him when Aaron and I first got back to Hawaii. Why?"

"He's a hottie," I observed quietly, glancing at Ty across the room. He looked up from his phone conversation and winked at me. He'd thought ahead to order a tray of sandwiches and fruit, but I wasn't hungry. I nibbled on the fruit anyway.

"Hey, mister. Don't get any ideas. Jus' 'cause I'm ten hours away doesn't give you license to be hookin' up with every hot FBI agent who jumps in your lap," Ren teased.

I hiccupped. "That's not gonna happen, my beautiful husband."

"How much have you had to drink?"

"Only one. Ty thought I needed it to calm my nerves. I feel drained of energy." Sleep tugged at my consciousness, but I didn't want to hang up.

"Here," Ty said, "Let me talk to Ren," and took the phone from me. "Ren, he's fine. He's in shock, is all. Have you heard what's happened here?"

"Only that the *Adelaide* exploded. No word yet on survivors."

"So, Aaron hasn't told you about Warren?" Ty asked.

"No, what happened?"

"As I was driving Terry and his security detail to the shuttle dock, we spotted Warren on the side of the road, coming out of a bar. We decided to follow him," Ty began. With the questions Ren and Aaron had, it took about five minutes to get through it all.

"We think Warren inadvertently caused the explosion on board the *Adelaide*, under the Malefactor's instructions. He was crazy at the end and we weren't sure if he had a gun. When he tried to punch in a code on the phone, we shot and killed him. But we were too late. Half a minute later, the *Adelaide* was destroyed."

My eyes were droopy. I could hear Ren talking, but not understand what he was saying.

"The last thing on his phone was an outgoing text message that said *RIP —M*."

I heard an emphatic *fuck* from Ty's phone.

"We've got connections with the Coast Guard and the Honolulu Police Department," he continued. "When I know anything, I'll contact you. It's not looking good, though," Ty said, sadly. Then, "Sure, hang on a sec."

"Here, Ren wants to talk to you," Ty said and handed the phone to me.

"Are you okay, hon?" Ren asked.

"I wish everyone would stop asking me that. Hell, no, I'm not okay. But I will be. I just need sleep."

"All right. Well, we'll be landing at Joint Base Andrews in a few hours. Things are likely to get messy here, but don't worry, okay? I'll call you when we know anything. Ty promised to wake you when they find out who, if anyone, survived the explosion. I wish I could be with you now, but Aaron and I are going to end this nightmare one way or another tonight. I love you, Terry. More than I can possibly say."

"I love you, too." I handed the phone back to Ty.

"Okay, guys, I'll take care of Terry, so don't worry about him. Good luck, tonight. Do you want another drink?" Ty asked me when he ended the call.

"You trying to take advantage of me, mister?" I replied, trying to grin.

"Oh, if I only could," he teased. "No, I'd never. Just tell me what you want to do."

"I'd like to have a long, hot shower, brush my teeth and go to bed," I answered with a yawn.

"A'ight then, come on," he said and hauled me out of the chair. Then he led me to the bathroom and closed the door behind me. "Let me hear some noise in there, or I'm comin' in to strip you myself," I heard him call out, his voice muffled by the closed door.

"I'm good. Give me twenty minutes," I called back. I unpacked my toiletries, then brushed and rinsed my teeth before undressing to get in the shower.

The hot water felt wonderful. I sat in a ball with my eyes closed, the hot water flowing over me until I felt the cold lump of fear and worry in my gut begin to melt. Standing again to soap and rinse, my mind turned to Ren, remembering the last time we'd showered together.

I quickly diverted that train of thought.

Stepping out of the shower, I dried off and wrapped the towel around my waist. When I returned to the bedroom, Ty was sitting at the desk talking on the phone. He looked up at me with deep sadness.

"Thanks, Abbott. Yeah, I'll tell him. Talk to you soon." He ended the call and came toward me. "You feel better?" he asked.

"Mmm-hmm. Who was that? Abbott?" I asked. "What did he have to say?"

"Terry, you should probably sit. I've got some bad news. But here, put these on first," he said, and handed me clean underwear and a T-shirt from my bag before facing away to give me privacy.

"Thanks," I mumbled through a yawn as I dressed, then pulled a pair of shorts on top of the underwear. I sighed when he turned around, smiling at me, but the engaging grin couldn't crack the sadness in his expressive dark-brown eyes. "What's the bad news?" I asked.

He dropped his head for a moment, then raised his eyes to mine once more. "There were only two survivors, Terry. Russ Garrett and Glen Moreland. They're both in critical condition at Queens Medical Center in Honolulu. Dale, Mack and Alex died at the scene."

I sank into the chair, numb from the evil and hate that claimed so many lives.

Alex. Sweet, beautiful Alex. One of the most gentle and loving spirits I've ever known. How would Russ go on without him? Did Russ know about Alex? I looked up at Ty, about to ask that very question.

He shook his head. "No, Russ doesn't know about Alex yet. He's been unconscious since the rescue. Same with Glen. They both have major injuries. They've got a chance, but it's touch and go right now. It'll be twenty-four to forty-eight hours before we'll know—if they'll survive."

"How badly were they hurt?" He gave me a brief, but rather gruesome report of their injuries. I nodded, resting my chin on my chest. "When can I see them?"

"I'll see what I can do, but as I said, don't expect anything for a couple of days."

"Okay, but they need to know someone is here to take care of them. Ren and I will pay their medical expenses, so tell the hospital to do everything they can," I pleaded.

"Ren already told me the same thing, and I'll tell the hospital. Don't worry, they're in very good hands."

"You talked to Ren? When?"

"While you were in the shower. He said to tell you to go to bed and he'll talk to you in the morning."

"Huh. Have they arrived in DC?" I asked.

"Not yet, but soon. They've got a difficult few hours ahead of them. But we'll talk about that in the morning, okay? Do you feel like you can sleep? I can ask the front desk to send the on-call physician with a sedative, if it'll help," Ty offered.

"No, I'm going to lie down," I said, moving to the bed. He turned out the lights and sat quietly at the desk, concentrating on his phone.

~

Tyrel Singleton

FBI Special Agent

If it were me getting all that news at once, I'd have been keyed up for days. Terry crawled under the blankets and, moments later, the clothing I'd given him was shoved from beneath the blankets and off the side of the bed.

"Any word on Dunkin?" he asked sleepily.

"Not yet," I replied, but I doubt he heard me. He was already sinking into the dreamy huddle of his husband's arms. I sat at the desk, looking at the photos of the deceased victims Abbott sent me, while waiting for Terry to go soundly to sleep.

Albright had been in the engine room of the yacht, next to the hold where the explosives were hidden. His body was shredded and almost unrecognizable.

Matthew McDonald was on the bridge, high above the explosion, but trapped under water amidst the twisted wreckage when the yacht sank. If he wasn't killed by the explosion immediately, he likely drowned.

Alejandro Martinez was probably the luckiest. The explosion snapped his neck, killing him instantly. Aside from his clavicle protruding through his right shoulder, he looked virtually unharmed.

I'd deliberately kept this information from Terry. No need planting those images just before he went to sleep. I didn't skimp on the extent of Russ and Glen's injuries, however. They were both in very serious condition, but at least they were alive.

Glen's right arm and leg were shattered, and he had a serious scalp laceration, bruises to his face and neck and one eye so badly damaged it might not be salvageable.

Russ fared moderately better. He suffered a concussion due to blunt force trauma to the left front of his skull, just above his temple, and a shattered right elbow. He was also bleeding internally, undergoing emergency surgery right now.

Both men were on ventilators to help them breathe. For Ren and Terry's sake, I truly hoped these two friends survived.

Aaron had massive influence in the right circles. He'd arranged to get the bodies to the coroner's office as quickly as possible and expedite their autopsies, if needed.

Terry was breathing deeply; softly snoring. I put his phone on the charger, left a note on the nightstand with my number in case he needed to reach me and let myself out as quietly as possible.

CHAPTER 16

Connie Watson
Oklahoma City, Oklahoma

I agreed to meet Bill Murray at Ren and Terry's, so he could sweep for bugs again. I had something to do afterward, however, and intended to ask if he wanted in.

I'd followed the stupid bitch who'd tailed Ren too many times to count; she was back in the city and I wanted to know what she was up to. No doubt she'd been instructed to follow Terry—at the very least—but Terry had flown to Hawaii and she was a little slow on the uptake.

"Connie," Bill Murray nodded to me as I unlocked the back door to let us into the house. Bill Murray wasn't his real name, but since he wasn't in the habit of giving his name to anyone, I referred to him by the nickname Ren had given.

"Bill," I swept out my hand, indicating he could get started on the house, then pulled out my phone and placed a call to the Where You Bean, the neighborhood coffee shop.

"Yeah, she's here," my favorite barista acknowledged. "The guy she's been seeing just came in. Gotta go."

Bill did a thorough job of the house, as always, and twenty minutes later, he was ready to go.

"How would you like a cup of coffee?" I asked him.

"Do I need a cup of coffee?" A bushy gray eyebrow lifted as he asked the question.

"Depends. Are you aware of stalker bitch?" He nodded. "Well, if you want to catch up with her, you need a cup of coffee." I followed him out the door and locked it behind me.

"All right, but I'm driving."

"Are you one of those guys?" I glared at him.

"Probably. Come on." He pulled keys from a pocket and headed down the block where his SUV was parked. He unlocked the doors remotely, then dropped his gear into the back of the vehicle.

I didn't say much on the way to the coffee shop, other than to give him directions. Once there, we got out and walked in, still silent.

Sure enough, stalker bitch was there, with the guy she'd been seeing ever since she'd popped up in Oklahoma City again. What I knew that he didn't, however, was that she'd been seeing someone else, too, on the sly.

I'd told Terry I was working on a nasty adultery case. I didn't tell him there was no marriage involved—I figured he and Ren had enough on their plates already, and he'd have waved me off if he knew I was tailing her. I could handle this part. I'd run the license plates of a truck and a hybrid car; one owner was the jealous type—the other was the possessive type.

Stalker bitch liked playing with fire, looked like.

"That her?" Bill Murray asked softly, indicating SB with a discreet nod in her direction.

"Yep." He and I got in line at the counter to place an order. So far, SB and boyfriend number one were busy talking, their heads close together over identical lattes.

"Uh-oh," I mumbled when boyfriend number two walked through the door. He immediately zoned in on SB and BF number one, before taking three long strides toward their table and jerking number one from his chair.

"What the hell?" Bill breathed when BF number two started yelling at number one, while SB sat there with an amused smile on her face.

She was one of those; the ones who liked being fought over.

Number two threw the first punch, number one answered by decking number two. When number two fell to the floor, taking two chairs down with him, he managed to twist around and pull a small handgun from a pocket.

Damn.

Boyfriend one ducked when the gun went off, unsuccessfully, as it turned out. The bullet lodged in his chest and he collapsed to the floor, leaving a wide-eyed stalker bitch open behind him. Number two fired again and she dropped like a sack of buffalo dung, the wound in her forehead spraying blood and brain matter over a few screaming patrons.

"Stop right there," I snapped at number two, who was now attempting to scramble to his feet and run. I'd jerked my pistol from the holster sewn into my purse and pointed it at him. He raised his gun toward me and fired, but he was still awkwardly trying to regain his feet and his shot went wide. I fired once. He fell to the floor clutching his chest then lay still. A pool of blood swelled from beneath him.

"Call nine-one-one," someone shouted, as two customers rushed to the other two bodies.

Later, like everyone else in the coffee shop at the time, I was detained for questioning. The bodies were carted off by the medical examiner's office. I had a license for the gun, and my PI's license ready when requested. Based on the eyewitness reports of the others, plus my own statements, the police detective—whom I knew—determined I had fired in self-defense, killing an alleged felon after he committed a double-murder.

When I was released, I rejoined Bill Murray. He'd waited for me, surprisingly enough.

"You decided against coffee?" He grinned as we walked toward his SUV.

"I'm going home and getting into a bottle of Scotch," I said.

He shut the driver's side door and started the engine. Before putting the vehicle in gear, he sighed before turning toward me.

"I had the impression you didn't like guns."

"I don't. Doesn't mean I'm too stupid not to carry one in this business."

"Name's Max," he held out a hand to shake. "Max Robertson. Glad you decided we needed coffee."

~

Ren

Joint Base Andrews

When we landed at Andrews we were met on the tarmac by the ubiquitous, standard black FBI SUV and the standard special agent in a black suit and black sunglasses. They were accompanied by military security, as well. The FBI driver took us to an office building on base property where he presented us to the Tactical Team Leader, Helen Bishop.

"Hello, Helen. Good to see you again," Aaron said, then introduced me. "This is Darren Gifford, who I've been working with the past few weeks."

Helen reached to shake hands and nodded at me. "Nice to meet you, Mr. Gifford."

"Likewise, but please, call me Ren. May I call you Helen?" I replied, and she smiled warmly, nodding her head.

"What can you tell us?" Aaron asked.

"Let's go to the conference room where some of my team are waiting. We can get you coffee and something to eat, if you need it," she said, leading us along a short hallway.

When we were seated at the conference table, hot coffee in hand, she briefed us.

"Everything is quiet at the café. A few customers wandered in, but they were told the freezer was out and all the food had spoiled, so they were given a free cup of coffee and sent on their way. We're waiting for Blake Thompson's arrival."

"Do we have any details on that?" I asked.

"Yeah. He's landing at Dulles in," she glanced at her watch briefly, "eighteen minutes. He's already arranged for an air taxi to fly him to the Luray Caverns Airport. We'll arrive soon after by helicopter, courtesy of the United States Air Force," Helen informed us.

"Why not go ahead of time?" Aaron asked. She shook her head.

"Our team is small to avoid detection, and we'd rather not alert anyone in the area working for M that we're there; they might forewarn Blake. Our intention is to let him walk into the café on his own, then my team will detain him until we arrive."

"What then?" I asked.

Helen shrugged. "Then you guys tell us what you want to do," she said, looking at Aaron. "Have either of you heard from the psycho?"

Aaron and I shook our heads.

"I feel sure he's in that cavern, though. His computer systems were well shielded, but we managed to track him to this location," I explained.

"Yes," she said with a curt nod, "I'm aware of the circumstances. Would it surprise you to know that we found the hidden door leading to the tunnel to the cavern?"

Aaron looked at me with arched eyebrows, then said, "I'm impressed. Is there security? Is it boobytrapped?"

"There's the typical electronic security that requires a keycard or PIN, or both, to gain entry. We haven't detected anything dangerous, but we won't know until we're inside the door. What's your analysis, Aaron?"

Aaron closed his eyes in thought for a moment.

"This asshole is the most prepared person I've ever dealt with, and I have to think this entrance would be highly protected."

"Yes," Helen said, "we found several cameras throughout the café. No doubt he already suspects our presence."

"But unless he's got another way out, he can't blow this one without trapping himself in the cavern," Aaron continued. "He's certainly not stupid. I would expect he'd have another bolt-hole for emergencies. What do you think, Ren?"

"I agree. But he's also a cocky fucker," I said. "Uh, sorry, Helen. He has the family estate locked down tighter than Cheyenne Mountain.

He might just keep this place with minimum security so as not to draw attention to it. If it's a secret as well kept as he thinks, maybe it's never been an issue."

"Good point," Aaron said. "We've been researching the construction of the café and the development of the land around here. The café itself has been here almost fifteen years. This is probably his secret sanctuary."

Helen's phone vibrated. "Heads up, guys. Thompson's flight landed early and he's on the way to Luray. Let's go."

I glanced at my watch; six-fifteen. I hoped Terry was getting some sleep.

We boarded the helicopter and waited to hear from Helen's team at the café.

~

"Blake is in a cab headed to the café," Helen informed us through the noise-canceling headsets everyone wore. "When my team tells me he's entered the building, they'll detain him and we'll land close by. ETA, eleven minutes."

Helen reached out and touched Aaron on the shoulder. "Are you armed?"

He nodded. "Just a small pistol strapped to my ankle," he replied.

"Here. Take this, just in case," and handed him another pistol. He tucked the gun inside his waistband behind his back.

"Ren? Do you need a weapon?" she asked, offering me a pistol as well.

I waved it away. "No, thanks. I'll leave that up to the professionals." She smiled grimly and put it away. A few moments later, we landed in the nearby parking lot.

Aaron and I jumped out of the chopper when Helen indicated it was safe, then walked to the café with Helen and her team leading the way.

When we entered the café Blake was seated in a booth, held at gunpoint by four heavily armed agents. As we approached the table he stood and raised his fist to take a swing at Aaron, but an agent shoved a gun in his face, forcing him to step back.

"I'm gonna repay that sucker punch before this is over, fucker," Blake growled. Aaron grinned in reply, ignoring the threat, which only angered Blake more.

"Shall we see what's behind door number one?" Aaron said, cheerfully. Then he turned to two of the agents and said, "Cuff this asshole, please. Make it tight and painful." We waited until Blake was shackled before proceeding into the storage room in the back of the café.

"Ren, you know how many dimensions of hell you'll unleash if you open that door, don't you? Even if you manage to overpower the boss, which I think highly unlikely, it'll trigger a chain reaction of death and destruction like you've never seen," Blake breathed.

"Seriously, Blake?" Aaron taunted with a *tsk-tsk*. "Why all the melodrama? You're as curious as we are to see who *the boss* is; don't deny it. Why'd he bring you here, anyway? Do you think maybe he's getting scared?"

"I don't have anything left to lose, Blake," I lied. "M tricked Warren into blowing up the yacht with everyone on board, and Warren was killed by local FBI agents trying to stop him. Everybody's dead, Blake. *Everybody* I care about is dead," I seethed. "There's no one left for him to destroy."

"Ahhh. I hadn't heard the news," Blake purred with a smug look on his face. "My condolences. But you and Aaron may have one or two surprises still waiting for you."

Aaron and I looked at each other, then Aaron nodded toward the door before us. "Open it," he barked. A tech agent stepped forward to open it and Aaron turned to the rest of us.

"At a minimum, he'll be alerted to the door being forced. We don't know how long the tunnel is or what awaits us below. Everyone stay sharp. Oh, and put Mr. Asshole at the front in case someone decides to shoot at us." Blake was forced forward and through the door the moment the agent had it open.

But there was no tunnel. Instead, we stepped into a freight

elevator. It had one button. When the door closed, Helen pushed the button and we descended, probably around two-hundred feet.

When we stopped, the elevator doors automatically opened on both ends; the agents scrambled to swing their weapons around to cover both exits. We stepped onto a well-worn path and looked around us. I could see cameras following us, but saw no hint of guns or people. It was also very cold, something I hadn't anticipated.

I looked at Aaron. He looked at Helen. "What should we do now?" I asked.

"Follow the path, Ren. It will lead you to me," said a quiet voice over a speaker system. That was spooky.

Thirty yards along the winding path was another door, standing slightly ajar. As we approached, Helen whispered, "Hold, everyone. Let my team go in first," she instructed. We stepped out of the way so they could move ahead of us. She pushed gently on the door, opening it farther into the room, then motioned briskly for two agents to enter.

Moments later, they returned to address the Team Leader.

"There are two people tied up, but we found no indication of anyone else," one agent reported.

Aaron rushed past Helen, then, dragging Blake with him by the elbow. I followed immediately. Before Helen could react, the door slammed shut between us, and a heavy bolt shot closed to lock us in— or them out. I could hear them pounding on the heavy metal door, and muffled shouts.

I looked around the brightly lit room, built into the cave walls. There were indeed two people in the room. One we expected, the other not. Aaron rushed toward his wife, who was tied to a chair with her mouth taped shut. Her eyes were wide with fear and she shook her head violently, warning him to stay back.

"Stop right there, Jeffries," continued the calm voice through the speakers. "If you approach your wife, she will die."

Sitting next to Sophia, looking equally terrified, was NanC. Aaron looked at me, completely baffled.

Suddenly, an arrow from a hidden crossbow shot across the room and lodged in the wall just inches from Sophia's head. She yelped, but her cry was muffled by the duct tape.

"Need I warn you again?" Aaron stood still, then stepped back. His eyes narrowed in anger. He looked at his wife then and made a calming gesture with his hand.

"Take deep breaths, Sophie. Relax. This will all be over soon," he soothed.

"Drop your weapons, unless you want to watch these two women be riddled with arrows," the voice instructed harshly. Slowly, Aaron retrieved his ankle pistol and dropped it on the floor.

"I'm not armed," I said, my voice shaking.

"Uncuff him, Ren. Do it now."

"I don't have the key."

"Jeffries has one. Take it from him."

I looked at Aaron, who nodded, pulled a keychain from his pocket and handed it to me. When I dropped Blake's cuffs on the floor, he promptly stepped forward and punched Aaron in the face, hard enough to knock him down.

Aaron was slow to look up, rubbing his jaw with one hand. "Mother*fucker*," he shouted at Blake, who stood glaring down at him.

I reached out a hand to help Aaron regain his feet. He still looked stunned.

"I told you I'd get even, asshole," Blake growled.

Blake picked up Aaron's discarded weapon and trained it on us, motioning for us to stand closer together.

"Frisk Ren, Blake. I don't believe he's unarmed."

"Turn around and put your hands on your head," Blake ordered. He was a little too rough with the frisking, in my opinion.

"Nothing, boss," he said, sounding disappointed.

The pounding at the door stopped, making the sudden quiet in the room more ominous.

"Well, Ren. It's nice to meet you in person, so to speak. Too bad Terry isn't here with you. I'd hoped to make you watch him die," the voice purred.

Blake looked at me then, eyes narrowed with loathing. "You said Terry and everyone else died in the explosion," he accused.

I shrugged. "I lied."

"It'll be a pleasure for me to take care of Terry later, you piece of shit," he growled, hate spewing from his mouth. He raised the gun and pulled the trigger three times, in rapid succession.

The first bullet pierced my right shoulder, spinning me around with its force. The pain was instant and I thought I would faint. I'd have fallen if Aaron hadn't caught me. The second and third bullets missed me entirely. I held my left hand over the wound and glared at Blake, who looked to be lining up his next shot.

"Blake," the voice shouted through the speakers. "Stop. You are not to kill them until I tell you to do so."

Slowly, Blake withdrew a few steps and lowered the weapon. His eyes narrowed to pinpoints of anger and his face flushed red at the rebuke.

"Stop being a coward and show yourself," Aaron said to the open room.

"Well, if you insist, Mr. Jeffries," said a sweet, feminine voice behind Blake. He spun to look at its source.

NanC rose from her chair. Her shackles clanked at her feet as she gently removed the tape loosely covering her mouth, revealing a microphone.

"What the hell?" Blake said.

~

Aaron

The frumpy woman I thought was NanC removed a wig, revealing short-cropped brown hair. Then she tugged at a wisp of skin, which appeared to be made of plastic, at the corner of her eye. Slowly, she pulled, pinched, and scraped until her disguise was completely removed.

"Anne?" Blake said, incredulously.

Anne removed the microphone she'd been using to speak to us through the speakers.

Blake struggled to understand. Anne was a good fifteen years younger than she appeared in the disguise, masquerading as NanC, an elderly, somewhat eccentric clairvoyant.

"Keep the gun on them, Blake. I don't want anyone trying to be a hero," she ordered. Blake distractedly raised the gun in our direction again, but couldn't keep his eyes off Anne. "And the rest of you, remember, Sophia is still a target until I release her. *If* I choose to do so."

She pulled another device from her sleeve, probably a remote that controlled the hidden crossbows, and raised it so we could see it.

"What's going on, Anne? Why are you here? I don't understand. Why are you wearing that ridiculous costume?" Blake asked.

She twirled in a slow pirouette with a huge, self-satisfied grin on her face.

"Ren's been shot and needs medical attention," I shouted. I could feel Ren shaking in my arms, his legs starting to buckle. "The least we can do is bandage his wounds. It appears the bullet went straight through."

"Fuck him," Blake shot back. "He can bleed to death for all I care."

"No, Blake. I don't want him to die—just yet." Anne glared at me as she casually strolled to a desk across the room and pulled a first aid kit from a drawer, then tossed it toward me where it bounced and slid to a stop near my feet.

"Stop the bleeding if you can," she said. "Nothing for pain, however. I want to watch him suffer." She returned her attention to Blake.

"Why, lover? Why wear this ridiculous costume? To fuck with Ren, of course. He's the only *project* who's ever defeated me—and I blame you for that, Blake. You got lazy and relied too much on those brainless *associates* of yours. Oh, and speaking of brainless, Dava's dead," she tossed out offhandedly. "She screwed up in Arizona, nearly costing me the game. It seems she was caught up in a lover's triangle, and all three died in a coffee shop shootout." She paused to savor the thought, then added, "Love is a many splintered thing."

"So Dava's the reason that scene was so badly handled," I surmised. "It was pretty stupid to cut the dress and force it onto a dead body, but even more stupid not to destroy the phone."

"Speak again, and your bitch will die in seconds," she hissed, raising the remote with her thumb hovering over it.

"You're good," Ren said gruffly, slumping to the floor. "You completely fooled Terry, while winning his affection, by the way. How can you live with yourself, knowing how intensely you hurt so many people?"

"Seriously, Ren? I wasn't hurting Terry. I was hurting you." She came closer to us to gloat. "I knew you'd eventually see through the disguise, but your little puppy-dog husband is too goody-goody to see the bad in people. Any damage to Terry is just a bonus for me, for a job well done. Icing on the cake, as they say." Smiling, Anne took a moment to savor her accomplishments.

Ren's body coiled as he tried to launch himself toward her, but his wounded shoulder had no strength and he couldn't push himself to his feet fast enough. Blake took three steps forward and kicked Ren hard on the side of the head, and he fell over on his back, eyes glazing over.

"Leave him be," Anne shouted at Blake as she retreated, her entire body stiffened in anger.

Blake turned toward her again, face flushed with anger. I watched as her demeanor instantly changed; her eyes grew round, projecting innocence and beauty at Blake, trying to entice him. Then she started laughing, which escalated into a maniacal, disturbing scream that made me want to cover my ears.

Blake still struggled to understand. The woman he'd loved and the one before him were two completely different beings. Conflicting emotions maligned his face until, finally, he pulled the right thread to unravel his confusion.

"You're the boss. The *Malefactor*? How can that be, Anne? I've been in love with you for twelve years. The only reason I continued to work for, uh, you, is because you threatened to kill my girlfriend —also you."

"Delicious, isn't it?" she teased. She was supremely pleased that her deceit had held through more than a decade of their relationship. "It makes me, you know, a little horny," she said, lasciviously, speaking the last word in a seductive whisper as she strolled toward where Sophia was still tied to her chair. "You wanna do it right here in front of them, Blake?"

When she saw the look of disgust distorting his face, her demeanor changed instantly.

"Kill them, Blake. All of them. Start with Jeffries and his bitch; I want Ren to watch them die. Do it now," she commanded forcefully, loudly. But Blake was walking slowly toward her, raising the gun he'd taken from me, ignoring her demands. Anne backed away, suddenly appearing scared, but never broke eye contact with Blake.

Ren sighed, his eyes blinking shut. I scrambled to get to the first aid kit. Anne and Blake either didn't notice or didn't care.

"Come on, baby, don't be like that," she whined. "We can go to Europe or South America and disappear. Just the two of us, okay Blake? We'll stop all the projects, stop killing people and digging up their petty cravings. Doesn't that sound good, sweetheart? You know we're good together. Don't you want to get married?"

I pried open the kit to find it empty. I looked up at Anne and she looked at me, smiling wickedly, then faking a pout.

"Oh, my. No supplies? How thoughtless of me," she said with a giggle. Blake stepped toward her.

The farther she back-stepped, the farther he followed, until he stood directly in front of Sophia, just as Anne wanted.

He gripped the weapon, prepared to destroy the woman he thought he loved. With a rapid intake of breath, she tapped the remote. Four arrows flew across the room in rapid succession. Three pierced Blake's body; one through the neck and two through the side of his chest.

One arrow missed entirely and lodged in Sophia's neck. "Nooo," I wailed, as I rose to my feet.

The expression on Anne's face was one of orgasmic joy as she watched Blake slowly sink to his knees and topple forward. She stepped closer to watch the life flow out of him and sighed, fascinated by the spreading pool of blood that welled from beneath his body.

"Everybody freeze," came the shout from behind Anne. Helen and the tactical team swirled through a hidden doorway in the back of the room and spread out, weapons at the ready. Anne, still staring down at Blake, covered her mouth in mock surprise, fully believing she was still in control of the game.

A gunshot rang out, then, startling all of us.

A single gunshot.

Anne fell over backwards in a heap, with a bullet lodged squarely in the middle of her forehead. The remote control tumbled from her hand and across the floor.

Everyone stared at me with shock on their faces.

"Give me the gun, Aaron," Helen said to me quietly as she approached. "It's time to put this one to bed."

I handed her the gun she'd lent to me when we landed next to the café. "Ren's been shot in the shoulder. I think he'll live but he's passed out and losing blood. He needs immediate medical attention," I told her. "And my wife has an arrow in her neck."

Helen nodded and spoke quietly into the microphone clipped to her uniform, then to me. "Paramedics are on the way."

I looked at Sophia. Her head was slumped sideways at an odd angle and she was unconscious, but she was breathing. I went to her to examine the wound. The arrow had narrowly pierced the skin and lodged itself in the back of the chair.

"Don't move her, Aaron," Helen advised. "If you remove the arrow, she may bleed out."

I nodded. "Get those paramedics in here," I shouted. I removed the tape from her mouth so she could breathe easier and unbound her wrists and ankles.

One of Helen's team opened the door where we entered, and paramedics rushed in, two to Sophia and two to Ren.

CHAPTER 17

Terry
Honolulu, Hawaii

A week had passed since the *Adelaide II* exploded. A week from hell, while I waited for Russ and Glen to regain consciousness. Glen stirred during the night, which was encouraging, but Russ was still fully unconscious. The doctors said they were both out of danger, yet had a long way to go. They also advised that I not tell them about the ones who didn't make it, at least for a while after they awoke.

Ty came by frequently to check on them—and me. I think if I weren't with Ren, he'd have asked me for a date. As it was, he was professional and friendly; a comfort for someone who had no close friends nearby. No conscious ones, anyway.

This morning, he ducked his head in the door with a huge smile on his face.

"Why are you so chipper today?" I wondered aloud, smiling in response to his mischievous grin.

"Because there's someone here who wants to lick your face. And no, I don't mean me," he answered with a wink. Then he stepped fully into the room, leading Dunkin behind him on a leash.

"Oh, my God," I cried. I couldn't believe it. I fell to the floor and

Dunkin jumped into my lap, his tail whapping from side to side and his tongue covering my face with kisses.

"Where'd you find him? How in the world did he survive the explosion? I can't believe it." Tears welled in my eyes. I heard a grunt behind me. Glen was frantically waving one hand.

"Oh, I'm sorry Glen, he can't get up there with you, but I'll lift him so you can pet him, okay?" I said, rising to do so. Dunkin licked Glen's hand then, and I put him back on the floor.

"Some people found him wandering on the beach, believe it or not. Completely unharmed, from what we could determine," Ty explained.

"But how'd they know where to take him?" I pursued.

"Abbott and Costello found pictures online of a Norwegian Dunker and posted them all over Waikiki offering a reward. I'm afraid you're gonna have to reimburse them a thousand bucks for that," he laughed.

I was excited to tell Ren about Dunkin. He'd be delighted to see him, too. Ren would return in a couple of weeks. He was still finalizing things in DC. We planned to stay in Hawaii until Russ and Glen recovered enough to leave the hospital. We'd made no plans beyond that.

I was still unaware of what happened in Virginia, but Ren said he'd explain in detail when he was here and could tell all of us at once. All he would tell me was that the Malefactor was dead and Aaron's wife had been rescued, although she'd been injured. He also confirmed that NanC was dead, but otherwise—nothing. I think he was giving me time to heal, emotionally. My thoughtful, beautiful husband. I'd feel much better when I was wrapped in his loving embrace.

$$\sim$$

Ren

Arlington, Virginia, USA

The gunshot wound was superficial, as they described it, although I'd lost a good bit of blood and it hurt like hell. I'd never been shot before and felt lucky to be alive. I had a black eye and a bruise in the shape of Blake's heel from the kick to the head, but fortunately didn't have a concussion. After several hours in the ER getting patched up, I was released.

Terry would be furious when he found out. I'd deliberately withheld my own injuries from him, choosing to protect him from the mental anguish and worry about my safety. And I wanted him to stay with Glen and Russ until they were well on the mend. If I'd told him I was injured, he'd've come to DC immediately.

We spoke on the phone every day, but it wasn't enough. I needed him near me, touching me, holding me. My sanity rested in knowing that day would soon arrive.

I invited Aaron and Sophia to come to Hawaii with me for the funeral I'd planned for Mack, Dale and Alex, but they were exhausted and Sophia was still recovering from her neck wound. The arrow had narrowly missed her carotid artery. It would leave a scar, but no other complications.

When I left the hospital, Aaron insisted I stay in his and Sophia's home until the lead FBI investigator released me; probably in a few more days. They have a beautiful and comfortable home, and I spent my time relaxing in their guest room or walking the grounds.

I was sitting on the patio on a sunny, humid day, drinking spiked lemonade, when Aaron walked out with a plate of oatmeal raisin cookies Sophia had just removed from the oven.

"Mind if I join you?" He asked politely, placing the plate on the table.

"Gee, I don't know. This is your home, though, so I guess it's okay," I teased. "And you have cookies."

He sat, then, smiling. He motioned toward my injured shoulder, arm still in a sling, and asked, "How's the wing? You think you'll fly again?"

"I've no doubt. It hurts, but it's definitely on the mend. How's Sophia doing?"

"She's healing just fine. Good news about your shoulder."

We sat in silence for a moment.

"Jerry is on his way over. Evidently, he has a few things to share," he said cryptically, tossing an entire cookie into his mouth. Somehow, he managed to chew with his mouth closed and smile at the same time.

"Oh? No state secrets, I hope," I replied, helping myself to a cookie.

Just then, Sophia poked her head out the patio door and said, "Jerry's here. I left him in your office, Aaron." She smiled and waved at us, then disappeared back inside. I noticed the colorful, casual scarf she wore to conceal the bandage on her neck.

Aaron grabbed the plate of cookies.

"Follow me," he invited.

When we entered the office, Jerry was opening his laptop on a small conference table. He looked up as we entered, smiling. Aaron introduced us.

He stood and extended a hand toward me. "It's great to finally meet you in person, Ren," he said warmly, with a firm handshake.

"Same, here, Jerry. I can't thank you enough for all your help the past few weeks. I don't think we'd be alive now without it," I said sincerely.

"I'm glad I could help. I only met Beau once, but he was a tremendous help to me, and I know how close you and Aaron were with him. I'm sorry for your loss."

Jerry was a trim, fit, black man whom I estimated to be in his early-to-mid-forties, with salt and pepper hair. He busied himself with his laptop for a few minutes while Aaron left to get a pot of coffee.

"So, what's going on? Aaron said you have something to share with us," I said to fill the silence.

He leaned back in his chair for a moment, wearing a poker face. "I do. But let's wait until Aaron returns."

Aaron stepped back into the room with a carafe of coffee and mugs, and closed the door behind him. Once we were settled at the table, Jerry began.

"I've already told most of this to Aaron, but let me start at the beginning. First, though, Aaron assures me you are trustworthy and can keep what you hear in confidence. This is crucial."

He looked at me expectantly, waiting for my reply. I simply nodded.

"Good. Speak up if you have any questions." He sighed heavily, as if bracing himself for an uncomfortable task.

"As you know, I got involved at Aaron's request, primarily to track down the source of M's emails, to determine her location. PTT&R was the only tool I had that would accomplish that task."

"Sorry to interrupt so soon, but PTT&R?" I asked.

"That's what I call the Proxy Trace, Trap and Report program," he explained. "Her proxy servers are all over the world. As each server location was determined, the program basically set traps, waiting for the next email or data stream to pass through and analyze the proxy's algorithm used to determine which server to jump to next, and then trace it."

My eyes must have glazed over, because Jerry paused. "Never mind. The inner workings aren't important." I nodded, relieved.

"Aaron and I assumed the locations with the highest number of proxy servers indicated a more likely location to find her—M. For example, there were a dozen or so in her family estate in Turtle Bay, several in Europe, Texas and Australia, and a few smaller clusters in other countries. However, there were only two locations where there was just *one* proxy server. Cazenovia, New York, and the Luray Caverns."

"Why is that significant?" I wondered aloud.

Jerry shrugged. "Anne owned a home in Cazenovia, along the eastern shore of Cazenovia Lake, on Death Point." He paused to let that sink in.

The irony of it wasn't lost on me.

"And her lair, for lack of a better term, was in the caverns," Jerry continued. "I shouldn't have assumed a greater number of servers in one location meant anything. We might have found her sooner."

Aaron interjected. "Jerry arranged for the server locations outside the United States to be discreetly surveilled, but they were unmanned locations, serviced by contract employees completely ignorant of their purpose. It was up to me to check the locations within the United States.

"I ignored Cazenovia, which Jerry found a couple of weeks ago, because it had just one server. And, of course, we didn't know about the one in the Luray Caverns until the very end."

They remained silent while I thought it over. "Water under the bridge, guys. Hindsight is twenty-twenty. We can't armchair-quarterback the play. Did I miss any metaphors?" I asked. "Seriously, this is not an issue for me. What else have you got?"

"Well, once the last proxy server was located I immediately launched an attack on the firewall protecting her system, which was sophisticated, but nothing compared to what we have at our disposal. I feared little time remained at that point before she shut everything down, so I started blindly data harvesting. In less than fifteen minutes, the entire system crashed."

"By the way," Aaron added, "that wasn't our doing. When Anne realized what was happening, she evidently flew into a rage. Beneath the room where we confronted her, she had a bunker where her computers were kept.

"She physically demolished the router with a sledgehammer to break the network connection. Then she removed all the hard drives and ran them through a pair of magnetic drive Degaussers."

"All data destroyed, irretrievably," Jerry concluded.

"Wow," I said under my breath. "Talk about thorough."

"I did manage to collect some interesting information, though," Jerry added. I nodded for him to continue. "Well, you know how she had Glen employed for those five years, and what she required him to do? There were twenty-three other individuals doing the same thing, mostly in the US and Canada, but a few elsewhere around the world."

"Oh, my God."

"Indeed," Jerry nodded in agreement. "I couldn't get the results for all their *projects*, as Anne referred to them. But I got enough. She had a particular fondness for people sexually abusing young children."

"But how did this happen?" I asked. "What happened to her to make her like that? You can't tell me psychopaths are just born that way," I said, heatedly.

"There are divergent opinions on that topic," Aaron said. "Many ascribe it to upbringing, heredity, or a combination of the two. Continue, Jerry."

Jerry dropped his head for a moment before continuing, his voice soft and low.

"She was raped by her father from the time she was three years old, Ren. *Three*. And by her brother, while her mother stood by and did nothing. In fact, her mother did worse than nothing. She made sure Anne was always clean and well dressed, the way her husband wanted. When the brother was old enough, he was forced to rape her while her father watched."

My stomach began to churn.

"She was physically abused, too, not just sexually and emotionally. Records I retrieved show numerous hospital visits for broken bones, bruises, concussions, cigarette burns, and so on, from the time she was four years old. The cigarette burns were always in places not readily visible; soles of the feet, between her fingers and, uh." He stopped.

We fell silent. I mulled it over, for a very long, uncomfortable few minutes. Aaron and Jerry seemed content to wait in silence while I digested the information.

I looked at Jerry again. "Do you believe all this?"

He shrugged, gesturing toward his laptop. "Dunno. But I can show you personal records, hospital reports, photographs and whatever else that will convince you of how she was abused as a child and young adult."

I was revolted by the thought of viewing that information. I wanted no reason to excuse her actions because of mental illness stemming from a life of abuse. I'd spent too much time building my hatred toward her and I wasn't ready to let it go.

"Why are you telling me this?"

"Without some rational explanation for what's happened, we never get closure," Aaron replied. "In my opinion, this explanation is better than thinking a young woman was simply born a psychopath and unleashed such evil on the world just because she had the means to do so." He sighed heavily, as I had moments ago.

"Have you ever known someone who committed suicide, who never left a note or explanation?" I shook my head. "Well I have, over thirty years ago. He was a very close friend, and it still crushes my heart not knowing what happened or why. So, this is my coping mechanism. I use the information and experience I have to reach a conclusion that helps me move on."

"So, what now?" I asked. "Do we just let Anne's mother, father and brother get away with what they did to her? Or, do we use the information Jerry has to try to prosecute them?" I was reluctant to drop it without *someone* being punished.

"I'm tired, Ren. So very tired. Jerry and I are working on some ideas how to handle this additional information, which, by the way, is not a part of the official investigation. I'll let you know when we're ready to share some ideas. Can we leave it at that for now?" he pleaded.

"Just one question, first. Why isn't this a part of the official investigation?" Aaron and Jerry looked at each other briefly before Aaron answered.

"Because what Jerry did was illegal. As a CIA employee, on duty and using government resources, he attacked a computer system inside the US. We can't use this information officially without implicating Jerry, and by extension, all of us."

"Okay," I grudgingly agreed. I, too, was very tired and suddenly felt deflated and ready to let it go.

~

Russ

Honolulu, Hawaii

I knew the moment I awoke that Alejandro was dead.

Was every bone in my body broken?

Machines were beeping, which irritated me.

People fussed over me, telling me I would be okay. I didn't care.

Someone took my hand then—not Alex—and I struggled to open my eyes. My vision was blurry, but I could see bright-yellow hair illuminated by brilliant sunshine streaming through the window. Terry. I'm so glad he survived.

I had so many questions, but couldn't string two coherent sentences together.

"Rest, now, Russ. Glen is here, in the same room. He's awake and says hi. I'll bring Dunkin up to see you when you're fully awake."

I think he was still talking when I slipped into dreams of happier times.

∽

Russ

Aboard the Happier Times

Hawaii, USA

Leave it to Ren and Terry to do a funeral right. They had all the class in the world, as far as I was concerned. They chartered a small yacht for the day, to take us out to sea one last time.

It'd been six weeks since the explosion. Most of that time I spent in recovery and physical rehab, forcing my body to recover while my mind was mired in grief.

Ren and Terry refused to let me wallow in self-pity. If I made a Herculean effort to do so anyway, they called me Glen. If that comparison didn't make me dig out, they'd start telling stories of Alejandro and his sunny personality, like how when they first met him, he had little blisters across his tummy and below from cooking bacon in the galley while naked. I admit, I smiled at the memory.

Today is different. Today is sad. Aaron arranged for Alejandro, Dale and Mack to be cremated, per their wishes, so we could bury them at sea. Ren flew Olivia here from Fiji for the service. I owed him thanks for that.

Poor Glen; he was worse off than I, with his head still wrapped in bandages and casts on his right arm and leg. But he gained permission from the doctors to be here for the day. Dunkin sat by his feet. Interestingly, Olivia sat next to Glen and held his hand. The sight brought a wistful, wishful smile to my lips.

Ren, Terry, Glen, Olivia, Dunkin and me. We were the only ones present to bid our friends, and my precious lover, farewell. One by one, we slipped them into the ocean. Mack. One by one, we saluted their passing. Dale. And finally, when we consigned Alejandro's ashes into the bosom of the sea he loved so much, my heart cracked.

~

Ren

Oklahoma City

Three Months Later

When Glen was released from the hospital in Hawaii, we brought him and Dunkin to Oklahoma City. He continued his physical rehab here. We also got him started in an out-patient alcohol rehab program, with a psychologist working with him—and us—in our home three times a week.

Glen hadn't had a drop of alcohol since the explosion, as far as I knew. It was as if it had blasted the desire out of him. Or perhaps it was our assurances that M was finally dead. However, he was still sullen and reluctant to talk about the Malefactor. Whenever the subject arose, most often he'd slip out of the room.

Glen had let his hair grow, so the one eye covered by a patch was hidden behind his bangs. He'd had multiple surgeries and the doctors thought he'd regain use of the eye eventually, although probably not one-hundred percent.

Russ stayed in Hawaii while he recovered and was healing well physically, but struggled emotionally. I certainly understood. I would be devastated without Terry. But Russ always rebounds. I envied that about him. I wouldn't have thought it possible after witnessing the depth of his sadness and grief when we said farewell to Alex a few months ago. We encouraged him to come to Oklahoma, but he wanted to stay in Hawaii for a while longer.

As for me, my physical wounds had completely healed, leaving only occasional aches and pains in my shoulder to remind me of what happened.

Terry had been furious with me for not telling him about it sooner. I admit, I underestimated his ability to deal with tough issues and I shouldn't have kept the information from him. Given the circumstances, though, he forgave me. We put it behind us on the condition that I would never withhold anything from him again. I readily agreed.

We found our dream home in northwest Oklahoma City, thanks to Brandi. Terry was supervising a makeover, but we expected to move into it within a couple of months. Our home in Mesta Park was purchased by a young couple with two children, but we'd arranged to rent it back from them until the renovations in the new house were finished.

Terry and I were looking forward to the upcoming vacation. When I mentioned to Aaron that we needed a change of scenery for a couple of weeks, he immediately suggested the Cayman Islands. I was burnt out on the South Pacific, so after running it by Terry, I agreed.

EPILOGUE

*R*en
Cayman Islands

It felt like it took forever to get this reunion arranged. Everyone had such busy lives, it was hard to find time when everyone was available. It finally worked out, though. And it helped when some of them found out Terry and I were footing the bill.

Aaron and Sophia were there. Russ and Glen were still recovering from their injuries, but were well enough to travel. And, of course, I was very grateful Terry was with me and doing so well. When I first started arranging the trip, he suggested we invite all our helpers over the last few months.

Billy from Phoenix, Ty from Hawaii and Abbott and Costello. Yes, those were their real names, although Terry insisted on calling them Bad and Loo. They took the teasing in stride.

Aaron had asked if he could invite Jerry. I agreed immediately and suggested he bring his family. Jerry's wife, Kristal, is a lively spirit and never lets the house grow solemn. His son, Lenny, is thirteen, more subdued than his mother and spends most of his time reading on his tablet.

~

So, on a sunny afternoon a few days after we arrived I asked all who were interested to join me at the gazebo for drinks and to discuss the Malefactor conclusion. Jerry sent his son inside and Kristal elected to keep him company. Sophia had heard enough, plus she was there when it ended, so she also declined.

I had to specifically ask Glen to attend or he wouldn't have. That left Russ, Ty, Aaron, Jerry, Bad and Loo, Billy, Terry and me. We had a tub full of beer, ice cold, bowls of fresh fruit and pitchers of lemonade, thoughtfully provided by Sophia.

As we took our seats under the gazebo, Aaron handed Terry and me a small package each.

"What's this?" Terry asked.

"Those are your personal phones, the ones I asked you to give me when we left Houston. I'll need the FBI phones back before we leave," he answered. "Government property, you understand," he added with a grin.

"Thanks, Aaron. I'd forgotten those," Terry admitted, then looked to me to kick things off.

"Okay, if I could have everyone's attention, please," I said loudly, and then waited for the conversations to subside. "I thought I'd start by remembering some friends who are no longer with us. Alex, Russ' partner, was one of the most fun-loving men I've ever known. He was always generous with his smile and his hugs. He will be missed."

"Thank you, Ren. I know he loved you, too," Russ responded, tears threatening to spill.

"Did you bury him at sea?" Ty asked.

"Yeah. He and I have always said that's what we wanted if anything ever happened to us," Russ replied.

"I also regret the loss of Russ' friends Dale and Mack," I continued. "They were good people and like so many others, didn't deserve the fate they were dealt."

"Russ," Terry said, "Have you heard from JT and Kat?"

Russ nodded. "I got an email from JT asking about working on the

Adelaide. It seems he and Kat are having problems, but I think once the baby is born, they'll work things out."

"What'd you tell him about the *Adelaide?*" I asked.

Shrugging, he said, "What could I say? It's gone, and I don't know if I ever want to sail again. It just wouldn't be the same without Alejandro. I don't know what to do, now."

So softly, I almost didn't hear Glen when he spoke. "Uh, any word from Olivia?"

Russ and I exchanged a thoughtful look, before he responded. "Yeah, li'l buddy. She's back in Fiji, and said if you're ever in the area you should come and see her."

Glen nodded and smiled. "I'd like that. Maybe in a few months, when I'm in better shape, I'll go for a visit."

Then, typical of Glen to abruptly change the subject, he said, "I wish we could've brought Dunkin here with us. I miss him."

"Where is he, by the way?" Ty asked.

"With Connie, a friend in Oklahoma City, until we get back. Did Glen tell you how Dunkin has survived not one, but two explosions? He's quite the miracle dog." I shared the story of how Blake and I found Dunkin on Glen's property after Glen's neighbor was killed in a suspicious explosion, which led to us adopting him.

"Does anyone have any questions?" I asked.

Billy raised a hand. "I haven't heard the whole story, and I'm still curious about that NanC person. She turned out to be the psychopath you were investigating? How'd she fool everyone into thinking she was a man?"

"Simple. Electronic voice modulation. No one ever saw him in person. Or her. All communications were by email, phone or text," Aaron explained. "If you'd seen the disguise she put together to make herself look much older and how well she perfected her NanC persona, you'd be amazed."

"That's what surprised everyone, I think," Terry admitted. "The NanC I knew couldn't hurt a fly. I was seriously convinced she was clairvoyant. She knew about the house for sale, where the cognac was stored, warned us when Aaron's hotel was going to explode and so on. It's embarrassing to think I was so naïve. She wasn't clairvoyant; she was the Malefactor and had either orchestrated or surveilled those things."

"Indeed," Aaron confirmed. "She was exceedingly talented at deception. Most psychopaths are."

"So, why'd she have the woman killed in Phoenix? The one who looked like her? Or rather, the disguised her, I should say," Billy continued.

"Ah, that. Ren and I think M wanted us to think NanC was dead. She probably thought it unlikely that anyone would question the body *not* being hers. If M's lackey hadn't screwed up and Terry hadn't gone to Phoenix to identify the body, we never would have known," Aaron explained.

"What I don't understand is how the phone in the hold was never detected by the bug sweeps," Russ threw out.

The *Adelaide II*'s destruction was traced to a relatively small quantity of explosives in the hold, that when triggered, blew the fuel tanks.

"I have a theory about that," Aaron answered. "I think we incorrectly assumed it was a phone that triggered the countdown because Warren sent a text message, and the phone had somehow been missed in all the bug sweeps.

"In my opinion, it was a simple computer module connected to the *Adelaide II*'s network by ethernet cable. It had no receiver and no Bluetooth, cellular or wi-fi transmitters, which is why it wasn't detected. It only served to start the countdown timer when it received a specific string of characters; in this case RIP –M.

"When Warren sent the text to a number, probably connected to one of Anne's computers, it forwarded the string of characters to the module's IP address."

"So, all that time, the module was using the *Adelaide*'s own satellite internet service." Russ stated.

Aaron nodded. "That's my theory, but I have no way to prove it."

"Amazing," Ty commented.

The conversation fell into a lull as everyone contemplated the scope of what they'd been a part of.

Finally, Jerry spoke. "Well, if there's nothing else, Aaron and I would like a word in private with Ren, Terry, Russ and Glen when you have a minute."

"Sure. Now's as good as ever. Let's go inside. There's no sense chasing everyone away from the beer and lemonade," I answered. We rose and followed Jerry inside, to his bedroom.

When we were all in the room, Jerry closed the door for privacy, then moved to the small desk where his laptop was set.

"Ren," Aaron started, "you know I got involved because Beau was a close friend and I wanted to solve his murder."

"Yes, and for that I will be forever grateful," I said sincerely. He nodded once.

"Remember my pledge to bring his killer to justice, even if I had to pull the trigger myself?"

I nodded, wondering where he was going with this.

"Well, I was as surprised as everyone else in the room when I fired the gunshot that killed her. By the way, her full name was Marie Anne Dekker," he lobbed out of the blue; typical of his style.

The light dawned on us then. M for Marie, not M for Malefactor.

"So, she really was related to Malcolm Dekker, and redirected his fortunes to fund her own bizarre interests," I summarized.

"Yes. It's my belief that she deliberately hijacked her father's wealth as punishment for her abusive upbringing. And that's the second part of this. We want to make sure it never happens again; especially with *that* twisted family, so Aaron and I have devised a plan."

"Go ahead," I encouraged. Jerry looked at Aaron and gestured for him to continue.

"Here's the deal. Did you wonder why I suggested we come to the Cayman Islands instead of the South Pacific, other than for a change of scenery?" Aaron asked.

"No, it didn't occur to me. So, why are we here?"

"Everybody gather around the laptop for a minute," Jerry said, scooting his chair forward to make room for everyone. "This screen shows the combined wealth of the Dekker family. Most of the cash is held in several banks here in the Cayman Islands, which is known for handling offshore accounts all over the world, mostly for illegal activities."

I squinted to see the screen. "Is that number real? Ten digits?" I asked, shocked.

Jerry nodded. "Yes. That's a real number. Almost one-point-one trillion dollars."

Russ let out a long, slow whistle, then asked, "All of that is in cash?"

"No, no," Aaron replied with a shake of his head. "Most of it is invested in corporations, land and other things around the world. But when the cash disappears, and they start selling or borrowing against assets to replenish their available cash, we'll siphon it off and give it to charity."

"Won't they change accounts when they realize what's happening?" Russ continued.

"Did Aaron tell you about the one time I met Beau?" Jerry asked. Russ appeared confused by the odd question he received in response.

"Only that Beau helped you with a computer software coding problem," I answered for everyone's benefit. "Why?"

I wandered around the room, feeling anxious. As Aaron continued, I glanced out the bedroom window. Several of the guys we left at the gazebo had taken up a lighthearted game of volleyball in the garden.

"Beau's coding solution is how I managed to eventually trace all the Malefactor's proxy servers to figure out where she was," Jerry explained. "And here's the juicy part. I've modified part of Beau's code. It'll completely drain the Dekker family's wealth, and I mean erase it from existence, over time. The bulk of it will go to a group of charities to help those in need; mostly children rescued from abusive homes. *Completely untraceable*," he emphasized.

"I've set it up so it will run concealed in the background; it'll detect any changes to the Dekkers' accounts and adapt. Of course, I'll have to monitor it occasionally, but it's mostly autonomous. It'll take some time, but it'll eventually redistribute their entire fortune to more deserving causes. If, by chance, the program *is* discovered, it will self-destruct, leaving no trace of its origin."

He paused with a thoughtful look in his eyes. "And, uh, some of the money will," he stalled.

After an uncomfortable pause, Aaron finished for him. "Some of it will go to us, is what Jerry's trying to say. We'll all be independently wealthy without fear of reprisal or discovery, *if we keep our mouths shut*. Separate numbered accounts have already been opened for each of us."

"It's only fair, in our minds, since Marie Anne Dekker ruined so many innocent lives. What do you think?" Jerry prompted.

We were all silent for a moment. Then Russ nodded and said he'd go along. I already knew Aaron and Jerry wanted to do it; they'd devised the plan. I looked at Terry as he observed me with those brilliant blue eyes, ready to go along with whatever I decided.

"Sounds like blood money to me," I said, finally. "What if I don't want it?"

"Then you can donate it to a charity of your choice, or I can distribute it to the group of charities already selected."

"How much are we talking about? For each of us, I mean?"

"One-hundred-fifty-million dollars each," Jerry said softly.

"Oh, my God," Terry exclaimed.

Aaron smiled and shrugged. "For all of us combined, that's less than zero-point-one percent of their total wealth. Even if we let the Dekkers keep their fortune, they'd never notice that small an amount missing. But it's meant to be punitive, guys."

"We have no way to prosecute the Dekker family," Jerry added. "M had plenty of time after I located her to wipe all her computers of incriminating evidence before she was confronted. If we want to make sure this never happens again, this is the best and only way I know to do it."

I sighed heavily, looking at each person in turn. "All right. I won't ask any of you not to go along with it, but I'm going to pass. Terry, I won't find fault if you want to do it. It just doesn't feel right to me."

When I caught his eye then, he winked at me, reflecting the proud smile peeking through the faint beginning of a blond goatee.

"I'm with you, hon," he said.

"What about you, Glen? You haven't said what you want to do." I asked.

"I, ah, I don't need that kind of money. I've still got plenty, and I don't want to touch any more of his, uh, *her* money. You know. What you said, Ren." His face flushed bright-red. "Blood money."

"Okay, that's settled," I said, turning to Jerry. "Skip the deposits for Terry, Glen and me, and give the money to your charity group." Jerry tapped on his keyboard for a minute, then looked at me with a soulful smile.

"It's all set, Ren. Since this is Beau's code that's going to take the Dekker fortune down, and to avenge Anne's senseless killings, would you like to do the honors?" Jerry smiled at me, gesturing toward his laptop.

I looked around at the group, finally resting my eyes once more on Terry. He nodded once. I took a deep breath and closed my eyes for a moment, awash in relief to finally be free of M Dekker's malevolent existence.

Then, with especially fond memories of Alex and Beau blurring my vision, I reached over to Jerry's laptop and tapped *enter*.

The End